Trapped in the Narrows

By
Charles Pulsipher

Providential Publishing

ISBN 978-0-9817042-0-3

Printed in the U.S.A.

Dedicated to my grandmother,
Cleone Pulsipher,
who fought the good fight,
and finished the work she had to do.

Author's Note

This is a work of fiction. However, the description of Zion National Park and the geography of Southern Utah and Nevada, including place names, historical facts, conditions, and the natural wonders and beauty of the Park are accurate as determined by research and first hand experience by the author, who considers Zion National Park to be one of the most spectacularly beautiful places in the world. With apologies to purists, the micro-geography of the Narrows hike is not entirely accurate, including the existence of a helipad above Big Springs. After all, the author needed to adjust the physical setting to make the story plausible.

Flood conditions and threats are also accurate; floods in the canyons of Zion National Park are dangerous as described, as is the case with all the slot canyons of the Southwestern United States. Lives have been lost in flash floods in the Narrows, including a catastrophic flood in 1961 that occurred as the author lived in Southern Utah and which partially inspired this work. However, the similarity ends with the date of that disaster; those killed by that flood were not members of the Boy Scouts of America. Twenty-one of the twenty-six hikers in the group were not in the Narrows section and were able to wait out and survive the flood. Also notable is the flood occurred prior to any rainfall in the canyon.

Beyond the natural and historical setting and a smattering of family history, the characters and events are entirely the figment of the author's imagination. The descriptions of police, National Park Service, hospital, and the Boy Scouts of America's policies and procedures are also fictitious, designed to make the plot as plausible as possible. Any similarity with any other person or event is entirely coincidental.

To anyone contemplating hiking in the Narrows, or any other of the wonderful places that God has provided for us to enjoy, please do not let this fictional account and the hazards described within it discourage you. The author has hiked the Narrows twice, and has not suffered any ill effect from the experiences. As with any proposed activity, planning, preparation, and good judgment will result in a fun and inspiring experience over ninety-nine percent of the time.

Acknowledgement

To all those who contributed their talent in helping to bring this effort to fruition, including Tracey Pulsipher, Alan Pulsipher, Annie McCall, Anna McDaniels, and last but not least, Peggy Pulsipher, thank you.

The cover is a photograph taken by the author in the Narrows and manipulated by David Heaton Photography to simulate flood conditions.

Table of Contents

Prologue	1961	9
Chapter 1	Return to the Narrows	16
Chapter 2	Unexpected Hikers	38
Chapter 3	A Revolting Development	46
Chapter 4	Unforeseen Events	56
Chapter 5	Kidnapped	66
Chapter 6	Conundrum	75
Chapter 7	Evacuation	85
Chapter 8	Ambush at the Fall	99
Chapter 9	Deep Creek	108
Chapter 10	Fight for Life	118
Chapter 11	Escape from Deep Creek	125
Chapter 12	Rain in the Canyon	136
Chapter 13	Death at the Grotto	144
Chapter 14	Pursuit to Big Springs	158
Chapter 15	Emergency in ICU	175
Chapter 16	Flight in the Narrows	180
Epilogue	Finish	197

Prologue

1961

"Stop! Wait for me!" David's plaintive cry was useless, it was instantly enveloped by the unrelenting rain, thrust into the river, and drowned before any sound could make its way far enough downstream for anyone to hear. There was not even the hint of an echo. More significant, there was no reply.

"Wait! Don't leave me!" David screamed again, this time drawing as much air into his lungs as he could and exerting his vocal cords to the limit. This cry was louder, but the tumult of rain and river still swallowed it as they both swiftly flowed down toward the converging walls of the canyon below. David desperately wanted to run after and catch up to his friends, but the water level in the river was to the upper thighs on his slight body, and he had to be satisfied with moving slowly and carefully, even with the staff he used to keep his balance. The water swiftly coursed around his legs, forcing him to concentrate on the rapid current and treacherously smooth rocks on the bottom of the waterway; a waterway that flowed relentlessly down and into the dark canyon before him.

David was utterly alone. He stopped, gasping for the breath lost by the combined exertion of yelling and picking his way down through the stream. He stood in the middle of the river and looked upward, trying to see the top of the two thousand foot high smooth red sandstone walls thrusting almost vertically up from the riverbed. The top of the plateau was indiscernible, lost in the clouds, falling rain, and water cascading from the high plateau above. Not only was David alone, but he was alone in one of the most dangerous places in North America during a thunderstorm, the narrow gorge through which the Virgin river flowed through Zion National Park.

Nine boys and two adult leaders of a troop of Boy Scouts began the hike the day before from a point on the North Fork of the Virgin River located on private property outside of Zion National Park. The going was easy at first, but as they had to ford the river repeatedly while working their way downriver, the trek became much harder. David was only twelve years old and was small for his

9

age, so working his way back and forth through the river was more difficult and slower for him than the others. He gradually lagged further behind as the day progressed, catching up to the others only when they stopped for the night.

That evening they camped where another stream, Deep Creek, converged with the river. Everyone else had eaten dinner and laid out his sleeping bag by the time David finally reached the camp. He ate while the others talked, but everyone was exhausted and soon had climbed into their sleeping bags. David followed. The water was deeper here, and the gentle murmur of the river lulled everyone into a deep sleep almost immediately.

They arose the next morning to a dark and menacing sky instead of bright sunlight. Clouds had massed over the park and over Cedar Mountain, which drained directly into the Virgin River and its tributaries, and it was clear that the predicted good weather was not going to materialize. The troop hurriedly broke camp and started down the canyon just as it began to rain.

Because of the possibility of flash flooding, troop leaders knew that it was imperative to get out of the canyon as quickly as possible if it rained. The alarm exhibited by the leaders infected the boys, and soon the young scouts, ignoring the pleas of their leaders, broke for the safety of the Temple of Sinawava, a rock formation where the road up the canyon ended, and where transport home was waiting. Soon the boys were scattered along the river, and it was every lad for himself. Each frantically rushed as fast as he could with the oldest and strongest leading the way, and the separation between the strongest and the weakest increased by the minute.

The adult leaders valiantly tried to get the boys to keep together. They reasoned, cajoled, argued, and in the end ordered the boys taking the lead to wait. Some of the boys responded; however, with the majority it was a vain effort. It was soon evident that fear was stronger than the authority represented by the Scoutmasters. In response, the leader in charge of the group sent one of the other leaders to catch up with the lead boys and force them to stop at Big Springs. He did not want them to continue through the Narrows if it looked like a flood was going to hit.

As the adult leaders could not persuade the older and stronger boys to stay together, they settled for splitting up and trying to monitor where everyone was and how they were doing. As they went forward, one of the boys that followed the Scoutmaster's instruction was specifically assigned to stay with David to make sure he was not left behind and forgotten.

It did not work. After a short time the boy became frustrated with David's inability to travel fast, and he went on ahead to try to keep up with the rest of the group. Soon David, bringing up the rear again, was on his own.

Now, as he stood in the river looking toward the malevolent sky above, the gravity of his plight began to sink in. David had listened to stories of terrible flash floods that swept down through the Park with a destructive ferocity that rearranged the canyon floor, sweeping away everything in its path, including uprooted trees and enormous boulders. He knew he faced certain death if a flood came.

His predicament brought him to the verge of panic. He had to get out of here! He had to fight his way down the canyon to safety! There was not a moment to lose! Why was he standing here wasting time when a flash flood could be hurtling downriver even now? "Run! Get going!" he viciously ordered.

Yet he did not, for in the midst of the confusion and fear, his mind caught upon advice given by his father, one of those lessons in life that are nearly universally applicable and valuable. "Don't panic, no matter how dire the situation. Nothing good will come from acting out of panic or fear instead of reason," he would say. The words came to him now, and David forced himself to calm down and think through his situation.

"Okay," he demanded of himself, "what should I do?" He carefully considered his choices. "I can try to catch up with the others – not likely. I can get downriver as quickly as I can, even if I do not catch up. (Either way, if I am caught in the Narrows by a flood I'm toast.) Or I can stop, climb to high ground, and wait out the storm." The first two options were attractive; David did not relish the thought of spending another day or two in the canyon waiting for the danger of a flood to pass; however, the danger he was in was palpable, and he recognized that it might not be worth taking a chance by continuing.

David wondered how much further he had to go. He had carefully studied a United States Geological Survey map of the park and so he knew the features of the canyon. Still he had not paid much attention to landmarks as he slogged downstream so he could not be certain of his location. Other than a few very narrow sections of the canyon above Deep Creek the day before, the canyon walls were closer than they had been the entire hike. Because he could only see a few places ahead with a slope gentle enough to climb up from the river bottom, David concluded that he was probably getting close to the point of no return.

David thought he knew approximately where he was; close to Big Springs, which was another of the many streams that cascaded down one of the many narrow side canyons feeding the river. There had been so much water added that it was much more than triple the volume that had been upriver the day before. He took some comfort in the knowledge that when he got to Big Springs the rest of the troop would be waiting for him.

From the map, David knew that Big Springs also marked the beginning of the Narrows. This is an almost two-mile section of the already constricted gorge where the walls converge. The canyon is so narrow that the walls are only an average of fifty to seventy-five feet apart at the bottom. Throughout the Narrows, the river's normal flow takes up almost the entire floor of the canyon, and indeed through several short sections covers the entire floor. The canyon is so thin that in at least one place the walls arch over the river to a point where if someone could elevate himself high enough, he could span the distance between the opposing walls with his arms. In the Narrows below Big Springs, there is no way to get to high ground in the event of a flood for the canyon walls are vertical, weathered, and devoid of opportunities to climb.

"I don't have to make a decision right now," David concluded, knowing that above Big Springs there would be an opportunity to climb out of harms way if he had enough warning. "I can continue on for now, and maybe the weather will clear up by then and I can safely continue" he hoped while the rain continued to beat down on him without any hint of abatement. David continued down the canyon.

It did not take long to reach Big Springs. Remarkably enough, the storm seemed to cooperate. It seemed like the downpour he just went through was the dying gasp of the cloudburst. Of course, he was still soaked to the bone, but he felt better.

When he reached the springs, David found no one there. For whatever reason, he was still alone in the canyon. He wondered if the rest of the boys had continued in spite of the Scoutmaster's direction, but he could not know and knowing did not change anything. He decided to stop and rest before he started the final leg of the hike into the Narrows.

The sky was still overcast, but David's anxiety about the danger of a flood faded away anyway. The setting was spectacular. Big Springs flowed into the Virgin River and created a small waterhole, and he could see trout swimming against the current. He watched, fascinated by their ability to maintain their position against the persistent downward force of the river. His mind wandered, and he momentarily forgot about the need to continue. As he watched the trout, he was even tempted to jump in and try to catch one with his hands.

Suddenly, the water in the river became clouded and murky, and he lost sight of the fish. David noticed the water level was rising; gradually, but fast enough to be discernible. In addition there was a lot of organic debris, including pine needles, twigs, and bark floating down the river. Up to now, the water had been clear and clean. Last, he could discern a faint low noise a long way up the canyon, which seemed to grow in intensity as soon as he recognized it.

Fear flooded back into his mind. Even though it had stopped raining in the canyon, he knew that floods sometimes came from storms miles away. It could still be raining on Cedar Mountain. Alternatively, the flood from the finished storm could have taken some time to reach the canyon in which he stood. It suddenly struck David that a flood was actually coming down the river, and fear seized his young mind. His terror was not just for himself, but also for his friends and leaders. He descended quickly to the mouth of the Narrows and called as loud as he could for the others, who had long since entered. As before, there was no reply.

The low noise had turned into a distant rumble, and now it was obvious to David that something unpleasant was coming down the canyon at incredible speed. His first impulse was to bolt downriver to try to catch up with the troop; he even took a few steps in that direction. However, he abruptly stopped as he forced himself to think about what he was doing. Realizing there was no way he could outrun it, he overcame his instinct to run and remembered that he had to climb as high as he could.

David looked around frantically, searching for the highest accessible place on the canyon walls. There, about fifty feet back up the river and about twenty feet up a steep but climbable slope of loose rock and dirt, he could see a solid ledge where he might be safe.

By now the rumble had become a loud roar. The water level was rising quickly. David threw off his pack and struggled through the now waist deep water to the far bank, still using the staff he used for stability against the swift current. Reaching the other side he ran as quickly as his short, tired legs could carry him, assisted by urgency and adrenaline. He reached the rock slope and started to climb up toward the ledge. Progress was difficult, because the loose rock and dirt gave under his feet. It seemed to him that he slid down two feet for every foot that he climbed, but his perception was false because the ledge above him was getting closer.

The roar was very loud and close now. David could hear what sounded like artillery as rocks and boulders, carried by the flash flood, slammed against the canyon walls. He climbed feverishly, even while thinking that he did not have a chance; he had started too late. There was no way he was going to beat the torrent. It was probably going to wash out anything lower than one hundred feet anyway, he thought. Still, he scrambled up the slope with all the energy he could muster.

By the time he had climbed to where he was five feet down from the ledge, the roar was deafening. A churning mass of muddy water at least fifteen feet in height, filled with rocks and plant debris, came crashing and tumbling around a bend in the canyon into his view. He glanced at it and realized he was not high enough. His fear propelled him in spite of his exhaustion, and he clawed the rest of the way to the ledge just in time. The wall of water passed by in an instant and slammed into the entry of the Narrows. His fear turned to exhilaration. He had made it!

The wall of water slamming into the constricted canyon walls forced a shock wave of water back toward him. Maybe he had not made it after all. He clung to the side of the rock face, petrified with fear, expecting the torrent to wash him from the ledge.

The energy of the initial backward shock wave quickly dissipated because of the tremendous downward inertia of the flood. The torrent seemed intent on grasping him, but was frustrated when its highest point was two feet lower than his ledge. Soon, the water level began to drop and David realized he was safe even as millions of cubic feet of water rushed past him a few feet below. He was safe, but he was also alone.

David knew that there was no way that anybody downstream from him in the canyon could have survived. He knew that all his friends were dead, and soon the shock of this realization sank in. He remained on the ledge for twenty-two hours in a stupor until a rescue party coming up the canyon looking for his troop found him, the only survivor of the disastrous 1961 flood that claimed so many innocent lives.

Chapter 1

Return to the Narrows

"Why are you driving so slowly? What happened to the wannabe Indy 500 driver?" Marie was not used to David driving conservatively through the gorge.

"Oh, I lost track of where I was. Sorry about that." David had always relished driving through the Virgin River Gorge since he first drove it. The short section of I-15 between St. George, Utah and Littlefield, Arizona winds through a narrow gorge cut by the Virgin River. When built, this section of I-15 was one of the most expensive of the entire Interstate Highway System; however, because the freeway follows such a winding course through the steep topography along the river, it is also one of the most fun sections to drive.

"What caused that? You always look forward to driving like a lunatic through this gorge." Marie was not exaggerating.

"Yeah, I know. I just got distracted is all."

"Well, if you're going to be distracted, pull over and let me drive. I like playing Parnelli Peterson too." Marie's reference to the famous racer Parnelli Jones made both of them laugh.

"No, I'll pay attention to the road. I won the toss fair and square, so I get to drive.

"I think he's lost his nerve," Rebecca chirped. Rebecca was sitting behind David, but he could see in the rear-view mirror that his daughter's eyes were still flashing the mischievous gleam evident when she wanted to tease her parents or brother.

"Let's not start arguing again." Marie, still frustrated by the protracted family fight earlier in the sport utility vehicle, wanted peace and quiet. Rebecca and her brother Austin had been snapping and snarling at each other since they had left Las Vegas early that morning and David and Marie had been sucked into the fight to prevent the conflict from escalating into the family equivalent of thermonuclear warfare. Marie had a headache, and could not rest during the squabbling. Getting up at three-thirty to prepare to leave home by four o'clock in the morning was bad enough without contentious kids. It was miserable with them. It was only since driving through Mesquite, a short fifteen minutes ago, that the argument had abated and there was peace in the car.

Austin had mostly been defending himself from his fifteen-year-old sister's teasing and attacks. Rebecca had finally become weary of the game and let him go to sleep. During the fifteen minute respite, Austin had sprawled himself across the rear-most seat of the car with his legs sticking out into the space between the middle seat and the door. He was asleep, or at least pretended to be, and Marie did not want Rebecca to do anything that would cause the fight to resume.

"I'm just joking! Don't have a cow!" Rebecca's eyes flashed with anger now. She had learned long ago that the best defense for indefensible behavior was a good offense. She was using this well-worn routine now.

Her mother was in no mood for it, though, and turned to face Rebecca. "I'm not having a cow... at least not yet!" she responded emphatically. "If I do, I guarantee that you will be the first to know! Be quiet, and do it now!"

Rebecca fell silent. Her eyes focused forward, and she successfully restrained the tide of venom she wanted to direct at her mother and steamed quietly. However, her anger quickly dissipated, and her eyes took to wandering across the passing landscape.

David looked at his daughter in the rear-view mirror. Rebecca was a medium sized girl of fifteen: blonde, thin, and beautiful, with azure eyes that were always expressive of her mood. With one glance of those eyes she could communicate a range of emotions from extreme anger to happiness and joy. A hostile glare from her could wilt lettuce. She had a mischievous streak, clearly evident on the road earlier in the morning, which was mostly directed at her brother, but her parents were also fair game for her semantical games. Her eyes would sparkle whenever she successfully angered her brother. Her eyes also betrayed her when she attempted to lie. Now, as she looked at the brightly colored mountains looming closer as they approached, David could see a mixture of excitement, awe, and fear in her eyes. It could have been the same look in his eyes long ago.

Rebecca was a gregarious and sometimes impetuous person, and David sometimes found himself worrying that she should be more protective of herself emotionally. She had always made and kept friends easily because she was so open and enthusiastic. That was generally good, but David worried that

17

someone with ulterior motives would take advantage of these character traits and hurt her. He had limited success in getting her to be more guarded in her relations with others.

Rebecca glanced forward and noticed her father looking at her in the mirror. "What do you want, old man?" This was a frequent and well-meant taunt, designed to playfully provoke her father into a verbal sparring match.

"I was just looking at you and thinking. I don't want anything. And I'm still young enough to grab you and turn you every way but loose young lady!" Her father had learned to not let her taunt bother him and knew what was expected. It was good that she was teasing him after the earlier confrontation.

Rebecca laughed at his expression, knowing she was in no danger whatsoever of being turned every way but loose. She had always been a strong willed person. Even when she was a baby she had fiercely resisted doing what her parents wanted in favor of any activity that could result in injury. Child-proofing their home had been the only way to keep her from killing herself. Regardless of how many times they said "no", one of her major goals as a toddler was sticking her fingers into electrical outlets. Then, when they would frustrate her in her effort to electrocute herself by putting plastic tabs in the sockets, she would try to undo their countermeasures. With her, the terrible twos had started at six months and had lasted, so far, for fifteen years.

The raging hormone stage, the impossible period that all children go through from about eleven to fourteen, hit Rebecca hard. At the onset of adolescence, David and Marie's relationship with their daughter strained, and came close to breaking, as Rebecca struggled for emotional coherence in spite of her economic dependence on her parents. She would be and gentle and caring one minute, then raging vociferously against the cruel injustices of her parents the next. It was like living with a Daughter Jekyll and Miss Hyde. It was a very trying period for the entire family.

In spite of Rebecca's seeming schizophrenia, family relationships were improving. Rebecca was finally becoming confident in herself, which in turn decreased her frustration with her family. During the last year she had started to mature emotionally, and seemed to conclude that, in spite of the antiquated notions of her parents, they might be right some of the time after all.

In fact, lately much of the time being around Rebecca had actually become fun. During the increasingly longer periods of time that she and her father were on speaking rather than yelling terms, they would play. David's favorite was to get his eyeball right up to her eyeball and have a stare down. It drove her crazy, which was probably why it was so much fun for David. Slamming, which involved crashing shoulders sideways to knock the other off balance, preferably when the other person was not expecting it, was a close second. Marie would often disassociate herself from them when David and Rebecca embarrassed her in public places as they slammed each other repeatedly, trying to get each other to lose balance, like two football players standing side by side scrimmaging. David had about an eighty-pound weight advantage and did not lose that game unless caught by surprise. Naturally, Rebecca always claimed she had won, or playfully accused her father of cheating.

Through it all, she retained her fierce independence and tenacious spirit. She did not let anyone think for her. Although he could not openly admit it for fear of having her react against what she perceived her father wanted, David was pleased. Emotional independence from her parents gave her a foundation for independence from her peer group also. The most obvious example of this was that she successfully resisted intense peer pressure to become involved in the self-destructive behaviors in which many of her friends participated. It seemed that most of the time the decisions she made were based upon what she wanted instead of what her peers wanted her to do.

"Are we there yet?" Rebecca asked for the umpteenth time, laughing as she asked the question. She had reverted to mischievous mode. David had just turned off I-15 towards Hurricane, Utah on his way to Zion National Park, a trip he had made with his family many times before. Rebecca knew that repeatedly asking the same question irritated her parents, and that alone was justification enough to continue asking, even though she knew exactly where they were.

"Almost," David replied softly, giving the unexpected answer. He was not in the mood for games now.

Marie just shook her head in disbelief, wondering what she had done to deserve such a child, but then took note of her husband's mood. He had been somber since they had left Las Vegas, and the sedate drive through the gorge reinforced her feeling that David was not his normal self. "What is so distracting that it takes your mind off this drive?" she finally asked.

"I just got thinking about the last time I hiked the Narrows. That was not the best experience of my life."

19

"Then why go?"

For a moment, David stared off into the distance toward the tops of the mountains within Zion National Park. Their destination was in sight. "I have to," he said simply. "I have to get over this childish fear. And I have to show the beauty of the canyon to my kids."

"Is it that important?"

"Yes, it is. You just don't understand how awe-inspiring it is. The Narrows is one of the most spectacularly beautiful places in the world."

"Perhaps. I love the Park too. But that is beside the point right now. Are you going to be all right? I'm just worried because you're not acting normally." Marie had been concerned about her husband and children taking this hike down the Narrows since David had first suggested it. David's current mood fueled her anxiety about their safety and whether David was ready for this hike.

"Since when has my father ever acted normal?" Rebecca seldom let an opportunity as good as this pass without comment.

"Not now honey." Marie shrugged off Rebecca's taunt, and kept her eyes fixed on her husband.

"I'm all right. It's just that it's been such a long time since I've thought about the flood and the loss of my friends. I'm just trying to be respectful of their memory."

Marie examined David's face and eyes carefully. He glanced over, and their eyes met briefly, but Marie was still not satisfied with his response, even with the assured expression in his eyes.

"You know I wouldn't do this if I thought there was any danger, don't you?" David had gone over the same arguments with Marie repeatedly. "You know how much attention I've been paying to the weather. Everything is going to be fine." He looked at her again, trying to reassure her.

"I'm just worried about you and the kids, that's all."

"I know, and I appreciate it. But it really is going to be fine. I scheduled the hike now just because this is the safest time. You saw the weather report last night."

Indeed, David had obsessively focused his attention on the weather reports in the weeks prior to the planned hike. He was understandably concerned that it not rain while they were in the Narrows. He had scheduled the hike deliberately in mid June to minimize the possibility of rain. This time of year is typically the driest, too late for the storms from the northwest typical of the prevailing winter pattern, yet too early for the storms from the south pushing up from the Pacific or Gulf of Mexico typical of late summer in the southwestern United States.

Moreover, the forecast called for perfect weather conditions. Last night's report showed a high-pressure system over Nevada and Utah. All the moist air coming up from the Pacific was being forced to the east by the high pressure system so the closest reported thunderstorms to Zion National Park were in the four corners area of Utah, Arizona, Colorado and New Mexico. This had been consistent with the weather pattern over the past few weeks, and Zion had not received any rain. Of course, Cedar Mountain, north of the park and the source of most of the water flowing through the Narrows, usually got some orographic precipitation after midday during the summer, but it was minimal and was not a threat. A visit to the National Weather Service's online web page the night before had also assured him that the weather would not be a problem.

"Yes, I saw it." Marie's skeptical tone was still evident.

"These conditions are as good as we can hope for. What happened forty-odd years ago couldn't happen now. With the weather reporting technology of today and the safeguards the Park has put in place it would be almost impossible. Thousands of people take this hike every year without mishap. It's been many years since anyone has been killed in the Narrows during a flood; what you really have to worry about is that I'll drown your son and daughter before we finish."

"Very funny. Fifteen thousand comedians out of work and you're cracking jokes?" Rebecca obviously did not appreciate her father's attempt at humor.

David and Marie laughed at Rebecca's reaction. The joke put Marie at ease. "You know, I probably wouldn't be so worried if I were going with you. It's just that with you and the kids going without me I feel helpless. If something were to happen, what would I do?"

"Hey, if you want to come, just say the word. I've wanted you to come all along, and it's still not too late."

"Someone has to pick you up tomorrow, remember? And besides, walking down through a river like it is a trail is not exactly what I call fun."

"You tell him, mom. I still think he's crazy. He's trying to kill himself, and he's trying to take us with him." Rebecca also did not miss an opportunity to lobby against the hike.

Trapped in the Narrows

David sighed and began his routine as Rebecca recognized what was coming and rolled her eyes backwards. "Rebecca, we've gone over this so often I've got the argument memorized. You need to see and appreciate the natural wonders of the world, and this is one of them. Besides, you made a deal. You go on the hike now, and we go to California later."

Ultimately, to overcome his children's staunch resistance to the hike, David resorted to a combination of persistence and bribery to get his kids to come. He pestered them for months on end, trying to convince them they really wanted to do it. They didn't buy it, but it did set them up for the bribe. Eventually a promise to take the family to Disneyland for several days later in the summer did the trick. Helping kids develop an appreciation for nature does not come cheap.

Rebecca continued to roll her eyes with the "here he goes again" expression on her face. "Blah, blah, blah. I can see the natural wonders of the world on PBS or National Geographic. I don't need to spend a couple of days away from my friends, computer games, television, the mall, and away from the comfort and convenience of my home to see them."

"You do if you want to go to California later this summer."

"But you didn't tell us that we wouldn't even get to eat hot food! Even cave men had it better than we will for the next two days."

"You didn't ask, and you still made the deal. We'll cancel California if you want to back out of it now."

David had her there. The bribe was just too much to refuse. Rebecca fell silent, yet again stewing to herself about how unreasonable her father was.

The car was gliding past the volcanic cinder cone on the ridge west of the Hurricane Valley. There was not a cloud in the sky, usual for this time of year in the Southwest, and very reassuring to the weather conscious driver. The east ridge across the valley with a scarp about halfway up came into view. About midway between the scarp and the crest of the ridge, a gigantic white painted "H" on the side of the ridge marked Hurricane High School's territory. The practice of painting the first letter of the local high school on the sides of adjacent hills is common in Utah, and the letters are maintained by yearly painting projects. The familiar letter seemed to jump at the driver as the car crested the summit of the west ridge and started down the other side into the valley.

22

The car started the decent from the west ridge into the valley and accelerated. "Must have smelled home," David thought, smiling to himself as he recalled the phrase his father had used so many years ago.

David, along with his brothers and sisters, lived with his grandmother for eighteen months when David was eleven and twelve years old. His father worked in Las Vegas, and came to Hurricane on the weekends to be with his children. He claimed that the old '56 Ford he drove could smell home when it came over this ridge and would accelerate itself to get home faster. The family knew that it was not so much the car as the driver, but they had a lot of fun with the joke anyway. The recollection set off a stream of memories, sweeping him back to 1961.

His grandmother had spunk. Her husband, David's grandfather, died in a hunting accident in Southern Nevada in 1932 at the height of the depression. With her husband's death, she became a widow with six children, the oldest of which was only six years old and the youngest not yet born. She had not remarried until her children had grown, which meant she had to care for her children and work to provide for them during what was a very lean time in the country's history. Not only did she accomplish this, but also she did it with little help from the community and none from the now familiar welfare agencies so common today. She learned to be a tenacious fighter for her family's welfare, and became quite independent and outspoken. David quickly learned not to cross her.

In Hurricane, there were many things for young boys to do. Hiking on the ridge east of town was always interesting. Molly's Nipple, a rock formation that looks exactly like a women's breast, was, for some mysterious reason, a favorite place for adolescent boys to hike. There are numerous small volcanic cinder cones surrounding the valley, and hiking around on the cones while imagining a volcanic eruption was imminent was fun and invigorating. In the summer, a short hike down to a swimming hole on the Virgin River was a great way to cool off in the heat. The river was not so muddy then, unless there had been recent rain in the mountains. In addition, during the summer there were orchards, melon patches, and strawberry fields to raid. Life was grand.

Zion National Park had been a favorite place to visit. His grandparents would bundle everybody up in the station wagon for a Sunday afternoon drive to the Park. They would drive either east up Pine Creek Canyon or north from the highway to Kanab along the road that turned off to the Temple of Sinawava. Each season presented a new view of the natural wonder, and the entire family never tired of making the thirty-mile drive to the Park. That was before the Park Service charged for admission, and so the only cost was the price of gas.

The drive through Pine Creek Canyon was fun because the family would go through the mile long tunnel and stop at the open lookouts called windows. These were small turnouts that three or four cars at a time could park in and get out to see the view. They would feed the chipmunks just below on the steep slope and look at the magnificent sandstone arch on the opposite canyon wall. David was disappointed when the Park Service closed some of the windows and prevented cars from stopping at the remaining open windows due to the death of a small child who fell from one of them.

The tunnel itself was an amazing technological feat, and driving through it as an imaginative child was a treat. It seemed like the mountain swallowed the car as it entered the tunnel. There were no lights, so the drive through the interior of the mountain was in darkness, with only the headlights of the car to show the way. An occasional flood of light from a window was the only evidence of the existence of an outside world.

When David's step-grandfather turned the car north to follow the road up the Virgin River floodplain to the Temple of Sinawava (named after a benevolent wolf god in Native American mythology), the grandeur of the sheer brilliant walls of the canyon rising abruptly from the canyon floor to a height of more than two thousand feet always awed him. The steep canyon enclosed the river and its floodplain, and the combination of rock, foliage, and river combined to create a spectacular setting.

The road meandered along the floor of the canyon. Halfway up the road from the turnoff was a lodge and the starting point for many of the trails in the park, including the hike to the top of Angel's Landing. The landing was a shorter promontory than the canyon walls that enclosed it, but it was still high enough when one was looking straight down from a narrow trail carved into the rock. It was a good cure for anyone's fear of heights.

Just up from the lodge was one of the most beautiful sights on earth. The Great White Throne is a massive rectangular mountain with rounded edges, independent of the canyon walls beside it, which starts at the base and thrusts almost straight up. The mountain is pure white Navaho sandstone from top to

24

bottom, unlike the other canyon walls, which are either red, layered with red and white, or a mixture of the two. In the afternoon, the direct rays of the sun hit the west face of the mountain, and it shined brilliantly, almost glowing. It was easy for David to imagine that it was God's throne.

Here and there on the sheer face of the white mountain, and on other walls throughout the canyon, small trees and shrubs were rooted in small cracks in the stone. Each time they made the trip to the Park, the plants remained, hanging onto the canyon walls, tenaciously clinging to life, and surviving under what seemed to be impossible conditions. David would gaze at the plants clinging onto the bare stone, amazed by the adversity that life could withstand and survive, and even thrive.

In the winter, mule deer, conditioned over the years to the protection they enjoyed in the Park, would feed on the canyon floor without concern for the human traffic that in any other setting would have sent them running for cover. Cars driving up and down the road could clearly see them, and the deer could also be approached on foot if one was careful. David once came to within fifty feet of a small buck before a menacing snort warned him to retreat. He was lucky the buck had not charged.

At the end of the road were the Temple of Sinawava and the trail that led upriver to the Narrows. This was a location shrouded in mystery and superstition. The Native Americans of the nineteenth century were afraid of the place, believing that it was the home of Wai-no-pits, a devil who lived where the sun did not shine. In fact, when first discovered by a young explorer in November of 1858, the Native Americans feared the entire area of the present day park. The Narrows in particular, where indeed there are places where the sun does not shine, was especially fearful. Though nobody in the twenty-first century was afraid of Wai-no-pits, the canyon demanded respect from those who would hike through it.

David's mind drifted through the memories of those years, remembering the close-knit community and the friends he made. Then the next year came the trip down the Narrows and the flood, after which there was an overwhelming response from the community. Even now, there were those in the community who remembered him and whom he considered his friends. Even though he had lived in Hurricane only a year and a half, it seemed like a large chunk of his life. Coming into the valley still felt like coming home after all these years. His grandmother had passed away several years earlier, but part of his extended family was still there, and he visited when he could. The quiet relaxed atmosphere of the small, closely-knit community was still there, and he looked forward to each trip to southern Utah.

"Did you call Larry before we left?" Marie asked. David, forced back to the present refocused his attention to his wife. David had arranged for his cousin to follow them to the trailhead at Chamberlain Ranch on the eastern side of the Park. From there Larry would follow Marie to the Visitor's Center where Marie would leave the car for David and the kids to drive to Hurricane the next day after they finished the hike. She was to stay with David's aunt, Larry's mother, that night in Hurricane.

"Yes" David replied. "He said he would be ready when we got there." It was great that Larry would take some time to help them in the middle of the week in spite of the demands and time that his furniture store placed on him.

Larry had wanted to go on the hike, but could not. The Park was especially significant to him because his father's family had a homestead at the mouth of the canyon earlier in the century. The canyon was a large and very effective corral for cattle, and they farmed the canyon floor. Larry's paternal grandmother had been born there. Eventually the family sold the homestead to the Federal government in anticipation of the creation of the Park. This trip would have been an excellent excuse to take time off from work, but owning a business brings added responsibilities that an employee does not have.

Marie's question brought David's train of thought back to the hike. It had been a long time in planning. David had taken time off from his job with the City of Las Vegas and had prepared for the trip by buying or borrowing what his brother Paul thought they would need. Paul had made the hike several times and knew what to expect. He was an experienced hiker, and David trusted his judgment. It was surprising that Paul was not going with them. It normally didn't take much to get him to go hiking in Zion National Park, or anywhere else for that matter. However, he could not get away from work on the scheduled days, so David and his two children were going alone.

David had also carefully studied a detailed topographic map of the route. As a youth, and later as a geography major in college, he was proficient in the reading of maps. With apologies to Will Rogers, he had never met a map that he did not like, and did not need much of an excuse to study one. This excuse was better than most and he took advantage of it, poring over and memorizing every detail on the map. He plotted potential escape routes up side canyons in case the weather changed unexpectedly. All things considered, he was confident that they were well prepared for every potential predicament.

They pulled into Larry's driveway, and David got out of the car, walked to his door and knocked. Larry answered immediately and was ready to leave as he had promised. After a short greeting, they were soon back on the road with Larry following close behind in his car. David's mood became somber again.

"You know you don't really have to go." Marie once again observed his pensive mood and decided to inject herself into his thoughts. "You have been there. You have seen it. You don't have to see it again."

"No, not really. I was almost catatonic when they found me. I don't remember any part of the Narrows after the flood. I was too afraid of another flood coming while we were in the river. For me, this will be like seeing it for the first time. Anyway, the kids need to see it."

"The kids really aren't that enthusiastic about going. And they have seen it too."

"Are you talking about us taking the paved trail going up the river from the Temple of Sinawava?"

"Yes. The one at the end of the road."

"It's not the same. Where that trail ends, the canyon walls are a hundred yards apart. That is like going to Paris to see the Eiffel Tower, then not going to the top where the spectacular view is. The real view is upriver from the end of the trail."

"Why don't you just go upriver for the short distance necessary to see the Narrows instead of spending two days in the water coming all the way down from Chamberlain's ranch?"

"The Narrows is not just one specific place---It's a whole section of the canyon. We would have to go upriver several miles."

"Even then it seems like that would take a lot less time."

"It might take less time, but it would be much harder. Hiking upriver would take about ten hours up and back, and we could just do a day hike without sleeping overnight in the canyon. But struggling upstream against the current is hard, especially with the water level as high as it is this year." Rainfall earlier in the year was well above normal, and the result was higher than normal runoff

27

through the Park. "Hiking downriver from the ranch will be much easier, even though considerably longer. Besides, the day hike would not take us through the entire canyon, which is almost as good as the Narrows."

"Then why the gloomy face? You act like you're going to a funeral."

"Don't confuse a reflective and pensive attitude with gloom. This trip just has me thinking. I'm not gloomy or afraid. I'm just thinking about my history here and how it affected me. It's no big deal. I really want to go, and I want to have fun with my kids. They aren't going to be with us that much longer, you know."

"Don't remind me." Marie was not looking forward to the empty nest any more than David was.

David looked in the rear-view mirror to see that both of his children were now asleep. The early morning start had finally caught up with Rebecca, and she curled up in her seat, her head resting on a pillow propped against the car's window. Austin was still in the same position he was in before they reached Hurricane.

Shifting his gaze toward Austin, David remembered the birth of his first child. He and Marie were so excited when he had come. Remarkably, his behavior at birth was reflective of his attitude in life. When delivered by the doctor, he had cried only for about ten seconds before the sound of David's voice through the surgical mask had soothed him. He had not cried much since then either. He was almost opposite in demeanor from Rebecca, cool and calm, at least when his sister wasn't tormenting him, with the exception that he shared the same stubborn streak. However, that was no surprise to either of his parents. David and Marie both had to admit it was possible that genetics from both sides of the family may have affected how stubborn they both were.

Austin had always been a very steady person, not given to extremes. He would reliably do what he said he would do. He had helped his parents build their dream home when he was fourteen. Most young men that age would not work hard for love nor money. He, on the other hand, worked just as hard hammering nails, pulling electrical wire, and helping to hang sheet rock as anyone else, although living in a small mobile home during construction gave him as much incentive to complete the home as the rest of the family. He had completed the requirements to obtain the rank of Eagle in the Boy Scouts of America, which required commitment and perseverance. A local supermarket had hired him, and his supervisor spoke highly of his dedication and reliability. Currently that was a lot for a sixteen-year-old boy. His parents were as proud of him as they were of Rebecca, at least when they were not tempted to strangle him because of his stubbornness.

Austin also went through the raging hormone stage. It was a challenge for his parents. He had the tenacity of a bulldog. His determination was such that when he thought he was right no amount of persuasion could cause him to budge from his position. David expected his children to conform to the rules of the family while they were living under his roof. Naturally, this was a source of conflict between parents and both children, but Austin a little more so than Rebecca. Austin had confounded all their attempts to use reason to get him to obey the rules. David wished he had a nickel for every time Austin had said, "I don't care" when presented with unpleasant alternatives for punishment because of disobedience. Nevertheless, he also had grown out of it for the most part and apparently had reconciled himself to obedience until he left home. That was only two years away.

Being around Austin had also become fun. He was sixteen, only sixteen months older than his sister, but considerably larger. David did not play the slamming game with him quite as much as he used to. Austin, at five foot ten inches and one hundred eighty pounds, was three inches taller and only slightly lighter than David. The problem for David was that Austin's weight did not include fat. David could still displace him, but it was getting a lot harder. Playing catch with the football or baseball with him was more fun, and safer (for David at least).

Austin and Rebecca's relationship, though they had been close when they were very young, had been a lot like a cat and dog during their early adolescent years. It seemed that they were constantly trying to kill each other. Gradually, they had developed a grudging tolerance for each other and kept a safe pre-negotiated distance. By now, they had become friends again, at least most of the time, and often were affectionate to each other. However, they were both still very stubborn. Rebecca, mischievous child that she was, loved to bait her brother and, just for the sake of argument, lure him into fights that were ridiculous. Austin had to exercise considerable restraint when Rebecca would start teasing him as she had earlier in the trip. He was getting better at controlling his temper. His sister was giving him a lot of practice.

29

So, for the first time in five years, the children were not a constant source of anguish and contention. Even though it was still difficult dealing with headstrong personalities, emotional maturity added to the equation made it much easier. This was a relief to both of their parents. David and Marie were getting older, and constant bickering and arguing wore them down. Arguments meant noise. Bill Cosby had accurately observed in one of his comedy routines that parents did not want justice: they wanted silence. It was certainly true in this case, and they had precious little of it over the last five years. However, it was finally getting quieter.

Now, enjoying the silence, David began to think of what it would be like without the kids at home. He had spent the last sixteen years dreaming of the time the kids would leave home. He and Marie had planned many activities together, all of them involving peaceful and quiet pursuits. Now, with the time actually growing closer, he had mixed emotions. If only he could keep them around without the trauma and chaos that surrounded them. He was even beginning to wonder if silence would be better than a home without children. Nevertheless, he knew that no matter what he wanted, they were going to leave soon anyway, which after all was in their best interest. These thoughts had given David incentive to build stronger relationships with his kids, which was another reason for the trip. The looming departure of his children had been weighing on his mind for some time and contributed to the nostalgic, almost melancholy mood he had been in since leaving Las Vegas.

The trip to the park would take about thirty minutes from the time they left Hurricane. They continued through La Verkin and turned east toward the Park, ascending the faulted ridge on the east side of the valley. Soon they were speeding toward the park with nothing but clear skies and colorful mountains and mesas in view. The bright vista gave David's spirit a lift. The road followed the course of the Virgin River for some distance as it went through several small agricultural communities. Several locations in this area served as settings for movies many years ago, for good reason. The scenery along the road was a vivid picture of the arid west, a picture that was desolate and beautiful at the same time.

The drive was very familiar to David. He had been on autopilot since they had left that morning, and let his eyes wander across the striking landscape. The desert has a beauty that many who are unaccustomed to it do not appreciate, but he had lived most of his life in this desert, and was well aware of its splendor.

It was a land of contrasts. The red Navajo sandstone layers in the base of the mountains adjacent to the valley contrasted starkly with the layers of white sandstone higher up the same mountains. Both contrasted with the brown desert dotted with sage, short bunch grasses, and creosote. In addition to the green forested mountains in the distance, there were mesas where the tops of the mountain were flat, making the Spanish word "mesa" singularly appropriate. They were indeed table mountains. The mountains, mesas, and desert sloped down to meet a thin ribbon of lush green fields and wild cottonwood trees along the brown and muddy river that was the lifeblood of the agricultural communities along it.

The Virgin River was certainly misnamed; the water in the river that David could see was anything but pure. Every time he saw the sediment-laden river, he remembered that John C. Fremont's cartographer mislabeled it as the Virgin instead of the clear pristine river that flowed from Moapa Valley into the Virgin River just above its confluence with the Colorado. Therefore, the dirty river became the Virgin River, and the clear pure river became the Muddy River. Because Fremont did not correct the mistake, the incongruent names stuck.

By now, the monotonous drone of the car had put even Marie to sleep. However, the prospect of the impending hike kept David's mind in motion (not to mention the need to stay awake while he was driving). His thoughts turned to some of the major events of his life. He had been born in Las Vegas, as had his father, before it was the gaming capital of the world. They had moved to Salt Lake City, Utah when he was five and had lived there until his parents divorced six years later. After a brief time living in Hurricane, his father remarried and moved the family back to Las Vegas. He graduated from high school in Las Vegas in 1968 and joined the Marine Corps immediately thereafter.

Upon release from active duty, he went to and graduated from college. There he met Marie, fell hopelessly in love, and was married. She was the best thing that had ever happened to him. After they had both graduated, they moved back to Las Vegas where he got the job he had now with city government. Both Austin and Rebecca were born several years later.

The years had flowed by quickly, and now, before he had time to think about it, he was middle-aged with a wife and two teenage children. He had

31

turned gray on top prematurely, but at least he still had hair. His chest had fallen to stomach level, and he was twenty pounds heavier but was still in reasonably good shape. He exercised regularly and was pleased that he could do more pushups now than he could in Boot Camp. Nevertheless, those pushups were getting harder to do, and he knew he was getting old. He shook his head at the realization and wondered if this hike was a subconscious attempt to deny his age. As the car drove into Springdale, the small town at the entrance to the Park, he reasoned that it did not matter: he was going anyway.

They were not obligated to stop at Park headquarters this morning. David had gone to the Park Service website, reserved the campsite at Deep Creek, and paid the fees online, so he was free to begin the hike immediately. Even so, David wanted to check in anyway. He wanted more detail on hiking rules and wanted to see what the latest status report on the weather showed. He had planned to arrive at the Visitor's Center when it opened at eight o'clock.

They reached Springdale at about seven-fifteen, with just enough time to eat before the Visitor's Center opened. David stopped at a local restaurant for breakfast and woke everyone. For the first time that morning, he got no argument from his children. Marie, David, and Larry had hash browns, eggs, and toast, while the kids chose French toast. They still could not get Austin to eat eggs as he thought they were gross. The meal was excellent, and they left the restaurant with their hunger sated and vigor renewed.

They entered the Park, paid the entrance fee, and then proceeded to the Visitor's Center just up the road, arriving promptly at eight o'clock. There they confirmed their permit for the hike and reaffirmed the rules regarding trash removal, camping, and various park procedures. The ranger noted with surprise that David's permit was the only permit issued that day, a rare occurrence even in the middle of the week. The ranger also directed David to a wall, which displayed information about hiking conditions.

Posted on the wall was a chart entitled "Narrow Canyon Danger Level", which described four separate danger levels, ranging from low to extreme, with moderate and high in between. Low was a forecast for favorable conditions but still cautioned the hiker to watch for changes in the weather. A moderate classification alerted hikers to potential flooding or adverse conditions. A high danger level indicated a high probability of flash flooding. Under that condition the Park Service did not recommend travel. The last level, extreme, meant all the narrow canyons of the park were closed due to dangerous conditions.

As expected, the posted condition was low, indicating the most favorable condition. Had they been anything other than low, David planned to call off the hike; however, the rating was no surprise considering the conditions outside.

David returned to the desk and asked about the weather just to be sure. The morning report had not come in yet; however, on the strength of yesterdays late report the ranger assured him that the weather would be good for the hike. Overall, it appeared that their hike would be under optimum conditions. After buying a few souvenirs from the gift shop, they left the Visitor's Center at about eight fifteen and proceeded toward the east entrance to the Park.

The road eastward through Pine Creek Canyon was steep and dangerous. The only possible way to engineer a road up the canyon was with switchbacks, which angled back and forth to ascend a steep slope of loose red sand and rock. It climbed until it reached the solid red sandstone face of the canyon through which the builders blasted the mile long tunnel. Lower in the canyon, the small black circle marking the entrance to the tunnel could be seen in the sandstone, and grew larger with each glimpse of it as they wound their way up the nearly shear slope.

They reached the tunnel and drove through it, passing the remaining open windows and the concrete filled windows, which only had a small opening left in them to let in a little light and air. David saw just a brief glimpse of the views he remembered from his youth. Now, the arch was only visible for a split second through a narrow opening.

The remaining trip to the east boundary of the Park was colorful, but David was now focusing on the hike before them rather than the passing landscape. They left the park and a few miles beyond turned north on the road to Chamberlain's ranch. The road to the ranch was paved only for the first ten miles. The drive along the paved section went fast, but soon they were on a dirt road and had to slow down to minimize the dust thrown up by the vehicle's turbulence and the uncertain quality of the road.

There were no other cars except one old battered truck they met coming the opposite direction. A young man with close-cropped hair who looked at David with a strange expression as they passed drove it. At first, David was a little concerned. He remembered that they were the only group to get a permit to go down the canyon today. Then he remembered this road eventually wound across the plateau and up to the paved road over Cedar Mountain. Old battered trucks belonging to ranchers driving along the road would be normal. He put the unease he felt out of his mind.

It took a little longer than they thought it would to get to the Ranch. Heavy rains earlier that year had damaged parts of the road and David had to drive with caution. The drive was a pleasant one though, and they saw several wild turkeys along the way. They had started from Las Vegas early enough so they could begin the hike around 9:00 A.M. Mountain Daylight Time. Due to the time spent at the Visitor's center, it was 9:30 before they got to the ranch. "A minor delay," he thought to himself as they reached the departure point. "We will be able to reach Deep Creek easily by nightfall."

Chamberlain's Ranch did not look much like a ranch. The river, which at this point was only a small clear creek, wound through a thin valley about one quarter mile wide. The flood plain was brown with dried grass, and further out was the ever-present sagebrush with a scattering of juniper. The only evidence of human activity was a small dilapidated mobile home, the dirt road, and a fence with a gate they had to pass through to reach a point where the road crossed the riverbed. Vehicles were prohibited from traveling further down the floodplain from this point.

David stopped the car and woke everyone. Both children had been sleeping soundly, and were not happy about the interrupted nap. They both woke surly and cross.

"Come on kids. It's time to get off your cans and earn the California trip." David was trying to inject some levity, but it did not go over well.

"You think that's funny don't you?" Rebecca was not amused.

"Rebecca, lighten up will you. Dad is jerking our chains." Austin wasn't enthusiastic about a new fight erupting.

"Yes, I am jerking your chains, and I do think it's funny. So why aren't you amused?" Now that they were actually ready to start, David felt good and was now in a mischievous mood himself.

"Well, simple minds are easily amused. I guess I'm not that simple." Rebecca replied acidly.

David knew that he couldn't win this one even if he won, so it was his turn to bite his tongue. They all got out and removed their packs. Each of them inspected their gear one last time, checking to verify that everything they needed was packed and properly protected from the elements.

Austin surveyed the narrow valley. "Why are we starting from here?" he asked. "It looks like the road continues further down."

"Yeah, I know, but the Park Service requires hikers to start from here., so from here we will start." David would have liked to drive further too, but it wasn't worth antagonizing the owners of the ranch through which they were hiking.

The three hikers shouldered their packs and prepared to start. David debated with himself as to whether to cross the river here. Crossing at this point was actually a self-imposed hardship because just a short distance upstream the road crossed over the river on a bridge. However, the water was only ankle deep, and though there was really no need to get their feet and shoes wet this early, Paul had said something about it being a tradition to be photographed standing in the river at the beginning of the hike.

"Oh, what the heck", David thought, "Why not? We might as well get used to it." He called Austin and Rebecca to start, and began walking toward the river.

"Dad, wait a minute. Why don't we cross the bridge?" Austin asked.

"Sorry kids, but the tradition is to have the first picture taken while standing in the river."

"Tradition! Are you nuts? That's a stupid reason to get our shoes and socks wet before we need to. Besides, this isn't a river. This is a glorified stream." Austin wasn't taking the bait.

"I'm with you Austin. This crazy old man is trying to make this trip miserable. He thinks he can get out of his obligation to take us on a decent vacation if we back out." Rebecca wasn't buying it either.

"You guys whine a lot don't you? The water will be cool, and it's warm already out here. Come on, we need to get going. And don't forget your walking sticks. The river is shallow here, but before we get to Deep Creek you will need them."

It worked. Soon, the three hikers stood in the remarkably cold water of the North Fork of the Virgin River while Marie photographed David smiling and Austin and Rebecca snarling at the camera. Each of them kissed Marie good-bye and thanked Larry again for his help.

Suddenly Austin decided to have a fake fit of despair. "Mom, I'm going to miss you. No wait! Don't leave. I can't bear to be away from you for so long. Take me with you!"

David laughed and shook his head along with the others. But he had an excellent standard joke just for the occasion. "Austin, do you know why donkeys don't go to school?"

Austin knew this one by heart. "Let me see, I may have heard this one before. Could it be because no one likes a smart ass?"

"You guessed it. Come on, let's get going."

As the children followed David out of the river, it was quickly apparent why many people ignored tradition. "Dad, there is water squirting out of my shoes." Austin was exasperated.

David couldn't resist another joke. Mischievously grinning from ear to ear, he turned to Austin and replied. "Well if you didn't want to walk in wet shoes you shouldn't have stood in the river so soon, you silly goose."

"Funny. Very funny. Did you stay awake all last night thinking up that one?

David laughed, then hefted his walking stick and turned down the dirt road with his two children following closely behind, each muttering to the other something about stupid traditions.

In the atmosphere high above Nevada and Utah, the mountain of air that prevented the intrusion of moist air from the Pacific was breaking down; a southern shift in the jet stream pushed the concentration of air to the east. The high-pressure system was collapsing. Pacific air, lifted by warm convectional currents rose high above the Tropic of Cancer, cooled in the upper atmosphere, then descended and warmed again as it streamed north, accumulating evaporated water from the warm ocean surface. The air, now laden with moisture, would lose its ability to hold that moisture when cooled again. Any large physical obstruction, such as the mountains of Southern Utah, would force the air higher into the atmosphere where it would inevitably cool and drop the moisture as rain.

Meteorologists working for the National Weather Service first noticed the shift in the weather pattern early in the morning. Bulletins immediately went out to all agencies dependent upon weather information, including the National Park Service, that the danger level had been revised to extreme and that flash floods were possible in Southern Utah. Word reached Park Headquarters in Zion National Park that heavy thundershowers were approximately ninety percent probable the following day and that the Narrow Canyon Danger Level had been revised from low to extreme. The bulletin had reached the Park Service Staff at eight-thirty.

Standard procedure under these circumstances was to send the backcountry rangers to Chamberlain's ranch to intercept hikers before they started down the canyon. The rangers would inform all the groups of the change in the weather and the canyon condition. Fortunately, today only one permit had been issued. Even better, the ranger at the desk informed the Superintendent that the group had come to the Visitor's Center that morning and departed only a few short minutes ago.

This was good news. That meant the group was still in the Park heading toward the east gate. They could easily be informed of the development in the weather by the ranger working at the gate as they traveled out of the Park to take the road to the Ranch. This would save the group the time it would take them to get to the ranch. In addition, the backcountry rangers would not be disturbed from what they were doing by unnecessarily going to the ranch. The Superintendent issued the order to have the east gate ranger inform the party.

Park Headquarters called the gate at the east entrance of the Park, informed the ranger of the situation, and asked him to watch for a white Hyundai Santa Fe, Nevada license number 625 CAP coming through on its way to the ranch. The ranger assured headquarters that he would stop the group and give them the bad news.

About thirty minutes later, as the ranger was checking in a line of four cars waiting to enter the Park with his back to exiting traffic, a white sport utility vehicle drove quickly and unobtrusively through the checkpoint. A brown sedan followed it. Both cars disappeared over a rise. The ranger did not look up from checking in the vehicle entering the park.

Chapter 2

Unexpected Hikers

"Hurry up!" Bart was angry as usual. He had turned to see the line of four men behind him, all with shaved heads and numerous tattoos, strung out over several hundred feet. He was furious. They had started down the river at nine o'clock from Bullock's cabin, a long abandoned dilapidated structure at the end of the road, and already they were strung out over an unacceptable distance. He yelled again at the stragglers to close the distance between them. "We have to stay together! How many times do I have to tell you?

"Then don't go so damned fast!" Ed was the last in the line, and had the heaviest pack in the group.

"Are you swearing again?! You know I will not stand for profanity!" This made Bart more angry than usual. His coal black soulless eyes glared at Ed for daring to swear, especially at him. Bart had a short, wiry physical frame with brown hair, though the color was indiscernible because of his shaved head. His piercing, penetrating hate filled eyes, glaring from one person to the next, betrayed an intense fanaticism and antipathy. Ed had the misfortune of having Bart's ire directed at him.

"I'm sorry. I didn't mean to." Ed knew better than to swear anywhere near Bart and was instantly sorry for his transgression. He lowered his eyes. "But we can't keep up with you," he whined in as apologetic a tone as he could.

"I told you we had to be able to get down the river quickly. Did you think I was joking?"

"No, but do we have to go so fast now? We haven't seen anyone, let alone those rangers."

"Just keep up. Never mind who we have or have not seen." By this time the straggling line had closed the distance between them and was bunched together on the shore. They were all dressed in military camouflage fatigues and backpacks, fresh from a military surplus store, crisp, unwrinkled, inexperienced, and untested.

"We don't need to go so fast now," Bill interjected his comment softly, but with an unmistakable malevolent edge to his voice. Bill was the second in line, a large, burly man with brown hair and a dark beard.

"I say when we need to go fast and when we don't!" Bart shouted, agitated at any hint of someone questioning his authority. "Just because you're my brother doesn't mean I won't take you down!" Bart was in Bill's face now, screaming the words at him.

Though he hid it well, Bart was afraid of his brother. Bill was a ruthless sociopath who had no qualms about killing anyone. Bart knew that Bill hated him, and the only thing that kept him in line was fear. Fear of him and the rest of the family.

Bill was twice the weight of his brother and could have easily squashed Bart then and there but, as usual, he didn't. He forced a rising tide of resentment back down into his gut and turned away, but his lowered eyes could not conceal his smoldering hatred. "Everything will be fine," he reasoned to himself. "I can vent my anger on someone else."

Bill did not like anyone telling him what to do, including Bart, but especially all those government stooges and pencil necks that did not have the brains that God gave a stale soda cracker. He could never keep a job because he always thought he knew more than the people he was working for and was not bashful about telling them so. When fired from a job a fight with his employer was a routine result; he did not deal well with authority. He only accepted the leadership of his brother because he had to. He was conditioned to cater to his brother's whims from the time they were both young children.

"Let's get this straight! When I say jump, the only question I want out of any of you is 'how high?' I'll waste anyone who is insubordinate!" Bart was barely able to control himself, and he instinctively reached down into his waistband and held the grip of his handgun while fingering the trigger.

All the other men in the group had learned long ago when to be quiet. They all looked at the ground while standing at the river's edge, avoiding eye contact with Bart and waiting for him to calm down. Eventually his breathing returned to normal, and the weapon remained in Bart's waistband.

"Let's go." They all obeyed Bart's command without question, and started down the river again with Bart in the lead. The weight of the heavy packs pulled down on their backs, making walking a struggle, even while on the bank alongside the river. Nevertheless, they all kept up with him.

Bart and Bill were respectively the brains and the brawn of the group. The other three, Ed, Rich, and Archie, were followers. They were along for the thrills and adventure promised. The latter three were medium weight and physically strong, but intellectually speaking they had all come out on the short end of the stick, especially Archie. The intensity of Bart's extreme and fanatical philosophy had converted them to his beliefs. Seduced by hatred, which is always easier to understand than well-reasoned ideas, they let Bart think for them, and if they did not completely comprehend the reasons for what they were doing, they appreciated the fact that Bart wanted it and so made it their goal. Of course, fear was also a powerful motivator.

By now, they were deep into the canyon. They had started from the ranch at nine that morning, having driven as far down the road as they could. A sixth member of their group had taken their pickup truck to the end of the trail at the Temple of Sinawava. So far, everything was going according to plan.

"When are we going to find the rangers?" Archie was the only one in the group who could get away with speaking when Bart was still angry. His intelligence quotient was well below average, so Bart was more tolerant of his questions, most of which were about trivial things.

"I don't know. But when we do, I'm going to teach them a lesson they won't forget. They'll think twice about giving me a citation again. Those sonzabitches are going to pay!" Bart had shifted his rage back onto the objects of his ire. The others shifted nervously at his language; however, they certainly were not going to call any attention to his hypocritical attitude about swearing.

"Why didn't you waste the rangers when they gave you the ticket?" Archie had donned his standard confused look.

"Because I didn't have my gun!" Bart's reply was sharp considering that Archie was the object. Bart was still angry with himself for not bringing his gun with him on the trip when he had gotten the ticket. "But I fixed that. That will never happen again. I'll never go anywhere without my gun again."

"You're going to show them now," Archie had a silly grin on his face.

Bart smiled, nodding in agreement. "Yep. That's right. Just wait till we find them. We'll show them now. And they deserve it. Those government bastards are all the same. They're all conspiring to enslave us Aryans and put the Jews in charge. Every single government worker in America needs to be shot, along with all the Jews." Bart was beginning to get worked up for his standard soapbox lecture.

The others were not particularly enthusiastic about hearing "the" lecture again, but no one wanted to say anything that would shift Bart's ire back onto him again, so they all kept quiet.

"You know why we are stuck in this God-forsaken part of the country don't you?" Bart began, and as usual got progressively more emphatic about his message as he went on. "I'll tell you why. It's because the wetbacks have taken all our jobs! We can't work in America anymore because they have all our jobs! And the Jews control every government in the world! They've taken over our government and are plotting now to put us all in concentration camps! I have photographic proof! United Nations troops in black helicopters are in this country right now getting ready to round us up! We can't trust anybody! Not one of us is safe! But that is going to change! Starting today! Those government bastards that gave me a ticket just because I was hiking in this canyon, which I as a taxpayer own and have a God-given right to be in, are going to pay."

"I thought we didn't pay taxes. You told us we shouldn't pay taxes." Archie had that confused look on his face again.

"Of course we don't pay taxes. We are not going to support an illegal government, a government which has overthrown the Constitution and is trying to enslave us, with our own money."

"But then how do we own this park if we are not taxpayers?"

"You idiot! We are taxpayers whether we pay taxes or not! Besides, we pay taxes every time we buy a beer. Every can of beer in your pack was taxed."

"Oh, I understand." A light had come on in his head. Bart always explained things so well to him.

The exchange between Archie and Bart put the others at ease. They continued down the river without as much tension between them. In addition, the beer in Bart's pack was just as heavy as the beer in the other packs, so he was slowing down too. The others were able to keep up as Bart continued his diatribe.

"Just look at what the government did to the Weaver's. All he wanted to do was live peacefully without them bothering him. He moved to Ruby Ridge in

Idaho to get away from them. But they went after him and shot and killed his son and wife. They killed his wife while she had a baby in her arms! And this was just because of a firearms violation! Those sonzabitches are trying to get our guns! But they won't get mine; no-sir-ree, not without a fight." His fingers instinctively reached for the weapon in his waistband as his tirade continued.

"And what about Waco? They went in and murdered all those women and children. Did those people have a chance? No way! Those bastards killed them all because the Davidians wanted to be left alone!" By now, he had worked himself into a fury, and he pulled out his weapon and searched down the river for a target. However, they were alone in the canyon. No rangers were there to satisfy his frothing desire to obtain revenge for the long dead Davidians. He jammed the weapon back into his waistband and hurried down the canyon.

For some time nobody spoke while Bart cooled off. Even Archie knew better than to say anything when Bart was in one of his moods. However, eventually Bart calmed down again, and Archie was able to ask a question he had wondered about since they had started that morning.

"What if they aren't in the canyon?" He asked the question timidly, afraid of the response.

"What if who isn't in the canyon?" Bart was growing impatient with all the stupid questions.

"The rangers. What if the rangers aren't in the canyon?"

"They're here. I can feel it in my bones."

"But I haven't seen anyone at all, especially rangers."

Bart said nothing in response. Archie was right. In spite of his show of confidence, Bart was worried about the same thing. They had not seen anyone at all. His plan for revenge had counted on the rangers being in the canyon. This concern accounted for some of the anger that kept surging in him. The plan was in danger.

Bart had carefully conceived and organized his plan. He reasoned that his group of skinheads stood little chance of being caught if they bumped off a couple of rangers. No one was ever at the trailhead at Chamberlain's ranch; this was certainly true today. If they met the rangers as he did last time, the rangers could not communicate in the narrow canyon with millions of tons of rock blocking radio communication. They would waste the rangers, hide the bodies in a side canyon, and continue down the canyon to the truck. It was perfect.

After they were safely out of the Park, Bart would call the local press and courageously take responsibility for the execution of the instruments of oppression, anonymously and from a pay phone, of course. Then they could plan their next battle in the fight against tyranny. However, it was not going to work if the rangers were not in the canyon.

"I think Archie is right." Bill spoke for the first time since his confrontation with Bart earlier. "We could go completely through the canyon without seeing the rangers. Then what? Are we going to storm the visitor's center and kill everybody there?" His suggestion was only partly cynical. Bill wanted to kill someone, anyone. He could transfer the malevolent, deep-seated hatred he felt for his brother to anyone, and could snuff him or her with the vision of his brother's face in his mind's eye. If the rangers weren't in the canyon, the visitor's center would work .

Bart looked at Bill, trying to figure out whether he was taunting him or whether he really wanted to attack the center. Bill stared back at Bart, giving every indication that he wanted to do it. But Bill always gave every indication that he wanted to kill anyone whenever the chance arose.

"No, we are not going to storm the visitor's center. We are going to give those rangers what they deserve."

"But what if they are not here?" Rich, who did not say much at all, chimed in with the last comment. If Rich was worried enough to say something, there was definitely reason for concern.

"Will you be patient? We've only been on the trail for a few hours now." Bart was beginning to be anxious. "What if they were not here?" he asked himself. It would ruin everything.

"I think we should just kill the first people we see," Bill was still lobbying. "It doesn't matter whether they're rangers or not. We can send the same message no matter who dies."

"But we agreed to let any hikers just go past us." Bart did not share his brother's indiscriminate blood lust. "Other hikers are not the ones who are trying to enslave us. We already decided to non-government citizens alone."

"No, you decided not to." Bill was getting up some courage.

"Are you challenging me again? You're beginning to piss me off!"

Trapped in the Narrows

"No! But just think about it. Anyone that sees us will be able to give the cops a good description. It's not like we don't make an impression on people. We don't exactly blend into the scenery you know."

"But we don't want to turn the people around here against us." Bart had heard all these argument before but now that they were actually in the canyon, the prospect of capture was real.

"Look, after the bodies are found, they're going to track down everybody they know were in the canyon and ask what and who they saw. The only way to be sure we'll get away is to kill everybody that sees us. What is more important, getting caught, or killing a few of the hicks who live around here?"

"We are not going to get caught! The cops around here don't know their asses from a hole in the ground. We're too smart for them."

"But we can't give them so much information that they'll be led right to us! Besides, if you call in and take credit as planned, don't you think they are going to figure out who's responsible? So it doesn't matter if we piss off the people here. They're just a bunch of hick religious fanatics anyway. We'll blow this place and go somewhere else."

Bart considered Bill's argument. He knew Bill was right, but he was not sure he wanted to take his mini-revolution to non-government beings. He began to reconsider the entire affair. "Maybe we should forget the whole thing," he tentatively suggested.

The expressions on Archie, Rich and Ed's faces were immediately sympathetic to Bart's suggestion, but Bill was furious. "Forget the whole thing?! You're going to let those pencil-necked rangers get away with it?!"

"I'm not going to let them get away with it!" Bart snapped back, angry at the challenge. "They will pay! But maybe we should try another way."

"What other way? Where are we going to find them?"

"I don't know, but we'll find them!"

"But we're here now. We've planned this for a long time. Plus, I don't want to have to carry this stupid pack down this river again if I can help it. Now is not the time to chicken out."

"Chicken out?! Are you telling me I'm chickening out?"

"I'm saying you shouldn't!" By this time, all progress down the canyon had stopped, and the two were facing off again. Bart's hand, as usual, went for the great equalizer in his waistband while Bill stood shaking over his brother, exerting all his effort to control his fury. They stood in this posture for a minute or two before Bill suddenly turned away, stormed out of the water, and climbed up a flat bank.

The others remained in the water, waiting for a cue from Bart. He was motionless for a moment until his rage subsided. He looked at the vacant expressions of the three remaining companions still standing in the water. "Let's get out of the river and eat." Bart had suddenly felt hunger from the exertion of the morning. "We'll eat, and then figure out what we are going to do."

"Maybe we should just wait here for the rangers. My back is getting tired." Archie was not used to the physical exertion needed to negotiate the river.

"We'll eat, then rest awhile. I need to think this out."

The others nodded their assent, and the four scrambled up the bank to where Bill had climbed. They took off their packs and began to eat, washing the sandwiches they brought down with beer. They all ate in silence, not wanting to rekindle the argument. Bill sat apart from the rest, his back to them.

The meal was finished with the litter from it strewn around the area, but still the group did not move on. Bill was still off by himself pouting. Bart was silent, his eyes on the bank, deep in thought. The others waited patiently, wondering what would come next.

They didn't have to wait very long. "Bart, I think we need to make up our mind pretty quick." Rich's voice had a high, nervous pitch to it.

"Why?" Bart looked up.

"Someone is coming. Look."

Bart rose from his rock and looked upstream. Sure enough, coming down the river toward them they could see two figures. They were too far away to tell who they were. Bill forgot his tantrum and joined the others. They each strained, looking for an indication that the rangers were walking into the trap they had laid. Bart reached for his waistband, and the others also retrieved their weapons.

Just up the river, the two figures continued down toward the group, oblivious to the danger that awaited them a short distance downriver, while overhead wisps of thin clouds formed high in the troposphere.

Chapter 3

A Revolting Development

Feeling a distinct pang of regret, Marie watched her family disappear around a bend in the road. Now alone, she was not nearly so enthusiastic about them going without her. She did not like it when the family split up, and she especially did not like being left behind. For a brief moment she was tempted to run after them; she thought it might be exciting to make the hike a good activity for the whole family. However, it was too late now. David and the children were depending on her to take the car around to where they could find it after they finished tomorrow. Besides, she certainly was not equipped for a hike.

Marie was one of those people who compelled herself to worry. Much of the time, she had important problems to deal with that were of significant concern. However, if by some quirk of fate she did not have anything real to worry about, she would manufacture something out of whole cloth. Sometimes it seemed she was trying to give herself a stress-induced heart attack, or striving to get a record-breaking ulcer. David had tried to get her to lighten up a little but with little effect. She was in her manufactured-worry-mode at this point. "What if one of them breaks a leg?" Marie asked herself. "Or what if they all get lost? Did they pack enough socks?" An endless stream of disjointed questions forced their way through her thoughts. Her mind seemed intent on making her miserable while her family was gone.

Larry honked his horn. He was in his car just up the road waiting for her to start, so she had to go. Marie got into the car and backed around so she could double back along the road they had taken in. She missed her family already. This was normal; it was typical for her to go out on a date with David and want to come home early because she missed the kids. What was she going to do for thirty-six hours without them? She started back toward the Park, sighing and resigning herself to being without her family for a day.

However, after traveling down the road a short distance, she was soon comfortable with her role as a driver in the outing. She really did not want to go on the hike, and the initial pangs of anxiety faded along with the dust trailing the car as she sped along the graveled road. Besides, the way David had described the hike, it sounded much more like work than fun. She was confident that walking almost continuously through the river as if it were a trail was not natural. It certainly wouldn't be something she would want to do. She relaxed and began to enjoy the drive. It was a brilliant day with only a few high strands of clouds that had crept into the southern sky. By the time she reached the east entrance to the Park an hour later her initial separation anxiety was gone and she was ready to enjoy herself. She was even looking forward to her free day.

Marie pulled up to the ranger checking cars into the Park at the East entrance. Because David paid the entrance fee earlier that morning and Marie was holding out the receipt, she expected the ranger to wave her through. However, the ranger in the booth looked at the sport utility vehicle with a puzzled look, and then asked her to wait a moment. The type and color of the automobile had triggered the memory of an unfulfilled assignment. He was confused though because of the time and the direction the car was traveling. He quickly searched through some papers to the side of his workspace and retrieved a hastily scribbled note.

"Is your license number Nevada 625 CAP?" he asked.

"Yes," Marie answered.

"Did you pull a permit to hike down the Narrows?"

"Yes, my husband got the permit online."

"I hate to tell you this, but because of a change in the weather the Weather Service has revised the danger level for hiking in the Narrows. The danger level indicator for hiking in the Park has been upgraded to an extreme danger level, I'm sorry, but the permit has been cancelled."

Marie's jaw dropped. "I dropped them off at the ranch over thirty minutes ago! They are on their way down the canyon! What happened? When we checked in this morning at Park Headquarters, we were told that the weather was going to be fine."

"Apparently they got an update that changed the weather outlook. It must have been just after you left the Visitor's Center because they called me and asked me to tell you when you came through. That was no later than eight thirty."

"Why didn't you tell us when we came through?"

47

"I'm sorry, but I just got so busy checking people in that you just got by without me noticing. I don't normally need to worry about cars leaving the Park, so I'm not used to looking that direction."

"Is it common for you to miss passing on what may be lifesaving information?" Marie was irritated now, knowing that they should have been informed about the changed weather forecast over an hour ago.

The ranger was sincerely apologetic. "Standard procedure is to send somebody to the ranch to tell everyone starting the hike the bad news. Today was unusual. You were the only party going down today, and they knew you were coming through here, so they thought I could let you know about the problem here instead of waiting for you to get to the ranch. I'm really sorry."

"Well that is just great. So, because of your mistake, my husband and children are hiking without a permit in a canyon that may get a flood."

"It seems so."

What now? How can we tell my husband and kids to get them to come back?"

"I'm sorry ma'am, but I don't know what the Superintendent would want to do now. The best thing for you to do is to go to the Visitor's Center and try to get what information they have there. It's probably not as bad as it seems. Try to stay calm and drive carefully. The road is narrow and dangerous. I'll call the Visitor's Center and let them know you are coming."

"I can't believe this!" Marie was muttering under her breath as she accelerated past the station. "This can't be happening! Her mind was in the fully focused worry mode at this point and she had forgotten about Larry in the car behind her. She was racing down the road almost as fast as her imagination, or at least as fast as the narrow winding road would allow, with Larry struggling to keep up. When she did remember him, she realized that Larry probably had no inkling of what was going on, but she did not want to take the time necessary to stop and explain it to him now.

"This is the one aspect of the hike that David was most concerned about," she told herself. "That was the whole point of stopping at Park Headquarters this morning even though we didn't need to. Now an hour and thirty minutes later the information is one hundred and eighty degrees opposite what they told us. Either these people are incompetent or this has got to be a mistake."

Marie questioned if the ranger at the gate knew what he was talking about. Maybe he was mistaken about everything. But that did not make sense; if he was misinformed, how would he have known about their car and permit? Obviously, he had obtained that information from someone; after all, he had their license number waiting in the booth when she pulled up. Even though she did not want to believe the ranger, she knew he was probably correct.

She glanced up and to the left. The high cirrus clouds to the south now took on an ominous look. She knew that any storm would come from that direction. She accelerated again and continued to move as quickly as she could on the narrow winding road with Larry following in the sedan, oblivious to the development.

The first clear indication Larry had that something was amiss was when Marie pulled into the Visitor's Center. After parking, Marie quickly explained to Larry what the ranger told her at the East gate. Marie was no longer in denial. During the drive, she had plenty of time to accept the fact that the weather had turned, that the hike was off, and was now focused on how to get her husband and children back up the canyon as quickly as possible. Marie and Larry entered the Visitor's Center determined to resolve the problem, went directly to the information desk, and asked to speak to someone who could explain the status of the weather and hiking in the canyon.

The ranger at the desk expected them. "Good Morning. My name is Jason. Are you the party the hiking permit was issued to?"

"Yes," replied Marie, "but the ranger at the East gate told me the Weather Service changed the danger level and that the permit had been cancelled."

"Yes, I'm afraid that is correct. The latest weather report shows a high probability of severe thunderstorms late tonight and tomorrow morning. We have upgraded the hazard level in the canyon to "extreme" and we cannot allow hikers in the Narrows with that high a flood potential."

"But he didn't tell us until we had already dropped off my husband and two children at the ranch! They have been hiking for nearly an hour now!"

Jason frowned. "Yes, the gate told me. This is unfortunate," he said. "But they should be all right. When they see the weather tomorrow, they will know to get high and wait out the storm."

It began to dawn on Marie that as far as the ranger was concerned, this was the end of it. They were just going to let her family continue down the canyon without warning them. Jason had turned away to help another visitor at the counter.

This infuriated Marie. "Look," she said in a direct commanding voice, glaring icily at the ranger behind the counter whose attention refocused on her, "my family has no idea that there is a problem with the weather. Only three hours ago you told us the weather was fine when we stopped here for the sole purpose of checking on the weather. Next, your ranger at the east entrance did not stop us on our way out to drop them off at the trailhead. Further, you did not send anyone to the ranch to tell us of the development and stop my family from starting the hike. Last, my husband was the only survivor of a disastrous flood that hit this canyon in 1961. And now you are going to tell me that you are going to leave them on their own, without warning them in any way? It may not even rain in the park, and if it does not, they will not know to take refuge. What happens if they get to the middle of the Narrows before a flood comes?" Marie was so angry that she was trembling, but she maintained her composure in spite of her seething anger.

Jason listened politely to her argument and silently considered what she had said. "Did you say your husband was the survivor of the 1961 flood?" he asked.

"Yes."

"Do you have your copy of the permit?"

"No. My husband took it with him down the canyon. I didn't think I would need a copy."

"Wait over in one of those seats," he directed, pointing to a row of chairs against the large picture window to the left of the desk. "Let me talk to my supervisor about the situation." He left, disappearing behind a partition, and Marie and Larry sat down with their back to the window to wait as instructed.

Jason walked down a short hallway to a computer station where he accessed the permit record. Printing a copy, he then walked to a back office filled with old World War II vintage file cabinets with papers piled on top of them. He went directly to one of the cabinets and searched until he found a large folder filled with old news clippings. He thumbed through a short stack of articles until he found the one he sought, and examined the contents briefly, comparing the name in the article with the name on the permit.

Finding what he was looking for, he pulled out the article, re-filed the folder and went back toward the front to where the superintendent's office was located.

He stuck his head into the office. "Earl, we may have a problem here," directing his remark at the figure seated behind the desk.

"What is it?" Earl was exasperated; he had been interrupted so many times already this morning he was beginning to think he was never going to get anything done.

"The party we issued the permit to hike the Narrows is here at the counter."

"So what? Just tell them they can come back another time."

"The problem is that only the drivers are here. They dropped the hikers off at the ranch."

"What?"

"The gate called us awhile back and warned us that they had not passed on the message to the group until they were coming back from dropping them off. At first, I didn't think it was enough of a problem to warrant us sending Sam and Keith after them. But now I'm not so sure. We may want to make an exception in this case."

"I should have known better than to have trusted the gate. We should have sent Sam and Keith to the ranch in the first place."

"That's true. But what are we going to do now?"

"They're in the canyon. They'll just have to look out for themselves. Why do you think this should be an exception?"

"They also stopped in to check on the weather just before we got the updated report. We told them it was okay."

"We can't guarantee the weather. You know what park policy calls for. Hikers are on their own after starting a hike. There is no way we can guarantee the weather for even a relatively short length of time." Earl was right; those hiking in the canyon had to assume responsibility for their own safety. The Park Service did not have the personnel to baby-sit each of the visitors to the park. It would be impossible to expect rangers to chase after hikers whenever the weather changed, especially considering the number of trails that would need to be covered. Further, it made no sense and was not good public policy to endanger Park Service personnel in addition to hikers by sending them down canyons that might flood. The only sensible way to approach it was to put the responsibility for hiker safety on the hiker. All the literature distributed and hiking permits issued contained such warnings. Earl was irritated that he had to call this to Jason's attention.

"Just one more thing before you decide. This may be a little more complicated than normal. The lady tells me that her husband is the survivor of the '61 flood."

"No Way. You're kidding."

"No I'm not. I checked. The name is the same."

"Well, isn't this a revolting development. How could this be?" Earl was beside himself. The 1961 flood was the worst in the history of the Park, at least in terms of the loss of human life. There had been many floods that had repeatedly wiped out farms, livestock, and road improvements over the years, but in none of these had so many people died at once. Even worse, the scout troop hiking the canyon had little warning of the impending disaster. Now the only survivor of that flood was in the canyon again with the threat of a flood?

"Here, take a look. The names match." He handed the article and permit to Earl so he could inspect them for himself. Earl took the documents, quickly examined them, and shook his head back and forth in disbelief.

"Jeez, can anything else go wrong?" Earl did not think so. No wonder Jason was pushing the issue. "Let me see if I have this straight. They got a permit. They stopped in to check on the weather, and we told them it was going to be good. We did not stop them on their way out, and we didn't send anyone out to the ranch to warn them. And last, the guy is the only survivor of the worst flood the park has ever seen?"

"That sounds about right."

Earl buried his hands in his face and shook his head again. He knew he should have stayed home that morning. After a moment, he breathed a frustrated sigh and looked up. "Well, Murphy worked overtime to get this one to conform to his law so thoroughly. What do you think we should do?" he asked Jason, who was waiting politely for his decision.

"I don't think it would be a good idea to let them go. We made too many mistakes, and even if we had not, having the "61 survivor involved in another flood now would be an incredibly big story. We would get beat up in the press pretty badly. Of course, the chances of a real flood are slim, but I do not think we should take that slim chance. Your right, Murphy's law seems to be operative here."

Earl knew Jason was right. If ever there was a situation where whatever could go wrong would, this seemed to be it. "That's what I think too. But can Sam and Keith catch them? They have a pretty good head start."

"I'll see when they started down," Jason said as he started back to the front.

Meanwhile, Marie was getting more impatient by the minute. The ranger had been gone for what seemed like hours although it was really only five to ten minutes. Time seemed to stand still, and Marie imagined David and the kids had traveled several miles during the time the ranger was wasting time in the back offices. Looking out the windows, she could see the sky; the clouds moving stealthily up from the south had crept closer and were now visible from the window. Marie looked away.

Jason came out of the back office and approached them. "How long has it been since they started the hike?"

"Nine thirty." Marie was relieved that he seemed to be considering doing something.

Jason looked at his watch; it was ten forty five. He excused himself and walked behind the partition and back to the superintendent's office.

"It has only been and an hour and fifteen minutes. They can catch up if we get them over there right now."

"Good." The superintendent was relieved. If the '61 survivor and his family were caught in another flood, the political consequences could be disastrous, even if none of them were hurt. There certainly would be a national uproar against Park management and the mismanagement that lead to the family being caught in another flood

Jason returned to Marie and Larry who were still sitting impatiently in the lobby. "I've talked to the Superintendent of the Park, and he has agreed to waive our standard procedure in view of the circumstances," he informed the relieved mother. "We have two rangers who patrol the back country. If you wish, I can have them go down the canyon and try to catch up to your husband and children before they get too far. They know the canyon and are in excellent physical condition. They should be able to overtake your family easily. This means you will need to pick them up at the ranch where you dropped them off because they will be coming out the way they went in."

Marie agreed immediately. A feeling of instant relief washed over her when told that the rangers would find David and the children and bring them back.

The information was reassuring. With the rangers going after David and the kids, there was no longer a reason to be alarmed. There was also no reason for Larry to be here, so Marie told him to return to Hurricane. She would go back to Chamberlain's Ranch to wait for David and the kids to come out of the canyon.

Marie doubled back over the road she had already traveled twice that morning. Driving slower than she had on the way to the visitor's center, she arrived at the ranch and parked. She could see dust to the west from a vehicle that had apparently crossed the river and was going down the road beyond where she was permitted to travel. "Good," she thought, "the rangers have already started after them." With the expectation that her husband and kids would be coming up the trail in a few hours, she decided that this would be a good time to take a nap. She was tired from the early start that morning and from the mental stress of the last two hours. Adjusting the seat to its reclining position, she laid her head back and soon was fast asleep.

Jason contacted Sam Parkinson and Keith Kowalski, the backcountry rangers, by radio as directed. Communication was tenuous in the park because of the terrain and lack of consistent cellular network in the vast wilderness stretches of the Park, but he had managed to get through and tell the two rangers what had happened. They accepted the assignment to find the party of three and have them hike out the way they came in, up the North Fork of the Virgin River.

Even though the task was unusual, they recognized that this was an unusual circumstance. Sam and Keith really did not mind the assignment although they were frustrated that they were now required to chase the family down because the knucklehead at the East gate did not do his job. At least they didn't need to walk as far as normal. Headquarters had informed them that the hikers had started walking at nine thirty from the river ford, and authorized the rangers to drive to the end of the road to reduce the head start the family had.

The rangers anticipated catching up with the family soon for several reasons. Although the family had a good two and a half hour head start, they could shave a lot of time off the chase. First, they were able to drive from the river crossing to Bullock's cabin where the road ended. That alone cut an hour off the lead. Second, they were experienced hikers who were familiar with the most efficient route down the river. In addition, the family should be taking it slow down the canyon, enjoying the scenery. Last, they expected that the family would stop for lunch, and that would allow them to close the distance even more while the hikers stopped and ate. After all the addition and subtraction of time, the family's lead could be cut to an hour. Sam and Keith both thought an hour would be easy to make up.

They were already in close proximity to the ranch, and soon had crossed the river and were driving down the road through the ranch toward Bullock's cabin. They quickly covered the few miles between the river crossing and the end of the road. They parked their four-wheel drive vehicle just below the cabin and prepared to start down the canyon.

Sam and Keith had their emergency packs and walking sticks. They did not think they would need anything for such a short trip and took the packs only as a precaution. They also took their cellular phone even though it was very unlikely that the phone would work in the canyon. Electronic signals could not make it through the millions of tons of rock. It was difficult to anticipate any problems that might arise to complicate the expedition. They expected to catch up with the family quickly and double back.

Soon they were fording back and forth across the river, maintaining a rapid pace in spite of the high water level. They passed the same landmarks as always and mentally checked them off to measure their progress. This hike was routine for them. They also paid close attention to the sky, particularly to the north over Cedar Mountain, looking for evidence of the coming storm. At this point, there was nothing other than cirrus clouds approaching from the south.

Chapter 4

Unforeseen Events

David, Austin, and Rebecca hiked along quickly together for the first two hours. The river meandered through the narrow valley as it flowed gradually downward. They were walking on the south side of the river almost due west with the morning sun at their backs. The road also wound around the narrow valley, rising a little here and there, but overall descending steadily downward toward the unseen canyon. At this point the floodplain was a large and beautiful meadow that extended nearly the width of the valley. They followed the dirt road for about two miles without the need to cross the river again.

As they walked along in their waterlogged shoes, each down step forced a small jet of water from every opening in their shoes, making a squishing noise. Then when they lifted their foot, the vacuum created in the shoe sucked air in to replace the water. It was a strange sensation. Little by little, the steady repetition of walking forced all the water from the first ford of the stream out of their shoes. By the time they crossed the river again, their shoes and socks were nearly dry.

The heat was already oppressive. Their packs seemed to grow heavier as they progressed down toward the narrow valley. They had started with jackets on over their shirts, but as the temperature rose, the extra layer of clothing became intolerable. Taking off the jackets, they stuffed them in the double layer of plastic garbage bags in which everything that needed to stay dry was packed. They proceeded, but it was still uncomfortably hot. For the time of year, this heat is normal in the Southwest, but it still isn't fun. They walked along in silence.

David began to appreciate the advice Paul had given them about what to take to keep the weight of the packs down and to make the hike easier and more comfortable. If walking downhill on a dirt road with what they were carrying was this difficult, the most demanding part of the hike would be unbearable with excess baggage to carry.

They had brought only the essentials. Each of them had two changes of light clothing designed to help retain heat. Hypothermia, even in the hot summer, can be a serious problem because of the amount of time spent in the water and the lack of sunlight deep in the canyon. Because cotton products adsorb water readily, they had brought only synthetic fabrics sprayed with a water repellent coating. None of them wore jeans.

The food for eating along the trail was as light as possible, yet nutritious. They had quantities of beef jerky, trail mix, granola bars, candy bars for quick energy, snack desserts, and hard tack candy. Because of weight and the fact that all debris was required to be carried out of the canyon with them, they did not bring any canned goods. Empty cans were much heavier than paper or plastic waste.

In addition to clothing and food, they had each packed a Swiss army knife, first aid kit, water purifier, cameras, a fifty-foot section of rope, and four liters of water. Their sleeping bags filled the remainder of the internal frame backpacks purchased for the hike. They sealed all clothing and bedding, plus anything else they did not want to get wet, in a double layer of plastic garbage bags. Sleeping in wet clothing or a wet sleeping bag would not be fun. Even with the waterproofing, some water always found its way into what they were trying to protect; but not much so they should only be a little damp that evening.

The remainder of their gear was either worn or hand carried. They wore comfortable synthetic walking shoes with high tops ideally suited for the kind of hike they were attempting. The shoes were flexible enough for walking in water, but sturdy enough to support their ankles and would dry quickly. Each hiker had a six-foot section of the round two inch dowels used for closet construction. These made efficient walking sticks and were necessary for fording the river, especially through deeper sections.

David had been tempted to bring his nine-millimeter handgun. His practice was to take a gun on expeditions such as this, and not having this protection concerned David. He had been taught at a young age the importance of self-defense against all animals, both the four-legged and the two-legged kind. Ultimately, while hefting his firearm and its considerable weight, he had decided not to. Besides, he understood that the Park Service strictly regulated who goes down the canyon, so bringing the gun seemed unnecessary. "It's probably illegal to carry the weapon in the park anyway," he thought as he replaced it on the shelf of his closet the night before. Reading the rules earlier at the Visitor's Center had confirmed that firearms were prohibited in the Park.

"But how does the Park Service regulate who is going down the canyon?" he asked himself, returning to his thoughts about security. He realized that they had not spoken to a ranger since they checked in at the Visitor's Center early that morning. No one had been at the turnoff to Chamberlain's Ranch, or at the drop-off point. With a little apprehension, he concluded that anyone could start hiking down the river, with or without Park Service permission. "Still," he thought, "what criminal is going to work so hard for basically nothing?" It could not be a very lucrative criminal practice. Tourists on the Strip in Las Vegas would be much easier targets in a considerably less hostile environment.

Occasionally they passed old and weathered human artifacts. Traveling further down the valley they eventually reached a small clearing in which sat an abandoned cabin, which was identified on David's map as Bullock's cabin. Its wood frame was dried and cracked, all visible metal had rusted, and the roof had collapsed into the interior of the cabin. It seemed small and lonely, and belonged to another century. Further down were a collection of old abandoned farm implements, also rusted and useless. A dilapidated fence ran along the side of the valley, its builder and purpose forgotten. The area appeared to be devoid of any contemporary human presence other than the well-worn road upon which they were walking. For that matter, they had not even seen any cattle since starting the hike.

David thought that the area might be too lonely. He had expected to see other hikers along the way, but they were the only group making the hike today. He was a little concerned about getting out of, or getting help into, the canyon if they had an accident. If other groups were in the canyon, it would be easier to communicate news of an emergency downriver. "But," he thought to himself, "there were three people in our group, so even if one of us is injured, one can stay with the injured person while the third goes to get help".

The overhead sky was still clear, but David could feel an increase in the humidity. In addition, the air was getting hazy. He let himself worry briefly about the weather again, especially because of the increased humidity, which tends to rise with an influx of southern air and is often accompanied by monsoonal thundershowers. However, he quickly dismissed the thought and accused himself of being unduly paranoid. Thus assuaged, he allowed himself to proceed. He did not mention his anxieties to his children for fear of seeming overly obsessed with safety concerns.

For her part, Rebecca was wondering again, "what in the world am I doing here? Why did I let my dad talk me into this?" She was hot, sticky from the increasing humidity, and getting angry. The early morning wakeup call was catching up to her and she was beginning to think that nature was not all it was cracked up to be. Apparently, there were cattle in the valley because occasionally they would come across large cowpies in the road, some of which were fresh with flies swarming around them. "Eeewww! Gross!" she said the first time her nose was assaulted by the smell. She would hurry past them as quickly as she could.

Rebecca had grudgingly agreed to come. The deal to go to California was too much to pass up; but now she was regretting it and beginning to think that her father had conned her. He had not told her it was going to be hot, miserable, sticky, dirty, and exhausting. They had not even gotten off the road yet and she was miserable! Her feet were already killing her because of the stupid wet shoes she was walking in, and she had broken a nail when she stuffed her jacket into her pack. Her father had said that this was going to be fun. Fun? Hah! I'd have more fun in a torture chamber. "I should never have agreed to come," she tersely muttered to herself.

"Are you okay Rebecca?" her father asked kindly.

She turned to him and said, "Of course. I'm fine," and gave him her "It's okay," look. Her father still thought he could read her mood from her eyes. She still wanted him to think he could even though he did not have a clue. The deception was useful at times for getting what she wanted.

She desperately wanted to turn around and go back, even though she knew her dad would have a hissy fit if she did. However, she knew her mother was not back at the drop-off point. Her father had planned the perfect crime. The only way she could get back to the comfort of civilization was to go through the gauntlet that was the canyon. If her friends at school saw her like this, she would be so mortified that she would have to kill herself.

What was the point anyway? They could have seen everything on television from the comfort of their home and not have had to walk around in squishy shoes. And why had they stood in the middle of the river back there? She couldn't believe how old-fashioned and out of touch with reality that her father was. He had actually made her stand in the middle of some freezing river in the middle of nowhere because of some stupid tradition. She had long been convinced that the Marine Corps contributed to the mental derangement of her father. This was just more proof of it.

Her resentment grew more intense by the moment as they proceeded down the road. She could be having fun with her friends, watching TV, playing video games, or doing any one of a number of fun things if she were at home. The fact that she constantly complained at home about there being nothing to do and that they never did anything interesting was immaterial. This couldn't be anyone's idea of fun, except maybe a masochist. Obviously, her father was.

He was a control freak too. He never allowed her do anything she wanted. He had so many rules (all of which she was expected to remember and obey, as if that were possible) it was ridiculous. What he really wanted was to control everything she did. They (her mother was a control freak too!) would not even let her go to the Prom last year because she hadn't turned sixteen yet! It just was not fair. All of her friends got to go. She might as well be in prison. Her parents were such worrywarts. Just because she went to a school where gangs and drugs were everywhere, they wanted her to be suspicious of everybody. They just did not understand. By now, she was so upset that a dark cloud seemed to form directly over her head.

Austin's attitude was much the same; he also wished he hadn't come. He was tired of hiking all over the countryside. To get the hiking merit badge in the Scouting program, he had gone on enough hikes to last a lifetime. Now here he was on another one. Moreover, he wasn't even going to get a merit badge for it! He wished he had not taken the time off from his job. He needed to save enough money for a car more than he needed to take this trip.

It wouldn't have been so bad if his best friend could have come with them. Wayne, with whom he had been friends since he was nine years old, was fun. He was a tall, athletically gifted African-American and his presence would have made the trip at least bearable, and maybe even pleasant. However, Wayne's mother said he couldn't come. She thought it was too dangerous. Austin had originally agreed to come on the hike only because he thought Wayne was going to come with them. Now it was just himself with his dad and sister, and he felt as though he had been cheated.

The small and increasingly sullen and worried group continued to descend the road until it ended where the valley gradually narrowed to a wide canyon. The meadow was gone, replaced by sagebrush and junipers, and red sandstone walls rose nearly vertically from the floor to fifty or sixty feet in height only a short distance downriver. The floor of the canyon narrowed to a few hundred feet, and the river meandered along the floor from slope to slope to wall.

For the first time since they left the car, they were forced to ford the stream immediately after leaving the road. Then after another fifty yards or so they were forced to ford it again. The shock of the icy water, no longer just ankle deep, on their nearly warm and dry feet and legs forced a soft intake of air from all of them. Both Austin and Rebecca were now firmly convinced that this trip was a major mistake and it would be their father's responsibility if they died of exposure and exhaustion. The children dreaded the thought of how bad it was going to be in this freezing river for the next two days.

The vision of the couch at home in front of the television was looking better even to David as he crossed the river. Maybe he was too old for this sort of thing. But he couldn't say anything to the kids that would make it seem like he was anything other than happy. He could feel the tension from the children, and Rebecca's "It's okay" look and verbal assurance had not fooled him. Behind the false facade, he could see that she was aggravated, as was Austin. If they thought their father was having second thoughts about the hike after getting them past the point of no return, they might be tempted to pull their ropes out of their packs and string him up. "Maybe I shouldn't have put so much pressure on the kids to come," he thought.

Peering down the canyon, David could see that from here on, much of their time would be spent in the river. The canyon had become increasingly constricted as they descended, and of course, he knew it was going to get worse. Looking down into the maw of the canyon, he sensed danger, a premonition warning him not to continue. For a moment, he paused and considered turning around and going back to the ranch.

"This is ridiculous," he thought. "Get over it!" he said angrily to himself, thinking he was still trying to avoid the canyon out of his historic fear. He tried to banish the thought of danger from his mind. He did delay continuing however.

It was early for lunch, but he was already hungry and decided it might be a good time to sit down and eat. Here the canyon still provided level areas good for stopping and resting. Such places might be harder to find later. It took no persuasion to convince the kids to stop. Even though they were both surly, they were hungry enough to get enthusiastic about eating. David wisely refrained from asking them what was wrong, knowing they were having second, third, and fourth thoughts about the hike. A little break might put them in a better mood.

They climbed a short distance up the slope on the south side of the river to a large pinion pine under which they shed their packs, and removing the lunches of jerky, trail mix, and water, they ate and drank at a leisurely pace. David was not going to encourage communication at this point; fearing that a conversation would result in an argument about going back. Therefore, they ate with only a minimum of essential communication. None of them were in a hurry to get back in the river. Anyway, they were on schedule for reaching their assigned campsite at the confluence of Deep Creek and the North Fork of the Virgin well before it got dark, so there was no rush. After eating, they rested for about fifteen minutes before proceeding.

By the time they finally finished repacking the remainder of their lunches and the small amount of garbage generated, forty-five minutes had gone by. Resigned to their fate, they started down the canyon again. David silently and gently cursed himself for coming when he had to again ford the river; the water came up past his knees and was so cold that it took his breath away. He was not alone; his kids were reacting to the cold water as well. They were also silently and not so gently cursing him under their breath. However, the initial shock quickly wore off as their bodies adjusted to the chilly water swirling around their legs.

The water rapidly cooled them. As the canyon constricted the layer of air just above the river, chilled by the water, retained an invigorating briskness that was ideal for hiking. Now protected from the summer heat, both Rebecca and Austin's resentment abated somewhat. They were no longer miserable. It was not so bad after all. They were discovering the fun of walking downriver with the current gently pushing them along in cool and beautiful surroundings. After awhile, walking in the water no longer felt unusual, but felt like they were coming home to an environment some ancient ancestor had crawled out of eons ago. They were starting to feel comfortable in it.

Rebecca was now feeling some remorse for the harsh thoughts she had about her father earlier on the road. She wished she would not get angry so easily. Even when she was furious with him, she knew her father really only wanted what was best for her, and when she judged him harshly for actions he took, which were clearly in her best interest, she felt guilty. She had great parents, and she knew it, even though they did not often do what she wanted them to.

Rebecca also concluded that what she thought she wanted was not always what she really wanted. Some of her friends had started dating early and were pressured to please the boys they were dating. As a result, they were now the mothers of small children, and the fathers had left them for greener pastures. Rebecca was determined not to fall into that trap. For the purposes of appearances, she blamed her parents and their rules for her lack of a one on one romantic relationship, but secretly she relied on those rules to do what she wanted to do anyway. Her parents were her best excuse to stay out of trouble and achieve her goals. Besides, her dad was fun even though (or perhaps because) he cheated when they played the slamming game.

They forded the stream constantly now as the gradual sloped canyon gave way to ever-higher sandstone walls that steadily constricted until the floor of the canyon was only seventy five to one hundred feet wide. The river had little room to meander now. Opportunities to walk the banks alongside the river decreased, and they spent a greater percentage of their time in the water, at one point passing a marker showing they had entered the Park.

The river was extraordinarily noisy now. At first, it sounded like a gurgling brook, but as the stream became deeper and narrower, the rapidly rushing water drowned out most other sounds. David, Austin, and Rebecca could only communicate with each other by speaking loudly.

Fording also became more difficult as they got further down the canyon. The water was deeper, frequently up to mid-thigh, but occasionally up to the waist. Crossing the river became a battle between them and the current while trying to negotiate their way over the moss covered rocks. Walking over the jumble of large rocks on the bottom was treacherous. It was easy to place a foot down only to have it slide, making it hard to maintain footing. In addition, the current was strong enough to take an adult down. Bracing themselves with the walking sticks they brought enabled them to cross, albeit slowly and carefully.

David had not remembered the hike to be this difficult this early. Even though he had been much smaller the last time he passed through this part of the canyon, he did not remember the water going up to his waist. He knew that the water level was higher than normal due to all the rain early in the spring, but he had not considered the implications of it. The hike was becoming much more strenuous than he remembered. He was tiring more than he thought he would have, and at this rate, he would be exhausted by the time they got to Deep Creek.

David began to trail behind his children, who had more stamina and were more impatient to get downriver. Wanting to get to the campsite as soon as possible, they focused on getting back and forth across the river. David was getting tired, both because of the strenuous hike and because he had already been awake for many hours. In addition, he was slower because he stopped frequently to photograph and enjoy the beauty of the canyon.

The view was now truly spectacular. At one point, an arch high above the canyon floor, spanning about three hundred feet, captivated him for several minutes. Pulling out his camera from its watertight plastic container, David took a picture of it, and when he started back downriver his children were no longer in sight, having gone around a bend in the river. He was upset that they had gone so far ahead of him and decided to scold them when he eventually caught up to them. Even so, he smiled to himself as the incongruity of the situation dawned on him. "I must hasten after them," he thought, "for I am their leader."

When he finally got around the bend, he could see his children about a hundred yards downriver. He was about to call for them to wait, which would have been an exercise in futility because of the noise from the river, but then saw that they had caught up with another group of hikers and were talking with them in a small clearing on a slightly elevated bank. "Good," he thought with delight, "someone else is on the trail today after all." He figured the kids would talk to them there until he caught up.

David started toward the group. He could see that there were five hikers in the other group, all of whom appeared to be male. They were standing and talking among themselves, although the river drowned out any other noise.

They apparently had not seen him. Then he noticed that they all had shaved heads; instinctively he was alarmed.

"Skinheads? What are skinheads doing here?" he asked himself.

"What are you asking?" he retorted to himself. "They have just as much right to hike the canyon as you do." In the past few years, a number of skinheads had migrated to Southern Utah, seeking refuge from less tolerant areas of the country. Though the people of Southern Utah were not wildly enthusiastic about a group composed of a significant number of paranoid racists in their community, they tolerated them because they kept to themselves and did not cause problems. The attitude of the area in general was to live and let live, so the sight of skinheads in the canyon was nothing out of the ordinary.

Then David remembered that his was the only group who had taken out permits to hike the Narrows that day. These people must be going down without a permit. The lack of control over the trailhead at the ranch above probably encouraged many to hike without permits, so he figured they were guilty of ignoring rules, a common occurrence in an over regulated society.

Just as David's unease began to decline, all the men in the group except one suddenly backed away from Austin. David could now see that he was pointing something at his son. The hand jerked backward as a weapon discharged and Austin crumpled to the ground. He saw Rebecca scream, but neither the sound of her cry or the report of the handgun reached him; along with the roar of the river it was swept downstream, toward the Narrows.

Chapter 5

Kidnapped

Bart could see the two people coming down the river toward them clearly now. They were both young, and it looked like and man and a woman. The couple was working their way through the river and had not seen them standing on the riverbank yet.

"Let's hide." After thinking of his brother's warning about hikers identifying them, he was inclined to try and make sure nobody other than the object of his anger saw them. He started to move up the slope, but after looking around, he could not find anything that would cover them.

"You're wasting your time." Bill had a smile on his face that stretched from ear to ear. "It's too late. They are going to see us, and unless you want to waste the entire trip, we have to kill them." His voice could not contain his excitement at the prospect, and Bart's uncertainty about what to do was delicious revenge for his earlier slapdown.

"Maybe we'll just forget about the whole thing." Bart was very nervous about the entire plan now. Too much could go wrong.

"It's easy Bart," Bill encouraged. "We'll take care of them, and then we can just wait for the rangers like Archie suggested."

Bart looked at the figures in the water. By now, it was evident that they were just a couple of teenagers, and one was a strikingly beautiful girl. "But it's just a young couple. They haven't hurt us."

"That's even better. We can have some fun waiting for the rangers."

Bart was initially repulsed by the thought of assaulting the girl, but as he watched her and considered the possibilities, he became aroused and began to rationalize Bill's suggestion. "Bill may be right. If any witnesses identify us, the chances are good that we'll get caught."

"Now you're talking! Let's do it."

"I said maybe. I haven't made up my mind yet."

"And just when do you plan on making up your mind?"

"Soon!" Bart snapped the last comment at his brother. "Sit down and we'll see what happens."

The entire group sat down and waited. The two were very close now but still had not noticed them. The couple continued downriver, using their staffs against the current, too busy to look up. The boy was in front with the girl close behind. Bart looked upriver searching for anyone else. He could see no one.

The skinhead's camouflage clothing blended well with the shadows in the canyon, and the two hikers had drawn even with them before noticing them on the bank. The first to see them was Austin. He was at once alarmed at the sudden appearance of five skinheads in camouflage sitting by the side of the river.

"Hello," Austin said as casually as he could. He just wanted to go by as quickly as he could, so he kept moving.

"Hi," returned Bart. He was eyeing the girl who had stopped just below the bank they were resting on to see to whom her brother had spoken.

"Nice day for a hike." Austin instantly regretted his comment. He did not want to say anything that might lead to a conversation, but it was too late and the words were already out of his mouth.

"Yeah, it is." Bart was still debating within himself what he was going to do. "The canyon looks great this time of year."

"This is the first time I've been here, so I wouldn't know how it looks any other time." Austin was still moving and had just passed them. Rebecca had not spoken, and had started again after her brother. She did not like the way these guys were gawking at her, especially the short guy with beady eyes. He gave her the creeps.

"Why don't you stop awhile and talk?" Bart was still looking at the girl. The more he looked, the more he reasoned it would not be a good idea to let them go.

"No, we have to move on. We want to get to our campsite before dark." Austin was even angrier with himself now. He did not think he wanted these people to know they were camping in the canyon. However, the packs on their backs probably told the skinheads that already. Still, he decided not to say anything else.

"Come on, stop and talk for awhile. We haven't seen anybody else all day. Have you?"

The question brought to Austin's mind the fact that they were the only ones who had permits to hike that day. These guys were in the canyon without a hiking permit. He was even more nervous now.

Even more alarming to Austin was the skinhead's observation that they had seen nobody else. "Why did he say that?" Austin wondered to himself. He suddenly felt exposed and vulnerable, and wished he had not gotten so far out in front of his father. He was extremely worried now, and was determined to get past the group as soon as possible.

"No. Just our group. Nobody else. But we really need to keep going. See you later." Austin quickened his pace, hoping desperately that they would not see them later. Rebecca had independently come to the same conclusion as Austin, and now was trying to catch up with her brother.

Bart watched them. He could see that the two were scared, trying to get away from them as fast as they could. That clinched it. He made up his mind. If these two kids talked to the cops, he and his followers would be history, especially with the long look the girl had taken. She could pick every one of them out of a lineup. His hand went to his waistband and pulled out the nine-millimeter while he ran forward on the bank until he was even with them again. Brandishing the weapon, he said, "I really want you to stop and talk." His tone made it clear he was no longer asking.

Austin looked back and his heart sank when he saw the gun. His eyes briefly darted back down the river, away from the skinheads, and he briefly considered making a run for it. But it was hopeless. It was impossible to move fast enough in the water to get out of range before Bart would shoot him. Even if he could, he could not leave Rebecca who was behind him.

Bart saw the desperate glance downriver and made sure the young man knew he was serious. He fired a single round into the water just in front of the boy. "Don't even think about it. Get up on the bank. You too," he said, motioning to the girl. Rebecca had screamed when the gun fired, and she was terrified.

Austin and Rebecca came out of the river and up onto the bank. Immediately the entire group surrounded them. Only the one giving the orders had a visible weapon; the others seemed to be taking their cue from him. Rebecca stood behind Austin, trying to keep him between Bart's now ruthless eyes glaring at her.

"Why didn't you want to talk?" demanded Bart.

"We're just hiking down the river. We wanted to keep going," Austin's voice cracked with stress.

"It seems to me that you were being rude. I just wanted to talk to you."

"I didn't mean to be rude. I am sorry, but I didn't mean anything by it. Look, can we go?"

"I don't think so."

"What do you want?"

"I want my country back! I want all the Jews to walk into the ocean and die! I want a nation led by good white people who will not cave to those who conspire to enslave us! I want a lot of things, but I don't think you are going to help me get them!"

Austin was shocked by the sudden irrational verbal assault. "What do you mean? What does this have to do with us hiking in the Narrows?"

"You stupid kid. The government is taking over. They are going to send all of us to concentration camps. One-world government conspirators are in cahoots with our government, and they have decided to enslave us. Every government stooge in the country is in on it."

"Are you kidding?" Austin allowed himself to be distracted by the stream of venom. "My father works in government. He would never do anything like that."

"Your father works for the government?" Bart's eyes widened dramatically and assumed an even wilder look. "Then kid, not only are you not a part of the solution, but you're a part of the problem." He raised the weapon even with the boy's chest. "Do you know what else I want?" he said in a menacing tone.

"No!" Austin's response was not to answer the question; he was in a panic, trying to will the skinhead to put the gun down.

Bart took it for an answer though. "I want to kill you." And with that he pulled the trigger, shooting Austin once in the chest at point blank range. Austin went down in a crumpled heap and lay motionless on the ground.

Rebecca screamed again and instinctively tried to collapse onto her brother. This was fruitless, for immediately two of the men grabbed her arms, one on each side of her. She resisted ferociously, kicking, twisting, and throwing her body from side to side as violently as she could to try and break free. "Daddy!!! Help!!!" she screamed as she struggled.

Bart turned to her, pointed the weapon straight at her mid-section, and said in a low, menacing voice "Hold still or I will shoot you." One look at his eyes told her he would. She gave up, sobbing uncontrollably, still calling out desperately for her father.

"Daddy?" thought Bart. He looked at the teenager lying motionless on the ground and quickly concluded he could not be her father. He frowned. That meant that there was someone else he had to deal with, who could not be far behind. Looking upriver, he saw a figure coming toward them. Obviously, this was the father. Was he armed?

Seeing the man propelling himself toward them as rapidly as possible, Bart reacted with characteristic suspicion and fear. "We can't stay here now," Bart said, concluding that the father could have a weapon if he was charging toward them instead of running away. He had to have seen his son go down and knew they had shot him. The father could not possibly be stupid enough to come after them if he was not armed himself.

Bart quickly concluded there was too much risk in meeting the father's charge head on. They were not yet within pistol range, and Bart decided to keep it that way until they could get odds that were more favorable to them in a firefight. Bart concluded they could run ahead of him and take care of him later. "We will have to postpone our fun till later. The girl's father is coming down the river and he probably has a gun. He wouldn't be charging us if he didn't"

Everyone else grumbled, even so they quickly put on their packs and started downriver. They put Rebecca as close to the middle of the group as they could, with three in front of her and two behind. In a moment, they were around a bend in the river traveling as swiftly as they could with the distressed girl.

Out of view of David, Bart stopped and grabbed Rebecca's arms. "You know I will shoot you if you make my life difficult in any way don't you?" he said in as menacing a tone as possible. "You come along without any fuss or fight or you will die. Is that clear?

Rebecca shook her head, but she was only vaguely aware of what was said. She was in shock. In a few short seconds, her life had been turned utterly upside down and inside out. Her brother was dead and she was being taken against her will. Her father was behind her and couldn't help. She was alone among vicious malevolent people who obviously had no qualms about killing. The gravity of her predicament forced her mind to stiffen and think.

As they headed downriver, the skinheads angrily berated Rebecca because her father worked for the government. She listened silently to their scathing remarks about how evil the government was, knowing that any argument could result in harsh punishment. The skinheads ranted on about how they were not going to sit still and watch while good people and their rights were trampled upon, and how Blacks, Jews, Hispanics, Environmentalists, and who knows how many other groups, had succeeded in taking over the government. A fanatical tirade, logically disjointed and contradictory, it continued for some time until the skinheads themselves grew weary of it. Unable to elicit a reaction from Rebecca the killers turned their attention to the difficulty of the hike.

Rebecca had paid little attention to the political diatribe. She was thinking about what her captors had said back on the bank and the implications began to dawn on her. What kind of "fun" was he talking about? She began to suspect that the skinheads had malicious intentions from the time they saw her and Austin. "They had probably intended all along to shoot Austin and have 'fun' with me," she concluded. The realization infuriated her. Her expression hardened. She was determined to escape and exact revenge upon these murderous monsters.

"Aren't you a cute one?" one of the men said as he put his arm around her from behind. He started to put his hand up her shirt.

"Bill, leave her alone! We don't have time for that now, you moron!" Bart commanded. "We need to get far enough ahead of her father to set up an ambush. We can't have any loose ends hanging around." At first, Bill instinctively rebelled against the command of his brother. However, he soon realized that Bart was right, the father was just upstream, and he would have to postpone his gratification.

Rebecca, shaken again by the man's overture, was even more alarmed by Bart's statement. They were going to ambush and kill her father! She realized that when she had called for him in her panic she had given vital information to her abductors without thinking about the implications for her and her father. "Don't panic. Say nothing. Don't tell them anything else!" she whispered to herself. If she had not called out for her father, they might have thought she and Austin were alone.

On the other hand, the reason they were heading downriver instead of remaining on the bank to have "fun" was undoubtedly because of the potential threat her father posed. The leader had said they had to "postpone their fun" when talking about her dad coming toward them because they thought he might have a gun. She understood that she had temporarily saved herself at her father's expense. "What have I done?" she asked herself. But after thinking it through, she realized it wouldn't have mattered anyway. They could kill her father there or downstream in an ambush because he had nothing with which to fight back.

Rebecca speculated as to whether anyone could know to send help. She knew that her family was the only party scheduled to go down the river and would not be missed until late afternoon the next day. Even then, no help could be sent until the next day, and it would be too late. "A search party will not find anything except bodies. These jerks have planned this well," she concluded to herself.

The hopelessness of her and her father's situation began to overwhelm her. The urge to escape and warn her father suddenly overpowered her reason, and, without thinking of the futility of the attempt, she turned around and tried to make a run for it back upriver. The current doomed the attempt; it was much too strong to walk against, let alone run. The only thing she accomplished was to run into the arms of the same man who had attempted to fondle her earlier.

"I wouldn't be in a hurry if I were you," said Bill. His eyes gleamed with a sinister light.

Rebecca twisted and broke loose, turned back and moved downriver again. Bill laughed at her helplessness. The tone of his voice had frightened her and made her realize that she was one of those loose ends that could not be left hanging around. They were going to kill her too, but not until they'd had their fun.

"Maybe I can outrun them, get far enough ahead to hide and let them go past me," she thought desperately. It was certainly a better idea than going against the current.

Rebecca bolted again, this time forward. She angled away from the direction her captors were traveling and managed to get ahead of two of the three skinheads in front of her. However, Bart had been watching and quickly and successfully moved to intercept her. Her break for freedom lasted only a few brief seconds.

The others were laughing at her failed escape attempt, but Bart was not amused. "If you try that again, I will kill you where you stand!" he hissed. Rebecca had the presence of mind to not say or do anything. He then pulled a rope from his pack and roughly tied it around her waist, with each end tied to the men in front and back of her. She had no chance of escaping now.

The group continued silently down the canyon for another hour. Now exhausted, Rebecca could not have escaped if the skinheads had allowed it. The men also were weary from the constant crossing of the stream. The deeper and swifter water was getting more and more difficult for all of them to cross. They had reached the section of the canyon where it occasionally narrowed to as little as fifteen feet; in these sections the water was deeper and more difficult to navigate.

In one of the narrow sections, Rebecca got sloppy with her staff, and suddenly slipped on a large rock in mid-stream. As she went down, the current caught her and started to sweep her away until the rope abruptly tightened. The force of the water against the rope was excruciatingly painful, and it felt like it would cut her in two. Moreover, the powerful current pushed her face down and under the water. Submerged for several frantic seconds, she finally found her footing and came up coughing, choking, and gasping for air.

The two men tied to the ropes bellowed at her for being clumsy and nearly causing them to loose their balance. Nobody laughed at Rebecca's clumsiness, a sight that normally would have been comical to the insensitive louts, for they were too tired. In order to give themselves a rest, they let Rebecca catch her breath for several minutes before they continued downriver.

They finally reached the Fall. Here the river flowed between large boulders wedged between the canyon walls. Trees, rocks, and mud caught between the rocks over countless years of flooding had formed a dam that created the short but powerful waterfall.

The weary group rested briefly while Bart led two of his men, Bill and Rich, to a rock outcrop on the south side of the river that shielded the view behind it from anyone approaching from upstream. He spoke for a short time to them. Rebecca could not hear what they said, but she didn't need to. Bart returned alone and the remainder of the hiking party started downriver again, portaging around the Fall past Bill and Rich who were now waiting behind the outcrop with weapons drawn.

Rebecca knew what this meant, but she was too numb from fear, exhaustion, and resignation to dwell on its significance. She could do nothing to stop them anyway. In her semiconscious state, the river crossings blended into a continuous painful blur. She wanted to stop moving, but also knew that stopping meant pain, degradation, and death. Resigned to the inevitable, she plodded along slowly with the others.

The shadows in the canyon were lengthening toward the east. It was late afternoon and the water was no longer a cool respite from the summer heat. The air was cooling rapidly. Rebecca began to shiver.

Chapter 6

Conundrum

David stood paralyzed from the shock of what he had witnessed, waist deep in water, too stunned to breathe. The implications of what his eyes had seen were too awful for him to accept. It could not be. This had to be a surreal dream, a trick his imagination was playing on him. Had he really seen what he thought he saw?

David rubbed his eyes, hoping that maybe they misperceived the light and images that entered them. He looked again. He could not see Austin. He could see Rebecca screaming and resisting two men who had grabbed her. The man who had shot Austin pointed the handgun at her and she went limp in their arms. He had seen it – was still seeing it! Horror set in. He had just witnessed his son being shot, and his daughter was soon to follow! "Stop – leave her alone!" he yelled as loud as he could. "Rebecca!" He continued, but no one heard him above the din of the river. His first impulse was to charge. He had to get to his daughter and stop them from hurting her! Then he realized that he could not stop them from hurting Rebecca, nor defend himself against that handgun any more than his son had been able to. He was unarmed and helpless!

Nevertheless, he had to do something. He started to rush forward, regardless of the futility of his attack on the armed men. After only a few yards, he stumbled on a rock and went down. Completely soaked, numb with cold and grief, he drifted several yards fighting both the current and his buoyant pack until he could right himself. Standing back up in midstream, he wiped the water from his eyes, but he could no longer see his daughter. The entire group, including Rebecca, had disappeared, apparently around a slight bend in the canyon immediately downriver. Had they shot Rebecca while he was underwater? Had they taken her with them? He had to get to the riverbank as quickly as possible.

He crashed forward, stumbling and falling repeatedly, desperately trying to reach the dreadful bank. The river helped a little, dragging him along as he stumbled. He used his staff more as a pole to vault over obstacles than as a support against the current. With all the energy he could muster, the river's downward pull, and a powerful dose of adrenaline pushing him along, he covered the distance rapidly, hurling himself through the water, slamming against the boulders along the side and bottom, oblivious to anything but the drive to reach what he could not bear to see.

Exhausted when he finally reached the bank, David forced himself to clamor up the five feet to the shelf above the riverbed. There was Austin, lying silent and still on his side; he was motionless. He quickly scanned the remainder of the outcrop; Rebecca was gone. His mind was still churning in anguish; he couldn't accept the reality of what had happened. "Rebeccaaaaa...!!! Where are you?!" he screamed at the top of his lungs, but the sound was swept away by the pitiless river. There was no hope of a response. Panic set in again. He needed to react, but was paralyzed by indecision and assaulted by a torrent of fragmented impulses.

"Dad? Is that you?" Austin's weak voice penetrated his disjointed mind.

"Austin! You're alive!" A wave of relief swept over David. His son's voice jarred him from the paralysis that had stricken him. David rushed to his side and was terrified with what he saw. Austin was bleeding from his mouth and could barely speak. His breathing was labored and raspy, and was frequently interrupted by fits of coughing that expelled blood.

"I'm sorry Dad. The guy was nuts. He shot me for no reason."

"I know. I saw it."

"They took Rebecca. There was nothing I could do."

"Of course there was nothing you could do. They shot you son."

"But I played dead hoping they wouldn't shoot me again."

"And it worked, didn't it? You only have one bullet hole in you, right?"

"Right. But what really worked was your charge. They think you have a gun. They didn't think about me after they saw you coming."

"Well, maybe that perception can help us later. But enough about that for now. We have to treat your wound. Where did it hit you?"

"In the chest. He aimed point-blank at my heart. I can't believe he didn't hit it."

"Okay, let me look at the wound. Don't talk unless you have to. Your lungs don't sound so good."

"They don't feel so good either."

David rolled Austin from his side so he was facing up, his pack propping up his upper torso in an inclined position, with his head bent slightly backward. A single stream of blood pumping from his left side had soaked through his shirt and had flowed down his side, and a large circular patch of blood was expanding to cover his pack beneath the wound. Austin had already lost a lot of blood. Grabbing Austin's T-shirt at the center of the bloodstain, David swiftly tore the shirt apart. A small hole was visible about two inches above and slightly to the left of Austin's left breast where blood was steadily and rhythmically being pumped through the wound, except that with each breath the bleeding stopped while the wound made a gruesome sucking sound. This was perilous; the bullet had penetrated the lung. No wonder his speech was labored.

"Austin, can you put pressure on the wound while I get a bandage?"

"I think so." Austin slowly brought his hand up and David guided it to the small hole in his chest.

"You've got to push down as hard as you can." David was pushing on Austin's hand slightly to ensure a complete seal of the wound. "Your lung is sucking air and you're bleeding pretty badly. If you release pressure, the wound will keep sucking air and bleeding."

"Come on dad, don't sugar coat it for me." David smiled at Austin's weak attempt at humor. But when David lifted his hand, Austin's hand kept enough pressure on the injury.

"Okay, I'm going to check your back now."

David rolled Austin to the side again and felt for an exit wound on his back. His fingers immediately found another hole almost level with but larger than the wound in front. He could also feel small but sharp shards of bone protruding from the puncture. The bullet had completely passed through Austin's body; it was obviously a large caliber weapon. When David found the exit wound, Austin groaned with pain.

"Sorry son. We have to take off the pack so I can get to this bullet hole in your back." David unsnapped the buckle to the pack and pulled the strap over Austin's left shoulder. That action moved the pack off the wound, and David saw that Austin's T-shirt was completely soaked in blood. He tore the shirt away and saw that the wound was rhythmically pumping blood.

"That is just great. Arterial bleeding. Just what we need." David thought to himself as he slapped his hand over the wound to stem the flow of lifeblood.

David said nothing to show how gravely concerned he was. But now every second was critical to his son's survival; he had to stop the bleeding as fast as possible.

David concentrated on what he could do to accomplish that. With his right hand, he kept direct pressure on the exit wound. Fumbling about with his left hand, he opened Austin's pack, which contained his first aid kit. With his free hand, David unceremoniously dumped the contents of the pack on the bank, scattering them until he found the kit. Seizing it, he opened it with his teeth and found four large cotton gauze bandages. Grabbing the first, he tore off the wrapping, again with his teeth, and released pressure on the wound just long enough to slap the bandage over the bullet hole. He reapplied pressure immediately.

The bandage was instantly soaked through with blood, so he quickly took two of the remaining bandages, removed the wrappers, and slapped them on, keeping direct pressure on the wound as much as possible. He dried the blood from around the wound with a dry part of his son's T-shirt, then applied adhesive tape to hold the bandages in place. Only then did he release the pressure on the wound.

"Wha...What...is...happen...?" Austin could barely get the words out.

"I treated the wound in your back and now I'm going to work on your chest."

"I'm....so....dizzy. I don't...think...I..." Austin's voice trailed off, and David saw that he was unconscious.

In spite of the setback, David forced himself to focus on treating the front wound. He moved Austin's hand, and repeated the treatment, folding then slapping the remaining bandage on the wound, then tore and folded what looked like the cleanest and driest section of the shredded T-shirt from Austin's pack to make up for the lack of bandages. David had more bandages in his own first aid kit only twenty feet away, but didn't want to take the time to retrieve it.

The blood soaked through both of the dressings rapidly but was no longer flowing or dripping. The outside edges of the bandages began to darken; the wounds began to clot. No more blood was pumping from either wound, an encouraging sign. Still, would it make any difference? Austin had lost so much blood that he was now unconscious, and that was only what David could see externally. He prayed that the bullet had not pierced the aorta or some other major vein or artery. If so, Austin would bleed to death internally.

Striving to recall his first aid training, David treated Austin for shock, removing his wet trousers, shoes, and socks. He untied Austin's sleeping bag from the pack and tore the garbage sacks from around it. The bag was still dry. Austin had been sure-footed the entire trip and the plastic covering had worked even though the river level had reached the bottom of the pack. David unrolled and unzipped the bag and gingerly rolled Austin on his side while sliding the bag under him. He covered Austin with the bag, zipped it up, then elevated Austin's legs.

"Now what?" David's mind was racing. "What else can I do?" A feeling of helplessness set in as his mind frantically ransacked its recesses for any knowledge that could improve the odds of his son's survival. He couldn't find anything. He checked Austin's pulse. It was still pumping, but he imagined that it was weaker. But it did not matter. Nothing he could do here would improve the strength of the pulse. Gazing somberly at his son, he recognized that Austin's survival was now in God's hands. He could do nothing more than pray for a miracle.

While unrolling the sleeping bag, a small but heavy object had fallen to the ground. After making sure Austin was as warm and comfortable as possible, David went back to the place where it had fallen and retrieved the bullet. It was a copper jacketed projectile, slightly over one hundred grains, and was now grossly misshapen and flattened by the obstacles it had encountered as it passed through Austin's body, especially the rib in his back. It was still slightly warm. After ripping through Austin's body, it had spent its remaining energy plowing through a layer of the sleeping bag.

David looked at the distorted projectile that was responsible for his son lying on his back bleeding and dying. It was amazing that such a small, unobtrusive object could do so much damage to a human body. He looked at his son and back to the projectile, and wished that he that had taken the bullet instead.

For the first time since he had seen his son shot, other than the brief surge of joy upon finding him alive, he felt something other than denial and panic. Anger began to well up from deep within. Looking at the bullet, he saw an inanimate object that could do nothing by itself. Another human had deliberately fired it into his son's body. He was seized by an impulse to catch the person who had perpetrated this heinous act and make him pay. He dropped the bullet to the ground and started toward his pack.

No sooner than he started, he stopped and agonized over the unconscious body. "But how can I leave my son?" he asked himself. "What if a coyote, or even worse, a cougar smells the blood and finds him before I can reach help?" They can smell blood for miles and the unconscious teen would be an easy meal. He had to carry him back upriver to help.

David almost instantly realized this would be impossible. Even if he could carry Austin, which he could not, nobody was upriver. The only direction he could go and expect to find anyone was downriver, and that was many miles and hours away. In addition, there was a murderous bunch of skinheads between him and help down stream. A bunch of skinheads that also had taken his daughter.

"What now?" he asked himself. "Think this through. If I leave Austin he is going to die for sure. If I don't, those jerks will kill Rebecca for sure. They are not going to just let her go after what they did to Austin.

David sorted through his alternatives. If he stayed here, Austin may live, but for how long? He had seen no one else in the canyon. No other hikers were supposed to be in the canyon until the next morning, so he could not count on anyone else coming downriver today. However, even if he went back up the canyon he could not count on anyone being there to help, and it was a thirty-mile walk to the nearest phone. Even if he chose either of those alternatives, Austin could still die.

Even worse, if he went back upstream, Rebecca would undoubtedly die too. It was clear to David that they would not let her live to identify them after what she had witnessed. He also had a suspicion about why they had taken her in the first place, which was just as alarming. Rebecca was a beautiful young woman, and it did not take a rocket scientist to figure out possible reasons why they had shot Austin and taken her.

It seemed to David that going downriver was the fastest way to get help for Austin and perhaps save Rebecca by doing so. If he continued down the canyon, he might be able to free Rebecca and escape down the canyon to the ranger station at the Temple of Sinawava where help could be dispatched for Austin. He just had to get Rebecca and get by the skinheads without getting killed himself. The only weapon he had was the Swiss army knife he had brought. It was no match for a gun. Still, he had to try. It was the best chance for Austin and Rebecca's survival. "But not for my own," he thought.

David was torn with the realization that realistically it didn't matter. "I'm not going to be able to save either of them. There is no way I can reach help in time to save Austin with him loosing as much blood as he is. And five men, all of whom are likely armed, have Rebecca. I have no means of rescuing her. In fact, they are likely counting on me coming after them and will use that opportunity to kill me and that won't be hard. There is no place to hide in this canyon."

The choice was the darkest decision he had ever been forced to make, but he had to do something to save Rebecca. Her death seemed to be a sure thing unless he did something to stop it.

David leaned over and embraced Austin, kissing the side of his face. He then got up and walked over to where he had flung his pack only a few minutes ago, picked it up, and put it on. It was still wet from the frantic race down the river. Taking his staff, he turned and looked at his son for what was most likely the last time he would see him alive.

"I'm sorry son. I've done all I can for you. Until we meet again." he said. Saying a silent prayer for Austin's safety and for the safety of his daughter, he scrambled down the side of the bank and turned west, downriver, toward the converging lines of the canyon.

Shadows were lengthening and stretching eastward. It was now early afternoon. The humidity in the air thickened further, while several miles overhead, unnoticed by the frantic figure moving rapidly down the river, wispy cirrus clouds were creeping up from the south, obscuring the bright sunlight, silently portending the coming shift in the weather.

David moved downriver as hastily as he could. He had to catch up to the skinheads and the only way to do that was to ignore the beauty of the canyon. He focused now only on the quickest and easiest route through the river and down the canyon, not looking up at the canyon walls or the sky. He tried to anticipate downstream conditions and adjust his route to minimize the effect of obstacles. The water at midstream was still waist deep and the current stiff. The time spent in the river increased as the walls of the canyon gradually converged and the banks along each side grew shorter and shorter. He began to encounter very narrow sections of the canyon, although these were short and the canyon broadened afterward.

Occasionally he could see signs of the group that he was chasing, such as patches of evaporating water splashed on rocks and disturbed sand along the side of the river where they had emerged. Progress seemed painfully slow. The only comfort he could take was the knowledge that the group ahead of him was encountering the same difficulties.

"But, I am an old man." His daughter's frequent teasing came back to haunt him. The group of what appeared to be young men was probably fitter and more agile than he was, and so was probably moving faster. They had about a thirty-minute head start to begin with and were moving faster! His heart sank. He could not expect to catch up with them until they stopped for the night. It might be too late to save Rebecca by then.

"What do I do if I catch up with them? What can I possibly do against those odds?" he asked himself. At least one of them had a gun, and more than likely they all did. His mind searched for any possible means of defense against a handgun. The only things he could think of were the knife and his staff. Maybe he could surprise them and disable all of them before one of them shot him. Or maybe he could hit them with rocks. "Fat chance", he thought, knowing that getting close enough to them to use the weapons available to him without their seeing or hearing him was next to impossible.

David thought of Austin's comment when he first got to him. "They know I am following them, and they suspect I have a gun. Can I use this to my advantage?" he asked himself. Try as he might, he could not think of any way the perception would help him. In fact, it was more likely that he would be looking forward to an ambush. If the skinheads thought he had a gun they would try to kill him as easily as they could without endangering themselves.

David began to pay more attention to downriver conditions, looking for places where an ambush could be set up. This was difficult because the entire length of the canyon was one ideal place after another for a surprise attack. The large boulders along the stream and frequent bends in the river and canyon made nearly every nook and alcove on the river suspect.

David began to imagine seeing figures flitting between rocks downstream and hearing suspect noises behind him upstream. "This is ridiculous," he thought after continuing like this for awhile. "If I let the fear of an ambush hinder my progress, I'll never catch up with them." He put the imaginary sightings out of his mind and forged downstream again, adjusting his route to help a little in the event someone was waiting for him in the places ideally suited for the expected attack.

It was late afternoon now, and the temperature had dropped considerably. Occasionally clouds high overhead obscured the sun. It had not been hot since entering the narrowing canyon with the cool air along the stream. Now it was getting cold. He was soaking wet and every time he pushed his way through the waist deep water, it chilled him again. He was also exhausted. He had been awake since three-thirty that morning and had been working his body continuously since nine-thirty. He began to dream of reaching the end of the canyon, but he knew that many miles of arduous hiking lay ahead before he could rest. The thought made him even more tired.

As he worked his way downriver, his mind continually returned to the question of how he could rescue Rebecca. He began to formulate a highly improbable plan, hoping that the necessary conditions for it to succeed would by some miracle fall into place. If the perpetrators stopped that night instead of continuing down the canyon, and if they did not kill Rebecca that night before they went to sleep, and if he could find them, and if they did not set a guard, and if he could get close enough to them without their hearing him after they went to sleep, and if he could find Rebecca easily in the group, and if she could be reached without waking any of them, and if he could free her, and if he and Rebecca could escape undetected, and if they could beat the skinheads downstream that night, they might survive. "That's a lot of ifs," he observed to himself wryly. "This is not going to happen." However he racked his brain, he could not think of any other way to accomplish a rescue other than finding a way to kill them in their sleep. So he concentrated on developing his idea as he continued along, plotting and scheming for success and trying to anticipate problems and develop contingencies for them.

Up to this point on the hike, he had not recalled much from his previous hike down the canyon so many years before. He remembered the arch earlier where he had lingered so long that he was separated from the kids. The remainder was a blur. Besides, he was only focused on getting downstream. However, he was now approaching a place that he remembered.

The Fall. Here the canyon was wider but large boulders on the canyon floor constricted the water into a narrow gorge. Rocks, logs, and driftwood from floods over the years had piled up behind the boulders to form a twelve foot Fall in the river. The river was forced along the sheer canyon wall on the north, with a bank and rocks on the south. Even as he was approaching, from above the roar of the Fall was much louder than the background roar of the river to which he had grown accustomed.

He had planned to skirt around a large boulder on the south side of the river, then up and down a slit between another large rock lying off to the side of the first to portage around the Fall. A well-worn trail demonstrated that this was the normal route. However, he noticed that wet tracks emerged from the river at the same place. He looked forward, seized with fear, realizing that this would indeed be an ideal place for an ambush. His eyes continued up the trail and, sure enough, saw that the tracks separated with some continuing around the portage but others headed directly toward a rock outcrop just off the trail.

David knew that if he followed the portage skinheads hiding in the rocks would shoot him at point blank range. He had to find a different route. However, he could not go back upriver even if he wanted to. Moreover, there was no bank whatsoever to get by them on the north. They would either chase him down, or continue to wait here until it was too late for him to help Rebecca.

He looked at the river. Was it possible to get to the Fall and somehow climb down it to get around them? Maybe he would luck out and they would be asleep. In any case, this was his best hope. He continued downriver keeping next to the river's edge, approaching the Fall from above until he was a few feet above it, standing to the side of the river studying the main current sweeping over the mass of wood and rock. He could see that this was a hopeless route; there was no way he was going to be able to climb down this impossible jumble of material with tons of water falling directly on him.

The next instant he felt a searing pain in his left arm. The sound of the discharging gun reached his ears a split second later, and he grasped that he had not lucked out after all. The impact of the bullet twisted him around to his left and he fell into the water. As bullets splashed around him, the river swept him backward over the Fall.

Chapter 7

Evacuation

Sam and Keith had been hiking for just over an hour. They had started looking ahead, hoping to get a glimpse of people in the river ahead of them. They were still moving as swiftly as when they had started.

Just past the arch high up the canyon wall, they came upon a bank with what appeared to be someone camping on it. Even though there were no designated campsites this early in the hike, they were still relieved to think that they had found the hikers so early. Yet, when they climbed the bank, they discovered only one person in a sleeping bag in a debris field. Calling out, they got no response from the figure in the bag. Sam walked to and knelt over a boy and, pulling the sleeping bag down, saw that the bag contained the motionless body of a teenage boy with a blood soaked bandage on his chest.

"What the...?" Sam asked aloud in surprise. The two rangers surveyed the situation with alarm. Sam pressed his finger against the carotid artery in his neck. "He is breathing and has a pulse, although it's weak," he indicated to Keith.

"Look," said Keith. "Some type of wound has been dressed and he's been treated for shock."

"Look at the bandage. The blood in the center of the bandage is still red, so the dressing is probably less than thirty minutes old. But what is the wound from?"

"We can't remove the bandage to examine it. If we do he'll start bleeding again."

Both of the rangers suspected the wound was not an accidental laceration, and they looked briefly around the site for any clue that could help them figure out what had happened. A pack was lying on the ground, the contents unceremoniously dumped and scattered on the ground. It apparently belonged to the unconscious boy. A first aid kit and the debris from it used to treat the boy also lay in disarray. A walking stick was also nearby. Last, there were many empty beer cans just up from where the boy lay. They continued to search until Keith saw the glint of metal. "Here it is!" he shouted triumphantly, his suspicions justified. The spent nine-millimeter shell casing that was lying on the ground fifteen feet from where the boy lay told them all they needed to know. The boy had been shot.

Taking care not to get his fingerprints on the casing, Keith picked it up with a small twig. It was bright with no corrosion on it. He sniffed and smelled a faint trace of gunpowder. He was confident the casing was from the bullet that wounded the boy. A moment later Sam found the bullet. The casing and bullet were evidence, so he took a plastic bag from his pack, put the bullet and casing in it, and then replaced the bag in his pocket.

"So, who did this?" Sam asked.

"And where is he now?" Keith returned. "Whoever it was, he must have gone downstream. Maybe the kid's father drank way too much beer, flipped out and shot his son. Neither he nor his daughter is here. Why wouldn't they have stayed with him?"

"That's possible. Still, that doesn't make much sense. If he went nuts he would have killed them both wouldn't he? Plus, someone treated this wound, why would he shoot his son and then take care of him?"

"Not necessarily. Maybe the boy got out of hand and he shot him, then treated him because he didn't really want him to die. All we can do is speculate. Who knows why he might have done anything. Right now, who did it is unimportant. We have to try to save this boy. We have to get him to a hospital as fast as we can if he's going to live. A gunshot wound to the chest means there's probably internal bleeding, even if the wound has been treated and the external bleeding staunched."

"Let's see if we can get through to headquarters," Sam suggested. "Maybe we can get someone else to help us." They attempted to call the Visitor's Center, but as expected, there was too much intervening rock. Even if they could have communicated, they would still need to carry him out to where a helicopter could reach them. There was no getting around it; they would have to carry the boy out.

"Which way are we going to take?" asked Keith, already knowing the answer. The easiest and normal route would be to go downstream to the emergency helicopter pad above Big Springs. However, this was not a normal situation. First, Big Springs was at least six hours away going downstream.

Second, if they reached Big Springs they still wouldn't be able to get through to anyone to ask for a medivac chopper. Third, the river would be much more difficult to negotiate as it got deeper, especially with them trying to carry what looked like almost one hundred and eighty pounds of dead weight. Perhaps most important, Keith knew that the person who had shot the boy had obviously gone downstream. They could not be certain of their own safety if they took the downstream route.

On the other hand, they were only an hour from their vehicle just west of Bullock's cabin. Still, that was an hour traveling uphill, against the current and without carrying the unconscious body of the boy. Even so, it was obvious that they could make it in much less time than it would take them to get to Big Springs.

"What do you think?" asked Sam. He had run over the same arguments in his mind and had come to the same conclusion.

"Going upriver will be hard, damn hard. But it will be faster. Besides, some trigger-happy loon is downriver, and I'm not excited about catching up with him. I want to leave him to the Washington County Sheriff."

"I agree. Let's make a stretcher to carry him back to the Jeep."

They hurried to make a stretcher for the wounded boy so they could carry him out. They took the two walking sticks they had brought and set them parallel to each other eighteen inches apart. Then they took off their shirts, buttoned them back up, and threaded the poles through the bottom of the shirts and out the arms. Rummaging through the pack, they found two T-shirts and a sweatshirt that they also put onto the stretcher, using the T-shirts to double the strength of their shirts on the poles and the sweatshirt to make the stretcher long enough to fit the boy's torso onto it. Fortunately, the boy did not look like he was so heavy that he would tear the shirts. They placed the stretcher next to the boy, rolled him on his side, and slid the stretcher under him with him still in the sleeping bag.

They rested a little before beginning, trying to psych themselves for the grueling task they faced. They knew how difficult the rescue they were attempting would be. To carry a body out of the canyon going uphill against the current would take all the strength and stamina they had. It had taken them about an hour to reach the bank where they had found the wounded boy, and it would almost certainly take twice that to get back out, if they could make it at all. Even though they had walked up and down this canyon so many times they could not count, they had never had to carry someone out like this. But the boy's survival depended on them getting him out soon enough to get treatment before he lost so much blood that he died. With the knowledge that this boy's life hung in the balance, they were determined to accomplish what they needed to do to save the boy.

They abandoned their packs, keeping only their canteens and cellular phones. The first time they picked up the laden stretcher, the poles bit into their hands immediately. This was not going to work; they needed something to cushion their hands. They set the stretcher down, retrieved additional clothing from the boy's pack, and wrapped the poles as best they could. Once again lifting the stretcher with the poles creaking and the fabric of the shirts straining and stretching, they balanced the weight between them. For a moment they thought that the cloth might tear under the weight of the body; however, the material was strong enough to hold, and they started the journey back up to their Jeep.

The shock of the cold water on their legs brought home how tough the trip back was going to be. They struggled to stay upright while fighting the current to get upstream. While in the water, they had to hoist the stretcher to their shoulders to keep it out of the water. Even doing that did not entirely work, soon the clothing covering the stretcher was wet and there was nothing they could do to prevent it. They pressed on.

Fortunately, the canyon was not narrow for very long. The banks along the side became wider and longer and the time spent in the river shorter, which made the effort much easier. They stopped for brief moments when they were so tired they couldn't continue, but hated to do so because picking the stretcher back up was almost as painful as carrying it for a hundred yards. At each rest, they would check the boy's pulse to ensure he was still alive. They continued on, gradually progressing up the river.

It seemed like the poles of the stretcher were cutting into their flesh even with the cloth padding. The only way to relieve the pressure on a hand or shoulder was to shift the weight of the load back and forth. They developed a routine; shifting the stretcher's weight from their hands to their shoulders, then to carrying it high with both hands. The intervals between these load shifts quickly decreased to a point where no matter what position they used it hurt immediately. The shoulders and hands of both men felt like they had been carrying an unbearable weight for hours on end. Finally, they had to stop and take a long rest.

Sam and Keith set the stretcher down and collapsed beside it, panting for air. They laid long enough to catch their breath with their eyes closed and aching bodies pleading for them to stop. Neither of them spoke a word to the other; it was unnecessary work.

After several moments, they roused themselves and each drank greedily from their canteens, gulping the cool precious liquid and letting it sate their thirst. They considered where they were and how long it had taken them to get here. An hour had passed from when they had started. Even with the heavy load and the uphill work, they had made a lot of progress. They had covered about two thirds of the distance to the Jeep, and they were encouraged with their progress. They rested ten minutes, and then lifted the stretcher and started again after taking another long swig from the canteens.

The water they had would be all they would get. Drinking water from the river was not an acceptable alternative unless as a last resort. Most of the streams in the Western United States have Giardia and other bacteria in them that do very unpleasant things to the digestive system, so even though they were surrounded by water they could not drink it without treating it first. And they couldn't do that as their water purification tablets and water filters remained in their packs back where they found the boy. The canteens were two thirds down and they knew they had to make it last until they got to the Jeep.

The effect of the rest wore off quickly. In no time, the poles again pressed into their shoulders and hands regardless of the stretcher's position. They did not stop again for a long time for fear they would not be able to start again, but after covering about half the remaining distance their arms and legs involuntarily collapsed, dumping the boy's body unceremoniously onto the riverbank. Though they were very close, they had no choice but to rest; their sore aching bodies would not let them continue.

They rested silently, drinking about half of the remaining water and trying to muster enough strength to finish the journey. Keith checked the boy's pulse again, almost hoping he would not find one. If the boy were dead, their agony would be over. They could leave him and go for help. The pulse was still there. After another ten minutes, they started again.

Trapped in the Narrows

The last leg of the hike was incredibly difficult, even though they were only infrequently in the water. What had started out as a hundred and eighty pound load now felt like it was six hundred pounds. They stumbled forward, saying nothing, now even too tired to shift the load off their tortured shoulders. They plodded on, focusing only on putting one foot in front of the other and dragging their bodies and the body of the boy forward. Time seemed to be suspended, as if they were trapped in a time warp that would keep them bearing this burden forever.

Finally, they struggled up a small incline gasping for breath and saw the Jeep about fifty yards in front of them. At last, they had made it. Seeing the Jeep and the end of their travail gave them just enough strength to cover the remaining distance. Setting the stretcher down, they opened the doors of the vehicle, and slid the body into the back seat with his legs dangling out of the window. They buckled the body in.

Sam examined the boy again. He was very pale now, but there was still a pulse. He was still alive. However, the pulse was weak and his breathing even more labored. Sam did not think he could make it to a hospital for treatment before he died. He was discouraged that in spite of their Herculean effort he was probably going to die anyway.

Though the connection was weak, the cell phone worked, and Keith contacted headquarters. He was able to communicate their situation and confirm the dispatch of the medivac chopper. He directed that the chopper inbound from St. George would meet them on the road where the pavement started. Because the Park was a de-facto wilderness area in which overflight was severely limited, the chopper would be approaching from the south to avoid park airspace. They could shorten the distance it would have to cover by driving toward it.

They jumped into the Jeep and started back up the road as fast as they could, while at the same time trying to minimize the impact of the rough road. They both drained the water in their canteens. It had taken them an hour and forty-five minutes to get the boy out of the canyon. As difficult as the hike out had been, especially toward the end, they both recovered quickly.

Marie woke to hear the sound of an approaching vehicle. "Good," she thought, "they're back." It was three o'clock in the afternoon. She had slept

90

fitfully, both because of the discomfort of sleeping on the seat of the car and the earlier stress of the day. She was tired and wanted to get to Aunt Audrey's to rest. Yet, as a Jeep came into view, she could see only two shirtless men in the front seat.

This was odd. "Where's David and the kids?" she asked herself. "And why aren't these rangers wearing shirts?" She thought of the answer to the first question immediately. The Jeep was not big enough to hold all of them. They must be walking up the trail. She was instantly irritated that she would need to continue to wait for them. The answer to the second question did not immediately occur to her; however, the question vanished when she noticed the end of a recognizable sleeping bag sticking out of the window on the driver's side of the Jeep. "Someone is in the bag," she thought as the Jeep drove up.

"Are you with the party hiking down the Narrows?" asked the ranger on the passenger side in a matter-of-fact, no-nonsense tone of voice.

"Yes. My husband and two children left this morning. What's going on?" Marie asked as she got out of the car. A lump was starting to form in her throat; the tone of the ranger's voice communicated an emergency.

"Can you identify this person?" asked the other ranger. He was getting out of the vehicle and walking around to open the door.

Marie was now very alarmed, and beat the ranger to the door. She opened it, saw the pale drawn face of her son, and nearly fainted. Gasping for breath, the sight of Austin's ashen complexion surprised her so much that she could not respond.

The ranger who had gotten out brought her back quickly. "Is this your son?" he asked forcefully. "We don't have a lot of time to get him to a hospital if we want to save him"

A weak "yes" was all she could muster. Bewildered by seeing her son in this condition, she was only dimly aware of what the ranger said.

"Follow us. A chopper is meeting us up the road where the pavement starts. You can fly to the hospital with him if you want."

The driver closed the Jeep door, obscuring Marie's view of Austin's face. The shock of losing sight of his face jolted her back to reality. Understanding what she had to do, she nodded and returned to the car as the ranger got back in the Jeep and started up the road. By the time she had turned the car around the

Jeep had a good lead and she was forced to drive faster than normal to catch up with them.

Her mind was racing again. "What has happened to Austin? Where are David and Rebecca?" she asked herself. Her mind frantically grasped for ideas, none of which were comforting. She imagined the worst. "David and Rebecca are dead and Austin is going to die." Her mind revolted against that thought. "They are not dead!" she insisted. "Everything is going to be just fine!" She did not believe herself though.

She followed as close to the Jeep as she could. Dust billowed up from the dirt road from the turbulence of the Jeep and choked her if she got too close. She stayed close enough to keep them in sight through the dust.

They arrived at the pavement, pulled off the road and stopped. The chopper was not there yet. Marie got out, locked the car, and went to the Jeep to be with her son. She worked her way in beside the pale figure lying in the back seat, and held his head next to her. Her mind was clear now and she had a torrent of questions to ask.

"What happened?" she asked.

"We don't really know," replied the driver. "We were looking for your family to warn them about the weather when we found this boy with a gunshot wound lying next to the river."

"Gunshot wound!?"

"It is definitely a gunshot wound."

"Where were my husband and daughter?

"He was alone. We did not see anyone else. Your husband and daughter must have gone downriver. We didn't pass anyone going down. We had to carry him out of the canyon about a mile and a half. Someone did treat your son for the wound. Whoever did that certainly saved his life, or at least prolonged it." The ranger winced at the error he had made in tacitly admitting the boy did not stand much of a chance of survival in front of his mother.

Marie refused to acknowledge the remark. "My husband must have treated him. He is trained in first aid." She wondered why David would treat Austin and then abandon him while he was in such bad shape. If the rangers had not come along, Austin would still be lying alone beside the river.

With this thought, she suddenly had the impulse to hug the two men who had brought her son out of the canyon under such difficulty. "Thank you. Don't forget", she said, looking at the two men with gratitude in her eyes, "you saved his life too. If you had not brought him out he would still be hours away from help." Mustering some hope, Marie was not yet willing to concede her son's death.

"That could be," the ranger said modestly, his attention distracted by a distant noise. The sound of a helicopter echoed in the distance as it approached from the south. He walked to the middle of the road and waved his arms as it came into view. The chopper saw the vehicles and landed on the pavement, whipping clouds of dust into the air from the edges of the road and making speech communication impossible.

The rangers pulled Austin away from his mother and the Jeep and put him into the chopper. Marie climbed in after him. The medical personnel in the chopper immediately began working on him, putting an IV in his arm and starting a blood transfusion. Keith spoke briefly to the pilot and gave him the spent cartridge and bullet he had retrieved earlier at the site of the shooting. The pilot took off, leaving the two rangers standing in front of the two vehicles. They were quickly out of sight.

In spite of the speed they were traveling, it seemed to Marie that the trip to St. George took forever. It was as though she was suspended in time as she examined the pale face of her son. The reality of the severity of her son's wound began to force her to accept the real possibility that he might die in spite of her will. That he was close to death was undeniable. She did not ask any questions of the medical staff. The grim expressions on their faces as they worked did not instill confidence in the eventual outcome of the battle they were fighting to save his life. Consequently, she sat silently, trying to stay out of the way and watching them work. She wondered if she would ever speak to the still figure lying on the stretcher again.

The chopper set down at Dixie Regional Medical Center. The body of her son, trailing tubes and IV pouches, was whisked from the chopper, onto a gurney, through the emergency room doors, and back to a waiting surgeon. Marie got out also and followed the gurney to the emergency room, but she was not permitted to follow Austin into the surgical unit. The nurse directed her to the waiting room. "He'll be okay," said the nurse soothingly, who looked like she did not believe her own words and certainly did not convince Marie.

Marie sat in the waiting room, the minutes slowly ticking by. Here she had time to think through what might have happened. She knew David did not have his handgun, so they must have met someone else in the canyon. That person, or persons, shot Austin, and if Austin had been shot, David and Rebecca may have been shot too. However, if that were the case, who bandaged Austin? David was alive at least long enough to treat Austin because it didn't make sense for the person who shot Austin to have then turned around and treated the wound, unless it was an accidental shooting.

But if it were an accidental shooting, David and Rebecca would have stayed to help carry Austin out. Why did they continue on the hike? The only logical reason Marie could think of was that after Austin had been shot David had treated the wound, and then had a more compelling reason to continue downriver than to carry Austin out. The only reason compelling enough for David to leave his wounded son would have been Rebecca. The implications of this realization dawned on her. David was probably alive, and was trying to help Rebecca. But from what? Or, more to the point, from whom?

"Excuse me ma'am. Are you the mother of the boy with the gunshot wound?" The uniformed police officer standing in front of her abruptly interrupted Marie's train of thought.

"Yes."

"I'm Sergeant Cooper of the Washington County Sheriff's Department. Can I ask you some questions about what happened to your son?"

"I'll cooperate in any way that I can. I think the rest of my family might be in trouble."

"That is a definite possibility, but first things first. How would you describe the relationship between your husband and your son?"

"They were close. Both of them are stubborn and headstrong, but they love each other, and show it often."

"Does your husband have a temper?"

"Sometimes. However, he never allows his temper to control his actions. If he is angry he normally waits until he calms down before he acts." Marie was irritated about the direction of the questions but decided to continue to give direct answers to get past the officers suspicions quickly.

"Does your husband drink, and did he take beer with him on the hike?"

"No to both questions. He does not drink, not even beer. And he deliberately avoided taking cans of anything to minimize the weight he had to carry."

"Does your husband own a handgun?"

"Yes, he has two. One is a twenty-two pistol he received from his father when he was young and the other is nine-millimeter semi-automatic he received for Christmas several years ago."

"Did you say a nine-millimeter?" the officer raised his brow.

"Yes."

"Where are the weapons?"

"At our home in Las Vegas. My husband was thinking about bringing one of them on the trip, but it wasn't allowed by Park Service rules." Marie was visibly upset now. "If you are thinking that my husband shot my son, I can assure you that is not what happened. My husband would never deliberately hurt his children." Marie forcefully expressed her opinion with all the conviction that she had in her being.

The officer looked at her closely. He saw the fire in her eyes and concluded that she was as certain of what she said as anyone could be. He decided to pursue a different line of questioning. "Do you have any idea who could have shot your son?" he asked.

"No, but I know it was not my husband. He bandaged the wound after it had happened. Why would he have shot him and then tried to save him if he was trying to kill him?"

"Maybe he lost his temper and then regretted it afterward."

"What obviously happened is that someone else shot Austin, my husband treated him, and afterward there was something more important for him to do downriver than carry Austin out. The only reason David would have left my son in his condition was if my daughter was in more danger than my son was! Do you understand the implications of what I am saying!?" The tenor of her voice rose during the exchange, and she shouted the last question at the officer.

Sergeant Cooper decided not to question Marie further. He had as much information from her as he needed right now anyway. He suspected that the father had shot the boy in some sort of domestic squabble. In his experience, those who were close and should be most interested in the victim's best interests most often committed these kinds of crimes. He always suspected family first.

However, telling that to the distraught mother was not the astute thing to do. Besides, her theory was plausible. Given the circumstances, it might not have been the father.

"It's possible," he agreed in a patronizing tone. "We'll send a party downriver to try to find your husband and daughter. I don't know how far they will be able to get tonight, and the threat of rain will make traveling in the canyon dangerous tomorrow. One thing is certain, whoever shot your son has to come out one of two directions, and we'll be waiting for him or her when he or she does."

The officer turned and left. Marie glared after him as the officer strode quickly down the hall and out of sight. She struggled to contain her rage. "How dare the police think David would shoot his own son?! He wants to pin the shooting on David to avoid a little work! What kind of a police department are they running here?" The angry mental tirade continued for some time after the officer had disappeared. It was clear to her what had happened and she was infuriated that any other possible scenario was being considered. Her wrath with the retreating officer was mixed with, or perhaps fed by, the overpowering sense of helplessness she felt knowing the predicament her entire family was in, and that as she sat here alone in the hospital, she could do nothing to help at all. For several minutes, rage, fear, depression, and grief, got the best of her, and she sobbed uncontrollably.

In due course Marie wrested control of her wits from the destructive emotions feeding her grief. She approached the nurse's station and asked how the operation was going. The nurse had not received any information from surgery yet, so Marie returned to her seat to watch the clock, wait, and wonder.

The Park Service has proprietary jurisdiction within the park for minor crimes and offenses. However, serious crimes were the responsibility of the County. The Park Service notified the Sheriff immediately upon learning of the apparent crime in the Park. Following the recommendation of Sgt. Cooper, the Sheriff assigned four members of the SWAT team to go down the canyon and find the person or persons who had committed the crime. This was dangerous, not only because there was some trigger happy lunatic in the canyon, but because of the weather. The prospects for severe thunderstorms the next day

96

were real, which added a new element of danger to an always-dangerous type of search.

The team was composed of a Sergeant, who was to lead the team, and three other officers, all of whom were well equipped for their jobs. One was a medic with enough gear to treat most medical emergencies, and another a communications specialist with state of the art satellite equipment for communicating in the canyon. The last officer was familiar with and carried detailed maps of the canyon. He was their guide. All the officers were armed with M-16's and nine-millimeter handguns. In addition to other gear incidental to their mission, they had wet suits to keep them warm.

Sergeant Cooper briefed the team; giving them all the hard information he had. A group of three, a father with his son and daughter, had started down the canyon this morning at about nine-thirty. Nobody else was supposed to be in the canyon. Shortly thereafter, the son was found with a gunshot wound from a nine-millimeter weapon by rangers looking for the three hikers. The father owned a nine-millimeter weapon, and although the man's wife insisted that he had not brought the weapon with him, he obviously could have done so without her knowledge. Someone had consumed a considerable amount of beer, which could explain why the father may have lost control even though the wife insisted that he did not drink. At this point, although Cooper was inclined to think the father was responsible, because the mother had adamantly claimed that her husband would not have committed the act, and that both her daughter and husband were in danger, the team was cautioned to expect anything.

An hour later, the SWAT team started downriver from Bullock's cabin, having been choppered to the site. The group was lightly equipped and planned to get downriver as far as possible that night, get up the next morning and sweep down the canyon picking up anyone they found for questioning. Because traveling in the canyon was so dangerous with the weather, an exception to Park Service rules had been granted, so the plan called for them to be airlifted out from the helicopter pad above Big Springs the next morning. Besides, they needed to get anyone they found out and to St. George for questioning as soon as possible. If all went well, they would be back in St. George by mid-morning the next day.

The group traveled swiftly. They reached the site of the shooting at seven o'clock and examined the area for evidence. There were too many footprints recently made to be able to tell what or how many people they might be able to anticipate. The rangers had made a mess of the site and the equipment preparing to carry the boy out. They could find nothing else and soon continued down the river after taking numerous pictures from assorted angles and bagging evidence.

Although they were making good time, they had gotten too late a start to expect to make it very far. As daylight waned and eventually failed, they continued into the night. The sergeant hoped to make it to the Fall and camp there for the night. Then they would continue in the morning.

They eventually reached their destination and quietly pitched camp above the Fall on a flat area which provided an adequate campsite. The group quickly fell asleep under the now starless sky, unaware of the solitary motionless body only a few hundred feet down the river.

Chapter 8

Ambush at the Fall

"Maybe he chickened out?" Rich questioned. He and Bill had been waiting at the Fall for just over fifteen minutes. Afternoon shadow had covered the bottom of the canyon, and close to the river the air was cool and invigorating. It was a serene and comfortable setting, but the two men were not concerned with comfort. They were both getting impatient and tired of constantly looking upstream, watching for the father to come.

"I hope not. If he went back upstream we are in serious trouble."

"He should have been here by now. What if he doesn't come?" Rich was plainly worried that the father had doubled back, in which case the cops would be there to arrest anyone coming out of the canyon tomorrow.

"He'll come. Remember, we have his daughter. I know these guys. His emotion will get the best of him, and he'll try to save her."

"But maybe he stayed to help the kid?"

"The kid is dead. Bart shot him point blank in the heart. He was dead when he hit the ground. You didn't see him move after he fell, did you? He won't be able to help the kid, so the only thing he can do is to try to help his daughter. And besides, he's probably so furious with us that he'll come just to get revenge." Bill grinned from ear to ear. "We'll use his anger against him. He'll be blind to us when he comes by." Bill was getting excited at the prospect of the kill.

"What if he has a gun? He won't try to get revenge without a gun will he?"

"Why do you think we're hiding behind this rock wall, you idiot! We are going to shoot him before he has a chance to shoot us."

"Oh, yeah, I forgot for a minute."

"Now when he comes, let him get to within a few feet before shooting. You wait for my signal. I'll put my thumb in the air like this (giving a thumbs up sign) and we'll both jump and empty our guns into his chest. That should take care of him and his gun if he has one."

"Yeah, that's great. He won't have a chance. I don't want to get hurt though."

"Don't worry; this is going to be safe, for us at least."

"But he's still taking so long. Are you sure he's coming? I mean maybe he just turned chicken on us. Maybe he ran back upriver."

Bill was irritated at Rich's constant circular questions. He had been pestering Bill like a nervous child, prattling on and asking the same questions over and over. This was very unusual; Rich was normally quiet. If Bill had known he was going to chatter on so much he would have had one of the others stay with him instead. Rich's last redundant question really set him off, and he glared at him as crossly as he could, while refusing to answer. Rich took the hint and didn't ask any other questions.

Bill reached into his pack and rummaged through the interior until he found a can of beer. "Time for a snack."

Rich took his cue from Bill and soon they were both pulling long chugs on their cans. They finished the first quickly, and then pulled out another. "How many did you bring?" Bill asked Rich.

"Never mind how many I brought. You're not going to get any of them. I carried them in and I'm going to drink them."

Bill tried glaring to intimidate him, but Rich wouldn't think of it. Bill briefly considered shooting Rich for his beer, but knew that Bart would go ballistic if he hurt one of his lackeys over such a trivial thing. He reached back into the pack and pulled out a can of sausage. Opening it, he began greedily devouring it with his fingers and washing it down with draughts of beer. Rich followed his lead, and they both ate and drank their fill, discarding the empty cans and other debris in the vegetation behind them. By the time they had finished, there was a sizable collection of refuse scattered in the brush. When they finished, they settled in to watch again.

They didn't have to wait very long. Forty-five minutes after Bart and the others left, a solitary figure could be seen coming down the river toward them, crossing the river back and forth as he focused on the route ahead. It did not seem that he was paying attention to what was downriver.

"This is great. He is walking right into the trap," Bill whispered, barely able to contain his glee. They cocked their weapons and prepared to fire.

The man continued downriver. He reached the point where the trail left the river toward the boulders and the portage. He stopped for a moment surveying the trail, then continued down alongside the river instead of coming out.

"He isn't following the trail!" Rich whispered worriedly. "Do you think he saw us?"

"No, if he saw us he wouldn't stay out in plain sight."

"Then why isn't he taking the trail around the Fall?"

"I don't know. Maybe he doesn't know about the Fall. Maybe he's just not paying attention."

"What is Bart going to do if he gets away?"

"Shut up! Don't worry so much. Just because he is off the trail doesn't mean he's going to get away. He's still too close for us to miss. Just wait for the signal." They fingered their weapons and crouched behind the rock wall, nervously watching David's progress.

It was clear that David did not have a gun in either of his hands, although he could still have one in his pack. He was only a few feet above the Fall now.

"Maybe he saw us and he is planning to jump over the Fall." Rich's voice had a very worried edge.

Bill agreed. If he was on to them and decided to jump over the Fall, it would take time for them to get down to where he was, giving the man time to take defensive measures. In any case, the man was not going to get any closer. Bill stabbed the air with his upward thumb, and they both stood up and fired as rapidly as the semi-automatics could, emptying both guns in the process.

The hail of gunfire erupting around the man had its intended effect. The force of the impact of a bullet spun the man around; he was obviously hit. He twisted to his left side, fell, and the river swept him over the Fall. In an instant he had vanished.

"YEAH!!!" Bill screamed at the top of his lungs.

Rich, caught up in the excitement, also shouted gleefully over their successful kill. "We got him! We killed him!" he repeated several times over.

"Yes we did. The world has one less government stooge to deal with now. Let's go find the body!"

They threw their packs onto their backs and climbed over the rock, then scrambled down the chute between the boulders that led around the Fall to come out just downriver from it. As they went, they popped out the empty ammo clips and reinserted full ones. At the bottom just below the Fall an old tree lay diagonally across most of the river, pointing in the direction of the Fall with the end closest to the fall submerged in the river. They climbed out onto the log as far as they could and looked for a floating body, first upriver toward the Fall and then downriver. They could see nothing. They looked directly into the Fall, trying to glimpse any movement past the white curtain of water. They could not make out anything.

"Where did he go?" Rich's voice had the same nervous edge as before.

"I don't know," Bill returned. "Maybe he is hiding behind the Fall. Let's put a few rounds into the water." They both shot several indiscriminate rounds into the pile of wood that constituted the bulk of the Fall. Still, no body came out from behind the curtain of water.

"Where is the damn body?" Bill was getting angry at the lack of a corpse.

"Could he have survived?"

"No way. I shot him three times. Did you hit him?"

"At least twice."

"If the guy has five slugs in him, he's dead. Besides, the fall from the top alone would have killed him. Look at all the rocks he had to land on. And if the bullets and the fall didn't take care of him, he drowned. He's dead. I'm sure of it."

"Maybe the river washed him down before we got here."

"That may be. How fast is the current?"

"I don't know, but it looks fast enough to take him away."

"Let's look for him downriver." Bill crept back along the log to the south bank, then worked his way downstream to catch the body, with Rich close behind. They traveled downstream for several hundred feet, each expecting to find the body behind the next rock or snagged on every log they saw. Finally Bill stopped, thinking intently.

"How could something that big not get hung up on any of these rocks or logs," he wondered aloud.

"The river is moving pretty fast."

"I'm not sure it would matter. I think we need to go back up the river. He might have survived the ambush after all. If he did, we need to catch him in the open."

"Bill, I'm beat. That's the wrong direction. Camp is downstream."

"We're going back!"

Bill's tone left no doubt as to what they were going to do. They both removed their packs and left them beside the river, taking only their guns. Crouching as low as they could, they crept slowly back up the river, watching closely for movement, and preparing to fire if they saw any.

Eventually they came back to the log below the Fall. Climbing out on it again, they searched for any sign of someone getting out of the water. The narrowness of the canyon was such that there were only a few spots to climb out of the river, including a huge boulder that split the water flow. All of these rocks were completely dry.

Bill stood on the log and swore as he searched for any sign of their victim. Rich said nothing. The tirade lasted for several minutes, and when it was done they both left, making their way back downstream to where they dropped the packs. Shouldering them, they continued down the river. In spite of the frustration at not finding the body, Bill was convinced that the man was dead. He was confident they would eventually pass the body downriver, wedged in the rocks.

Rebecca looked up to see they had emerged from another narrow section to where the canyon bottom had widened enough that the bank was wide enough for a large campground. She was too tired to notice another smaller river flowing from the north to join the river she had been in all day. She blindly followed the group out of the river to the left toward a small, flat, sandy spot with a yellow plastic marker that had the number "2" on it, a tent symbol, and a symbol indicating campfires were prohibited. She walked up against the canyon wall where she dropped to the ground, not even taking off her pack.

"We'll sleep here tonight." The others greeted Bart's announcement with relief. Ed and Archie dropped their packs on the ground and flopped down onto them.

"You two, get off your asses, get some firewood, and start a fire. It's going to be dark soon and I'm getting cold."

"But Bart, the sign says we can't have a campfire" protested Archie.

"You have got to be kidding. I've got news for you; if anyone comes, the campfire will be the least of their or our problems." Bart was peeved by the remark.

Ed and Archie groaned at the prospect of having to move their aching bodies. Still, they knew better than to argue any more with Bart, so they struggled to their feet and went off to look for dead scrub brush to burn.

After they were out of sight, Bart pulled Rebecca up, removed the rope and pack, and then tied her hands together in front of her. "I guess this is where the fun begins," she concluded absently, too tired and disconnected to resist. However, the man did not attack her. He pushed her to the ground against the canyon wall, took off her shoes, and tied her feet. He then left her to lay out his own sleeping bag, which he arranged between her and the trail to the river, after which he immediately collapsed on top of his bag. Almost immediately, the rhythm of his breathing signaled that he had fallen asleep.

It began to dawn on Rebecca that maybe she would get a temporary reprieve. The hike down the canyon had been harder than these guys had expected. Maybe all of them would be too tired to want anything from her tonight.

She sat quietly waiting for the others to return with the firewood, trying to change colors like a chameleon to blend in with the background and become invisible. "Out of sight, out of mind," she said to herself. It did not work though. She was still visible when the two returned with their arms filled with shattered pieces of wood left from previous floods. She did keep her head down and avoided eye contact with anyone.

Ed and Archie grumbled about having to work while the boss slept. They piled up some wood haphazardly and tried to light it, but it went out each time. They made so much noise arguing about how to get the fire started that they woke Bart.

"What are you idiots trying to do? Don't you know how to build a fire?"

"I don't," Archie admitted.

Bart swore at their incompetence, got up, and ordered them to construct a fire ring with some rocks. He built a teepee style fire, lit it with a lighter, and the men all huddled close to it to warm themselves.

The sun was low in the western sky and the entire canyon was in shadow. Rebecca was cold too, but the last thing she wanted to do now was draw attention to herself, so she remained silent and motionless where Bart had placed her. She had concluded that maybe she could postpone her torture and death until tomorrow, in which case she had the entire night to think of how to

get away. Her mind was beginning to recover from the exhaustion-induced stupor, and she began to plot
and search for a means of escape. Some heat from the fire radiated out to her, and her clothes began to slowly dry.

The three men ignored her and ate a light dinner of canned meat, trail mix, and beer. They did not speak at all, either because they were too tired to talk or because it was too awkward with her there. Rebecca was hungry, but she still said nothing. Apparently it worked. They paid no attention to her as they thought only of their own hunger and discomfort.

Several minutes after the three had finished eating, Bill and Rich arrived from the Fall with the news that they killed the father following them. They described shooting him just above the Fall and his body going downriver over it. They had not found the body, but they repeatedly assured Bart that he had to be dead because nobody could have survived the hail of bullets they put into him. Bill and Rich were also exhausted, and paid no attention to the bound captive whose body softly convulsed from the silent sobs that inevitably followed when she heard the news.

After eating, even though the sun had not yet set, the rest of the men laid out their sleeping bags around the fire and crawled into them with some effort. It was evident that their bodies were stiff and sore from the ordeal they had just experienced.

Bart came across the camp to Rebecca, pulled her sleeping bag out of her pack, and unrolled it. Throwing it to her, he observed in a malevolent tone that her ordeal would be over the next morning, and then returning to his own bag, he crawled into it. Soon everyone in the camp was fast asleep, and loud labored breathing signaled safety for Rebecca.

Rebecca knew that she was safe only for the moment. Nevertheless, she had a window of opportunity in which she could plan and execute an escape. Yet, even with this knowledge, the silence of the now dark evening was like a sleep inducing narcotic. The low rushing of the river lulled Rebecca into an almost dreamlike state. In spite of her perilous situation, because she was so weary she was torn between giving up and trying to escape. After all, she was tied hand and foot, exhausted, sore, and bruised from the ordeal in the river.

Rebecca was also alone. Her father and brother were both dead. Even if she got away, she did not think she could make it to safety without help and guidance. She was not even sure where safety was. She hadn't paid very much attention to the maps that her father had pored over and memorized. She had depended upon him to know the way.

Rebecca decided to try to climb into the sleeping bag to try to get warm. Her clothes were mostly dry now, but the cold air chilled her. The fire had gone down to a point where little heat reached her. She grabbed the bag and wiggled her feet and legs into it. Fortunately, Bart tied her hands in front of her instead of in back. She was able to slip gradually into the bag by holding it with her hands while she inched her way in. In a few short minutes, she was in the bag and began to warm.

Rebecca evaluated the obstacles to her escape, and allowed herself to be discouraged. To get away she would have to loosen the ropes that bound her. The cords binding her hands were tight, as was the rope around her feet. She could not reach the knot binding the rope on her feet because Bart tied it behind her, and she could not reach the knot on her hands with her fingers. That knot also was tied away from her face, so she could not reach it with her teeth.

Getting free from the ropes was only the beginning. Rebecca then had to get out of the bag, walk out of the camp, and proceed downriver on her own without waking any of the skinheads. Walking out of the circle could wake someone up; her pack would surely make too much noise.

Then there was the problem of walking out alone. She was not sure she could make it down the canyon, which would soon be very dark and forbidding. The very thought of traveling in the dark through the water without being able to see anything terrified her. The river was cold, unlike the now comfortable sleeping bag. She was tempted to give up and let tomorrow bring what it would.

Lying comfortably inside the bag Rebecca realized that in spite of the difficulty, she had to try to escape. No one was going to come and help her. She had to do it now and without any help. She mentally tried to plan each phase of the escape. If she could somehow work the knot on her wrists around to where she could loosen it with her teeth, maybe she could get the rope off her hands. Then she could easily loosen the ropes on her feet. She did not need the sleeping bag or pack. She was just going to leave everything. She would head straight downriver until she saw lights. Eventually she would reach safety.

Rebecca was as comfortable with her plan as she was with the sleeping bag. Her mind went over the scheme several times, each time losing more detail to the fog clouding her conscious thought. She just needed to lie here for a while to get her thoughts straight, but as she tried to sort through the increasingly muddled plan, her exhausted body won and she fell fast asleep.

Chapter 9

Deep Creek

The force of the water crashing down the Fall for uncounted years had scoured a small hole in the rock bottom, so when David came down it was water, not rock, that his body struck. In addition, the impact of the bullet hitting his left arm had twisted him to the left, and he tumbled over the Fall back first. So when David hit the water-hole at the base of the Fall, his pack bore the brunt of the fall. Even so, when he hit, the jolt nearly knocked the wind out of him. He would have drowned had it not been for the soft landing.

David's arm screamed with pain and his back felt like it was broken, but he knew he was dead if the men who ambushed him heard or saw him again. He had to resist the urge to get out of the water and try to treat himself. He had to hide, and he knew he had less than a minute to do so.

"Where can I hide in this canyon?" Glancing downstream, he couldn't see an answer to his question. There was nothing other than sheer walls on both sides of the river. While there were boulders lying on the canyon floor in the river, they could not possibly hide him. Then he looked upstream and saw the thunderous Fall. "I wonder if I can get behind the water." It was his only hope.

As he fell, he had unconsciously held onto his walking stick, which fortunately he still grasped in his right hand. He struggled against the turbulent current, first to regain his footing and then to push himself back upstream, all the while forcing his recalcitrant body to comply with his mental commands. He was successful in spite of the pain, and by leveraging his staff against the current he was able to force his body behind the wall of white water descending from above. He pressed himself backwards and to the side into a small alcove behind the Fall, trying to meld into the rocks and sticks protruding from the wall behind the cataract.

The pain was nearly unbearable and the sticks poking into his body made it worse. David's arm was in particularly bad shape, he could tell he was bleeding badly. The pieces of wood protruding from the dam made it impossible to get all the way behind the crush of water, so its force literally pounded down on his head and wounded shoulder. The pain was excruciating. He managed to break off several of the sticks blocking his way and was finally able to squeeze the rest of his body into the alcove, with the torrent of cascading white water crashing down in front of him.

David put his hand over the wound and pressed down on it to slow the bleeding as best he could in the position he was in, and then waited for the men to come. He could see through the water into the gorge, which was completely in shadow. He started to panic. If he could see through the water, surely they could see him! He had to suppress the urge to break and run; he would have no chance out in the open. He again squeezed back as far as the wall behind him allowed and prayed the failing light in the canyon and the sheet of white water would be enough to hide him.

He heard voices approaching the Fall from downriver. The men had climbed around and down the portage and now were backtracking to the Fall. As they approached, David realized how prudent he had been to stay away from the trail, "It was a good thing I stayed in the water," he thought to himself. "If I had followed the portage trail I would have been a sitting duck, without any place to hide. They would have been so close they couldn't have missed."

Two men climbed out onto an old dead tree lying diagonally across the river and down about thirty-five feet from the Fall. One was a large burly man who seemed to be in charge. The other had a medium build. Both had their weapons at the ready but apparently did not expect to use them. David could see they were talking, and though he could not hear anything, their attitude conveyed that they expected to see a body. However, nothing emerged from the small gorge.

David worried that they would come upstream to look for him. He tried to press closer to the alcove wall, but there was no more space between him and it. It would not have done any good anyway. There was no way they couldn't find him if they came in under the Fall. Nevertheless, they were apparently too tired to fight the current crashing down from above, deciding instead to take a few shots into the Fall to be sure he was not hiding behind the water.

As they began to fire, David was petrified with fear. He tried to pass metaphysically through the rock and tangle of wood to his rear. He was terrified as several bullets struck the wall to his side, one hitting about an inch away from his head and penetrating an old tree trunk. Fortunately, the wood was waterlogged and did not splinter. After expending several rounds, they stopped shooting. Amazingly, none of the randomly fired shots hit him. They waited on the tree for several minutes, undoubtedly hoping a body would float down to them. David did not oblige them. Eventually they conferred briefly, then scrambled back along the log to the bank and ran downriver.

David waited about ten minutes in the event they came back. He was cold, miserable, and in pain, but if they came back and saw him alive his misery would be over forever. Even though that prospect had some appeal just then, he gritted his teeth and waited. He finally concluded it was safe and decided to start down the river again. He struggled out of the alcove, the force of the fall knocking him down and under. His arm screamed anew with pain, and he allowed his pack and the river to sweep him downstream for several feet before he righted himself, still grasping his staff with his uninjured hand.

He righted himself and was about to climb out of the river over some small boulders when he again felt a premonition of danger. The feeling was intense, as if someone was whispering to him that he had to hide, and do it fast. At the same time, he was impressed with the importance of not climbing over the rocks in front of him.

David remembered the feeling he had earlier in the day, which he ignored, and realized instantly that if he had acted on the impulse and turned back, he and his family would be safe at Chamberlain's ranch, or better still in the comfort of Aunt Audrey's home. This time he heeded the warning and immediately turned and forced his way back up the river, once again struggling to get past the wall of cascading water to the alcove. Knocked over in the attempt, he was still able to push off from the rock bottom just enough to come out under the Fall. He pressed himself back into his alcove.

Just in time. He had no sooner squeezed back into the alcove when the skinheads returned. This time they approached silently and stealthily. For obvious reasons, or at least obvious to David, they had not found his body and now apparently suspected that he might still be alive. It seemed that they had hoped to catch him in the open. Had he not returned to the Fall, he certainly would have been discovered. David said a silent prayer of thanks to Him who had given the warning, and was grateful to himself for acting on it.

The two men climbed back out on to the log again, trying to see through the curtain of white water to where David was hiding. It seemed as if were looking directly at him. Even though the sun had descended to where no direct light was striking the river, there was still too much illumination, and he was convinced they were going to see him through the water. Nevertheless, they did not. David was not sure whether it was because of light, luck, providence, or a combination of the three, but he was grateful for whatever was hiding him in any case.

It was evident that both men were frustrated, especially the larger burly man. He seemed angry, as if annoyed that he could not enjoy the tangible results of the kill. He ranted for some time with his eyes darting in all directions, as if an angry lion denied his prey. He especially searched the rocks on both sides of the river, including the boulders David had stood before only a few minutes ago, looking for the telltale sign of water from dripping clothes. There was none. Nevertheless, he never approached the Fall to discover David's hiding place. The depth of the water as well as the swiftness of the current was apparently an effective deterrent. Eventually, after the angry man's temper cooled, they gave up looking and left.

David waited another fifteen minutes. He wanted to be sure that they would not come back again. In time he became confident they would not. Convinced it was safe to come out of hiding, he emerged and repeated the painful process of being knocked down by the torrent and floating downriver.

He struggled downriver for a hundred feet before climbing out of the river onto a huge boulder nearly flat on top that lay in the middle of the river. David's first priority was to examine his wound. To do this he had to take off his pack and shirt, while still trying to keep pressure on the wound. The effort loosely resembled a cartoon character trying to free itself from a sheet of sticky flypaper. Even though his arm was in pain, the effort was so funny that he could not help but laugh at himself and his comical effort. The intensity of his experience at the Fall had made him so tense that it was affecting his judgment, but as he was able to laugh at himself, much of the tension evaporated. He sat on the rock for a time, rejuvenated by the levity of the moment.

David continued to struggle with and finally succeeded in removing his pack and shirt. The bullet had first gone through the uppermost section of his pack and through his sleeping bag. This accounted for the tremendous force of the bullet when it knocked him off his feet and down the Fall. He examined the wound, which he could easily see; fortunately, it was only minor. The bullet had not hit bone, artery, or vein. Even so, it was astonishing how much it hurt.

He unfastened his pack and found his first aid kit, then treated and bandaged the wound as best he could with one hand and his teeth. The pain slowly subsided into a dull throb as he rested

"What now?" he asked himself. If he continued now it would be too dangerous. The experience with the ambush had emphasized how vulnerable he was. Chasing after the skinheads was a fine thing to do. However, what if he succeeded in catching them? Without a weapon, he was helpless.

He concluded that what he really needed to do was to try the plan he developed as he came downriver; that is approach them when it was dark and they were asleep, when he would have a chance to get close without the men discovering him. He also remembered that he was now very close to the confluence of Deep Creek and the Virgin, probably only an hour away with the river conditions being what they were. That was the best campsite in the canyon and is where they would probably stop for the night, if they were going to stop.

What if they did not stop? This thought was truly alarming. Still, it was also very improbable. These people had to be as tired as he was, and to continue all the way downriver tonight was nearly impossible, especially in the dark.

There had been only two men at the ambush. That meant that the other three had continued down the river with Rebecca. If they stopped at Deep Creek for the night, they would be there soon, except for the two who had just left. Was Rebecca still alive? If she were, she would probably remain so until morning. If she were not, it would not matter if he waited here to give them a chance to go to sleep anyway. He decided to wait and rest here.

David suddenly felt a twinge of guilt. Should he continue right now? He was not sure whether he had talked himself into waiting here just to give himself a rest. His body ached from the exertion of the day and from the pounding his body took going down the Fall. His arm, although it did not hurt as much, ached and throbbed. He was soaking wet and the late afternoon air chilled him. Given the situation, he worried that he was rationalizing to justify to himself staying here even though he should go on now. Yet, it did seem logical. The best time to try to get Rebecca away from the abductors would be when they were all asleep. He reaffirmed his decision to stay here and rest.

As he couldn't see any better place to sleep other than the boulder he was on, he didn't move from it. He changed into dry clothes, laid out the wet ones to dry, and arranged his pack so he could lie against it and use it as a pillow. Then he sat down, rested his body with pressure against the side away from the wound, and fell asleep without even looking up. Had he done so he would have seen clouds accumulating high overhead in the twilight.

David awoke with a start. It was pitch black and for a moment he was disoriented. Where was he and why did his arm hurt so much? The question triggered an avalanche of memory, and he was crushed that it had not all somehow been a bad dream that he had just woken from. How long had he been asleep? He looked at his watch and waited for his eyes to focus in the darkness. He saw that it was eleven o'clock. He had slept for almost three hours. He figured that this was as good a time to try his plan as he was going to get. Everyone in the group should be asleep by now.

David packed the now dry clothes he had worn earlier that day into the plastic bag that kept the sleeping bag dry, then carefully and gingerly shouldered his pack. He slowly started downriver again, forcing his lethargic and aching body to move while trying to minimize the use of his wounded arm. The pain in the arm had subsided while sleeping, but now re-intensified with use.

It was bitterly cold. The first time David had to ford, the water stung his now semi-warm body. That and the throbbing of the wound resulted in constant pain. He began to shiver every time he was forced to enter the river. "Why am I not home in bed cuddling with Marie?" he asked himself, wistfully thinking that if they had not come on the hike none of this would have happened. He wished he could remake the decision earlier in the day when he had felt the first premonition of danger.

David stopped. A wave of hopelessness was crashing over him just as forcefully as the Fall had earlier. What was the use in trying? This entire effort was an exercise in futility. Rebecca was probably dead now. He had failed her. He should never have left Austin. The only thing he would have accomplished by having chased after Rebecca was to ensure the death of both his children. He was tempted to end the chase, curl up, and go to sleep. He did not care if he ever woke up again. Waking was nonstop physical and emotional pain, and he was tired.

In almost the same instant, he was repulsed by his attitude. Guilt and shame overwhelmed him as he recognized that he was trying to furnish himself with excuses to give up. Then anger took over. He berated and recriminated himself severely for caring more about sleep than about his daughter. The anger worked. His spirits rose with the challenge, and he resumed the forward slog downriver.

David felt alone. "I'm not accustomed to hiking down through a river in the middle of the night without someone with me," he said to himself. After thinking about this observation briefly, he was struck with how stupid it was. "Well, duh!" he retorted, "Since when have you ever hiked through a river in the middle of the night?" He was torn between being so embarrassed with himself for even thinking the stupid thought and laughing at himself for it. Still, he had to make his way downriver without company, and he missed the companionship of and conversation with his children, strained though it was during their teenage years. "Of course, I'm going to miss the companionship of and conversation with my children for the rest of my life," he thought. The reality of the loss of his son and the probable loss of his daughter was setting in, and the recognition made his isolation that much worse.

It suddenly dawned on David as he plodded along that he was having a conversation, and he was the only participant. Talking to himself was normal, but he was both asking questions and answering them too. "Am I going insane?" he wondered. "I don't think so," he responded. "That I am asking the question is a good indication that I'm not," he argued.

Still, he was uncomfortable with the question. "The condition of insanity is obvious to all except he who is affected by it," he thought, "and with the events of this day, I would not be surprised if I am insane." Still, insane or not, he had to get to Rebecca. Insanity would not help him get there any faster, and neither would it help him after he reached her. He decided he could not possibly be insane after all simply because it was imperative for him to be sane to do what he had to do.

David continued down the river, stumbling more than walking. He could see almost nothing in the dark even though his eyes were as adjusted to the dark as they were going to be. Visibility was so low that he had to grope with his staff and feet for firm footing in the murky river while fighting to keep the current from sweeping him away. He was tempted to use the headlamp that he had packed, but if he did it would be a beacon to anyone looking or watching for him. That would mean instant death. He had to go on in the darkness without the light.

However, after falling and completely submerging because he stumbled on a rock that he couldn't see, he changed his mind and decided to use the headlamp anyway. When he pulled it out of his pack and turned it on, it glowed red instead of white. "That's great," he thought. "I forgot about the red light. Not only will it be harder for a lookout to see, it will also keep my eyes adjusted to the dark. I should have thought of this in the first place." David put the headlamp on and proceeded, and even thought the red light was dim, it was better than nothing. He did not fall again.

He did not feel quite as smart as he had when he had finally manipulated the kids into coming with him. The bribe had backfired and resulted in disaster. Austin was certainly dead by now. This thought brought tears to his eyes, knowing he would never see his son again, at least not in this life. Rebecca might be dead also, and very probably he would soon die too. He forced himself to continue through the gloom of his spirit and the night.

The darkness did seem very gloomy. He looked up trying to see familiar star constellations high in the heavens. The canyon wall obscured most of the sky, but there should be a portion of the visible sky with stars in it. He could discern sky from the rock walls, but could not see any stars at all. He wondered how cloudy the sky was and, for the first time since he had dismissed his concerns about the humidity early in the afternoon, wondered about the weather. However, it was too dark to tell what the atmospheric conditions were, and he convinced himself that some light clouds must have been covering the small section of sky visible in the narrow canyon. He again reassured himself that he had checked out the weather before starting the trip; besides, he had enough to worry about without fabricating additional problems. He continued downriver.

David was trying to make as little sound as possible. If he did find the skinheads, it was critical that he not wake anyone except Rebecca. He was most worried that the villains had posted a guard, which was probable if they were not convinced they had killed him. In that event, someone would be watching for David. In any case, his life depended upon silence and stealth. He traveled slowly and deliberately as much to minimize the noise he made as to reduce the chance of falling in the stiff current. He only partially succeeded; and every sound he made seemed to be amplified off the walls of the canyon like ricocheting bullets.

The black night hindered his progress, and contributed to the racket he was making. Try as he might, he could not control the noise. But he had to control it. He was sure he was getting very close now; a fact confirmed when David could faintly hear the murmur of another stream in the background.

Instantly, David stopped in midstream. The canyon had widened abruptly without him noticing, and visibility had improved. Directly in front, two hundred feet away, was a rock wall perpendicular to the direction he was heading. Lining the river to his left was a large sandy bank strewn with white rock. Light vegetation grew behind the shore. The floor of the open bank extended fifty feet to a rock face parallel to the direction he was traveling, which continued to within one hundred feet of the perpendicular wall. Even in the darkness, he could tell that the river was turning south where it was joined by another stream from the north. He had reached the confluence of Deep Creek and the North Fork of the Virgin River, where the rivers joined forces and their combined strength flowed almost directly south toward the Narrows.

David turned off his headlamp, amazed that it had not been noticed. He scanned the area, looking for any sign of a camp. To his left, tucked up against the rock face behind the scrub vegetation, he detected the dim glowing embers of an unfed campfire. He could not make out any people or tents, but he was confident that it had to be them. Other than Rebecca's abductors, he had seen no one all day. Seeing no movement in the camp, David was relieved that the noise he had made stumbling into the area had not awakened anyone.

As quietly as he could, he climbed out of the river and onto the bank. The smooth, water-rolled rocks along the bank gave way under his feet and made what seemed to him a horrendous grinding and scraping noise. He stopped abruptly, hoping he had not alerted anyone in the camp. Waiting a few minutes and holding his breath, David watched the campsite intently for any movement near the fire. Seeing none, he continued as quietly as possible until he reached the sand behind the rocks. There he walked quickly and stealthily, except for the water squishing out of his shoes, past the sleeping camp to the furthest point of the bank just below where the two streams converged. He took off and laid down his pack, whisked out the Swiss Army knife, and hefting his staff, backtracked to where he could access the camp via a narrow trail through the vegetation.

The squishing shoes and wet clothes rubbing together were making too much noise and David realized he would have to take them off. Even if the wet items had made no noise, he knew that he had to creep around a hostile camp and it would be disastrous to have water dripping from his soaked clothes onto the faces of those whom he did not want to wake. He disrobed to his underwear, shivering in the cold night air. Picking up the knife and staff again, he started up the trail.

He crept slowly and silently toward the embers. It was clear that there was no posted guard. Apparently, his foes were confident that no one would disturb them. In the dim light cast by the dying fire, David could discern six figures laid out in sleeping bags, most of which circled the fire. The number was right.

How could he distinguish which one was Rebecca? She would be smaller, and her sleeping bag was green. He carefully examined each bag visually, quickly working his way around the ring to a small green bag against the canyon wall away from the rest of the group. With an overwhelming sense of relief, David saw a shock of blond hair protruding from the top of the bag, which gently rose and fell with the rhythmic breathing of the figure inside.

Chapter 10

Fight for Life

The emergency team on the chopper worked frantically to keep the boy alive on the ride in from the Park. Austin's pulse had initially been so weak it could barely be found, and he was pale, cold, and clammy. He was in deep shock. The medics had immediately given him three units of blood, which had helped, and he was still alive when he got to the medical center.

Hospital staff was warned to prepare for the incoming patient when the helicopter was dispatched to pick the boy up. A surgical team was assembled and a room prepared. Both were ready when the chopper touched down, and Austin was whisked directly into surgery.

The scene inside the surgical unit was organized chaos. Some nurses hurried to prepare the instruments needed while others removed Austin's remaining clothing. The team of surgeons hurriedly scrubbed as the anesthesiologist gave him the anesthetic and arranged to monitor the patient during the procedure. A nurse placed an oxygen mask on Austin's face to force air into the undamaged lung. In no time at all, even more IV's were sprouting from Austin's arms. In a matter of minutes, they were ready to proceed and commenced the operation.

It was evident to the surgical team that their patient was probably not going to make it. He had taken a serious wound to the chest and had lost a large quantity of blood externally. In addition, the bullet had punctured his left lung which was now so flooded with blood that he was in danger of drowning. The left lung was no longer functioning, so the right lung had to work for the entire body. The wound was at least two and one half hours old: too much time had elapsed for the boy to have a reasonable chance of surviving.

The doctors in the emergency room at Dixie Regional Hospital did not have as much experience treating gunshot wounds as did their counterparts in the emergency rooms of major cities where gang and drug turf violence had transformed many urban hospitals into something resembling M.A.S.H. units. St. George was a small quiet community on the fringe of the Mormon culture region. It was not without drugs and the crime associated with them, but the scale of the problem and the violence associated with it could not compare with major metropolitan areas. This was good for the community but not so good for the teenager who now lay on the operating table, his life depending on the skill of the surgical team.

Performing the operation to the best of their ability, the doctors opened Austin's chest at the wound and followed the path of the bullet through his body. They located each area where there was significant bleeding and stitched it up - not an easy task, for the human chest, particularly the left side, is a mass of diverging arteries and converging veins. It was incredible that no major artery or vein had been directly pierced. However, there were many minor veins that needed repair, especially through the lung. Inserting a large suction needle, they withdrew as much blood from the lung as possible, trying to clear it enough for it to function. After that, there was nothing else they could do except to sew him up, pump antibiotics into him, and hope that they had done enough, soon enough.

Marie remained in the emergency room waiting area for at least an hour after the police officer left. Stricken by the events of the day, she struggled to think clearly through the emotional anguish that weighed her down. What should she do? Austin was still in surgery, there still was no word on his condition, and the nurse had no idea how long it would take to finish. Marie wanted to remain at the hospital until the operation was completed and she was confident that Austin's life was no longer in danger.

She also wanted to be at the canyon tomorrow when David and Rebecca came out. After struggling with despair at the thought of losing David and Rebecca, she resolved that no other possible alternative would be included in her plans for now. In order to be at the canyon tomorrow she would need the car, currently parked on the road to Chamberlain's Ranch. How was she going to get the car back?

Larry and Aunt Audrey abruptly came to mind. They could help, and Marie decided to call them immediately. She remembered that she was now long overdue at Aunt Audrey's and needed to call her anyway to let her know what was happening. Walking to the nurse's station, she obtained a phone book, found Aunt Audrey's number, and called. Aunt Audrey's cheery voice immediately answered "Hello" on the other end of the line.

The familiar voice brought a torrent of emotions flooding over her. Marie broke down and sobbed uncontrollably while Aunt Audrey first tried to figure out who was wailing on the other end of her line and then soothe her and figure out what was going on at the same time. It was awhile before she got enough coherent detail to piece together what had happened.

As Marie unleashed a flood of disjointed and alarming information, Audrey was shocked and worried, but knew that Marie needed her support and that she could not let circumstances overwhelm her. After talking with Marie for some time and sorting out the entire story, Aunt Audrey assured her that everything would be all right and that she would do everything she could to help. Eventually Marie's tears dried and she regained her composure. Aunt Audrey said she would send Larry to get the car, and Marie told her where he could find the spare key. Aunt Audrey was even able to get Marie to smile with a final assurance that everything would work out all right.

The conversation with her aunt lifted Marie's spirits, and she felt much better, as she always did after talking to her. Marie had established a strong bond of friendship and love with Aunt Audrey over the years, especially because she was so far from her own family, who lived in the Midwest. For the first time since seeing her son in the back of the ranger's vehicle, she had real hope for Austin's survival if only because of Aunt Audrey's attitude.

Soon after Marie hung up the phone, a doctor in a blood spattered green surgical gown approached her. Marie knew it was Austin's blood. She instinctively tensed, knowing that he had news of her son's condition, but almost unwilling to listen to what it was for fear it would not be what she wanted to hear. His brow furrowed and lined with worry, the grim expression on his face betrayed what he had to tell. Her renewed hope after speaking with Aunt Audrey was snuffed, and she expected the worst.

"Your son sustained a major injury to his chest," the doctor began. He spoke slowly and deliberately, carefully choosing his words. "It is incredible he was brought in here alive, but he was just barely alive. We have done everything we can, and the operation went as well as we could have expected. However, I cannot be optimistic about his chances for survival. He took too long to get here. He is in critical condition in our intensive care unit. I do not know whether he will live or not. Do you have any questions?" The doctor finished and waited for her reaction.

Marie was initially relieved; at least Austin had made it through the operation alive. The expression on the doctor's face had initially led her to believe that Austin had died in surgery. However, her relief was short-lived as she considered what the doctor was trying to tell her, both verbally and with his demeanor. He was essentially saying that she should not get her hopes up, and that Austin was probably going to die. Her heart sank again.

"When can I see him?" she asked.

"They are still working on him in intensive care," the doctor replied. "As soon as they have him situated they will come and get you."

"Is there anything else I can do?"

"We are doing everything we possibly can do. The only other thing anyone can do right now is to pray for him. That he has held on so long is at least a good sign. He is fighting for his life." The doctor's words gave her some hope to cling to even though his non-verbal signals were all negative.

"What did the bullet hit?" Marie asked.

"The bullet went through his lung. There was so much internal bleeding into the lung that it was not functioning at all. Because he only had one lung functioning he wasn't getting enough needed oxygen. We sewed up the damage in the lung and pumped as much blood out of it as possible."

"How much blood has he been given?" Marie knew that they had given him three units on the chopper and wondered how much he had lost.

"Between what he got on the chopper and in surgery, we replaced almost half his entire blood supply. We gave him three units in surgery in addition to the three he had coming in. That is a lot of blood."

Marie had no more questions for now and the doctor left her in the waiting room. She was alone again. She vacillated between praying fervently for her son's recovery and for David and Rebecca's safety and being overwhelmed with fear and recrimination. She berated herself for not going with her family down the river. Could she have prevented what had happened? The question kept gnawing at her. If only she had been there, her son might not be lying in intensive care on death's doorstep. She could have at least gone for help while David stayed to help Austin.

After swinging wildly several times between the hope and faith of prayer and the despair and self-recrimination of doubt, Marie began to think through the situation. Someone had shot Austin, and even if she had been there she

121

probably could have done nothing about it. If David had been unable to prevent it, how could she? Her mental turmoil eased somewhat, but she still knew that if she had been there, at least she would know what had happened, and she might have brought help to her son sooner.

Time crawled by. After what seemed like hours of waiting, but was really only about thirty minutes, a nurse came down the hall and told her that she could join her son. She followed the nurse briskly through a corridor and into a large room directly adjacent to the nurse's station. There were only three patients in the room, and they all had multiple intravenous tubes going into their bodies. Each also had multiple wires feeding into electronic monitoring units. The effect was frightening, and seemed to reaffirm the doctor's pessimistic assessment of the situation. One of the still figures with tubes and wires cascading down to his body had Austin's unmistakable mat of brown curly hair. Marie rushed to his side.

Austin's face was pale with almost a purple tint, and looked worse than when he arrived at the hospital. Four pouches fed two intravenous tubes pumping plasma, whole red blood cells, saline, and antibiotics into his body. Both arms were being utilized in the effort to replace lost fluids. Austin was also hooked up to two machines: a monitor to measure vital functions, and a ventilator to pump oxygen into his lungs. The mouthpiece of the respirator covered the lower half of his face, and was taped into place.

The combined effect of his unhealthy appearance, the tubes and wires converging on his body, and the ventilator essentially breathing for him pushed Marie even further toward despair, who had not prepared herself for the macabre sight. The scene could have been out of her worst nightmare. Her child was lying limp like a vegetable with his life sustained by a machine. She looked at the still, motionless body and wondered if her son was still in this physical shell lying on the bed.

"He is still alive," the nurse said as if reading her mind. "His heart is working on its own, and there is still brain activity. He hasn't left us yet." She apparently had done this before and was prepared for Marie's reaction.

Still, Marie was not comforted. She had little hope after seeing him in this condition. The "yet" that the nurse used to end her statement corroborated what Marie instinctively felt, that even if he were alive now, it was only a matter of time. She pulled up a chair next to the bed, sat down, and threaded her hand through the maze of obstacles in search of Austin's. When the tips of her fingers touched his hand, her pessimism deepened. The hand was cool and clammy to the touch, and seemed devoid of life. She caressed his forehead with her other hand. It also was cool and clammy, like lifeless rubber. The revulsion she felt was overcome only by her need to touch and comfort what remained of her son before he was gone.

Marie keeping a silent vigil by the bed for several hours, and still Austin showed no sign of life. Marie could not see nor feel anything to encourage her. Occasionally, she would look at his face and it would seem that his color was improving, but it was only wishful thinking on her part. In fact, when she was honest with herself, it looked and felt like he was getting worse. Still, she continued to pray and felt better when she did.

When Aunt Audrey arrived, she tried to encourage Marie, but the condition of her nephew took some of her natural optimism out of her. She and Marie speculated about what had happened in the canyon. Marie had not heard from the police since being questioned in the late afternoon, and it was now early evening. They should have had some word from the team going down the river. On the other hand, maybe not hearing from them so early was good. As it would take longer for the police to catch up with moving people, it was encouraging to realize that both David and Rebecca were probably working their way down the river. This decreased the likelihood that they were lying dead on a riverbank not far from where Austin had been found.

Audrey quizzed Marie as to when she had last eaten. Marie acknowledged that she was famished; she had not eaten since breakfast but she did not want to leave. It would be just her luck that as soon as she left, Austin would wake up just long enough to give her a farewell message of love before he departed permanently, and she would be in the cafeteria selfishly satisfying her appetite. Audrey insisted that Marie go get something to eat anyway, and would not take no for an answer. She practically ejected Marie from the room.

Leaving the intensive care unit, Marie found her way to the cafeteria, ordered dinner, and waited impatiently while the server placed it on her plate. She was jealous of the time she had to spend away from Austin, and waiting around for food was not justified in her mind even if it was only a few seconds.

Eventually she got her order and paid for it, then found a table in a corner of the room where she wolfed down her food. As she chewed, she watched others coming and going, wrapped up in their own lives and paying no attention to the distraught woman in the corner. She wondered how many times she had visited hospital cafeterias herself and not been cognizant of suffering people eating in corners. Finishing, she rushed back to find the Austin's condition unchanged.

After a few more hours, Larry arrived. He had driven the car to St. George, and parked it near the front entrance of the hospital. The three talked quietly about what had transpired over the day, trying not to draw attention to them. Only two family members were allowed at one time in the unit, so they tried not to give the nurses a reason to ask one of them to leave. But it was now late and quiet in the hospital, and the nurses did not object.

A few more hours went by, and it was now very late. Larry had to go home to get some sleep, and because he had driven Marie's car to St. George, he was dependent upon his mother to take him home to Hurricane.

Marie was exhausted. The stressful events of the day had finally caught up with her. Both Larry and Audrey tried to persuade her to come home with them to Hurricane that night and sleep, but Marie was adamant about staying. There was no way she would leave her son alone in the hospital in such serious condition. Audrey and Larry could see that there was no changing her mind and said goodnight after a final prayer. Marie was alone again with her fear.

Chapter 11

Escape from Deep Creek

David had found Rebecca still alive, but his relief turned to dismay because their situation seemed hopeless. His heart was pounding, and he was perspiring from fright in spite of the cold night air. His mind screamed for him to turn around and run. He knew it was impossible to get Rebecca out of the camp without waking any of the skinheads. The fear welling up inside him insisted that he wait and try something else later. Nevertheless, reason contradicted his fear. He would not get another opportunity like this one and in spite of the danger; he knew he had to act now.

There were five shaved heads protruding from the other sleeping bags arrayed between him and Rebecca. David forced himself to think rationally knowing that he had to find a way to get her out of there. This seemed impossible because the small campsite was hemmed in on both sides by rocks and vegetation, and the only way in or out was over the top of the maniacs who had killed his son and had wounded him. If the skinheads woke up, they would surely kill him.

Should he attack them as they slept? In the Marine Corps, he had been trained to kill efficiently and silently. He might be able to kill all of them in their sleep. He examined his new Swiss army knife and scowled at the small dull blade. This blade was not going to cut anything efficiently. Furthermore, if only one of them woke up while the gruesome work was in progress, he would not stand a chance against the rest. He dismissed the idea of trying to cut their throats as they slept.

Knowing the skinheads had at least three guns, David considered looking for and obtaining one of them. That would make the rescue very easy. If armed with a weapon, he could wake them all up and force them to lie spread-eagled on the ground. If anyone resisted, a quick round in a knee should be ample persuasion. Even if they all attacked at once, he felt he could kill most, if not all, of them before they got to him or had their weapons ready to fire at him. He was a good shot, and he only needed one round per person, especially at this

125

range. He could then have Rebecca tie the skinheads up while he held them at bay with the weapon. David's mind was ecstatic. This was a good plan! It could work!

Scanning for a gun, his eyes systematically combed the entire camp, searching for any sign of a weapon in the dim light cast by the embers of the fire. The packs were lying at the feet of each of the men. He examined the visible portion of each pack and sleeping bag, hoping he would get lucky, but it was no use; he could find no clue as to where a weapon was.

He was tempted to search the skinhead's packs. It was a long shot. He had no idea what was in each bag and how much noise he would make rummaging through them. He would possibly need to search all five packs and even then, given the situation, might not find a gun if they were all sleeping with their guns within easy reach, which was entirely possible. The quick euphoric high he had experienced when he thought how easy the rescue might be vanished. It was too risky. He had to think of something else.

What about attacking them with his staff? He could jump into the middle of the circle and just start banging heads. He knew where to strike to ensure death or incapacitation of the person he attacked. However, that would undoubtedly wake everyone up immediately, and it was unlikely that he could get all five before one of them got him. In addition, the fire was in the middle of the circle and its location would severely complicate any attack, especially in bare feet. This would not work either.

After straining his tired, barely functioning mind for several minutes, he concluded that neither a sneak attack nor a direct frontal assault was his best option. He would have to rely on stealth, wake Rebecca up, and sneak out with her without waking the others.

"How am I going to wake Rebecca?" he wondered. "Maybe I can hit her in the head with a small rock." He had always been proficient at throwing rocks, especially because when he was young it was forbidden, and that automatically meant that the behavior was irresistible. Laying his weapons on the ground, he looked around and found a few small pebbles. Taking one in his hand, he took careful aim and threw it at Rebecca's head.

It missed. He had overshot, and the pebble hit the rock wall with a report that seemed as loud as a small caliber gunshot. He stopped breathing and waited for any of the figures in the circle to stir. No one moved. He breathed a deep sigh of relief and worked up the courage to try again. He took another small rock and this time imagined he was in the bathroom at work throwing wastepaper towels through the narrow opening of the garbage can from fifteen feet. He never missed that shot. It worked. He hit her squarely on the head.

Rebecca did not stir. Either she had not felt the impact through her hair, or she was sleeping so soundly it did not wake her. He would have to go in and get her. Retrieving the knife and staff, he plotted a course through the circle of sleeping bodies that would allow him to avoid touching any of them. He began to thread his way through the group to the other side ever so carefully. He closely examined where he would place his foot before each step to make sure there was nothing that would break or make a sound. Moving slowly but steadily, soon he had quietly crossed to the other side without incident, and was standing directly over his daughter.

Now he had to wake Rebecca and identify himself before she screamed in alarm at seeing a partially clothed man crouching over her in unfamiliar circumstances. Placing the staff and knife down where he could quickly grab them, he knelt in the small space between her and the adjacent bag, and pondered how to do it. He could put his hand over her mouth and hope he could communicate who it was before she managed to get out a sound or wake the others with the noise of a struggle. No good. Too risky. Besides, most of her head was buried in the bag. Or he could softly call her name. That would not work either; she was normally a heavy sleeper, and the exertion of the day would make the present sleep even deeper than normal. The rock he had thrown a few moments before supported this theory. Besides, any noise could wake the others.

"Is there any way to wake her without waking the others?" he asked himself. Then he remembered that when Rebecca was younger he had a habit of softly caressing the side of her face to wake her. She had loved it until she was old enough to think it unfashionable. It just might work.

He gently pulled the sleeping bag away from Rebecca's face so he could touch her. She resisted in her sleep, pulling on the bag, her brow furrowed with tension, but he succeeded in uncovering the side of her face anyway. Gently and slowly, he stroked her cheek with the tips of his fingers until the stress lines on her face slowly eased and gradually the tension dissipated. After a minute, she opened her eyes.

127

Disoriented, Rebecca at first could not remember where she was. However, in a split second the previous day's horror returned and she started to panic. David put his finger to his lips and motioned for silence. Suddenly she recognized him. Her body convulsed with silent sobs, and he held and comforted her for a brief moment.

Rebecca was tied up. Although he couldn't understand why, David had not expected this, but he had the knife and retrieved it from the sand. It required several attempts with the blade to severe the rope binding her hands, after which she extricated herself from the bag with some difficulty for her feet were also tied. She was fully clothed in what she wore at the outset of the hike. Less anxious about the treatment she had received, David struggled silently and as swiftly as he could to cut the cords binding her feet.

There was yet no indication that any of the skinheads were awake, but David wanted to impress the gravity of the situation on his daughter. He pointed to the ring of sleeping bags then put his finger to his mouth to indicate the need for silence. He then placed two fingers to his temple and figuratively shot himself in the head to show what the effect would be if the skinheads woke as they tried to leave. Rebecca hardly needed to be told; she was conscious of the danger they were in, but the point could not be emphasized enough.

Motioning to Rebecca to proceed through the circle to the exit from the campground, he mouthed the words "Be very careful" and pointed to the places he had stepped while coming in. She understood without a sound, carefully tiptoed through the maze with amazing speed and agility, and waited at the exit down the trail. She made it look so easy, like she was playing hopscotch against an incompetent opponent. "I am an old man," he said to himself, wishing that it were that easy for him.

He had started after Rebecca when he saw she did not have her shoes on. He waved his arms to get her attention, pointed at his own feet, then at hers, and shrugged his shoulders to ask where. She understood and pointed to her pack that was leaning against the canyon wall. He saw the shoes beside the pack, with socks poking out of them, and scooped them up.

"What about the pack?" He briefly considered trying to bring it with them before dismissing the thought. "Picking it up will make too much noise," he observed to himself. "Besides, she can move faster without it, and we won't need the food. She can share mine and we'll be out of the canyon before dawn."

Clutching the boots, knife, and staff, he started to retrace his steps carefully and deliberately as before, slowly creeping through the circle to where Rebecca was waiting.

Suddenly there was noise and movement. The skinhead that David stood next to had shifted his position, rolling over in his sleeping bag. It was the large, burly, and foul tempered man that had sought David earlier in the afternoon. David's heart jumped into his throat, and he froze in place. While the skinhead's movement was slight, it was enough to put pressure from his back onto David's foot. David was petrified knowing that if the skinhead woke because he was leaning on his foot he would not be able to defend himself while holding Rebecca's footwear and his gear. David could see the terror on Rebecca's face, and she nearly started to cry. David motioned violently for silence, and she stopped. After that, all David could do was keep still and hope the man would continue sleeping without noticing the pressure on his back.

The seconds ticked away, and the regular breathing of the skinhead resumed. David knew that he risked waking the man by moving his foot, but he could not detach it and leave it there. Bit by bit he pulled his foot away from the man's back, and soon wiggled it free. The man shifted again, but his movement was away from David and the skinhead remained fast asleep. David resumed his course and proceeded through the remainder of the unconscious group.

As he stepped out he gave Rebecca a brief hug, and then checked for movement among the figures visible in the faint orange light. Other than their breathing, they remained motionless. David and Rebecca had made it through the most dangerous part of the escape without waking any of them. Motioning to Rebecca to continue, they both crept down the trail to where David had left his clothes. He quickly dressed while Rebecca put her shoes on. As he dressed, he couldn't figure out which was worse, the frigid night air on his partially clothed body or the freezing wet clothing scraping over his body like sandpaper. Rebecca continued to wear the clothing she started the day with.

Or was it today? "What time is it anyway?" he asked himself, looking at his watch. It was just after twelve o'clock. The day from hell had finally ended. David wondered if this day would be any better.

He finished dressing, pocketed the knife, and they quickly walked to where his pack lay. Silently shouldering the pack, they started downriver, instantly swallowed by the darkness of the sharply narrowing canyon under the dark and starless sky.

Entering the water at the confluence of the two streams, the cold water chilled him to the bone, and Rebecca's sharp intake of air told him the water had the same effect on her. The water coming in from Deep Creek was colder and deeper than was the water they had been traveling through most of the previous day. The water level was occasionally up to the middle of their waist. The canyon air, cooled by the water under it, did not seem much warmer than the water itself. Their bodies shivered to retain heat and keep warm, but David forced himself and gently encouraged Rebecca to carry on in spite of the cold.

The exhilaration from the success of freeing Rebecca physically helped, but it was wearing off fast. David knew they had to get to the ranger station before the skinheads behind them woke up, or at least open up an insurmountable lead. If not, the skinheads would chase David and Rebecca down and kill them. When the skinheads woke, they would know that David helped Rebecca escape from the signs in the sand and the severed ropes. They would be looking for both of them. So regardless of the bitter cold, numbing fatigue, incredible hunger, and pain, they pressed on.

When they had progressed about five hundred yards downriver, David felt they were far enough out of earshot to finally speak normally. He asked Rebecca to tell him what had happened back at the arch as they continued downstream.

"We found these guys sitting beside the river," she said, beginning the story. "At first they acted friendly, but they scared both of us. When we kept going, the leader pulled a gun and made us stop. They started this paranoid ranting about world government conspiracies and then shot Austin without warning when he tried to defend you." She began to sob softly.

"Defend me?"

"Because you work for a government agency."

"They were angry enough to kill over something that trivial?"

"I don't think so. I think they were waiting for anyone, and we just happened to be the first ones down the river. Our reaction just gave them the excuse they were looking for to do what they had intended to do all along. But our response really set them off. After they took me, they were constantly talking about reclaiming their land from the minorities and environmental communists who had taken over. I think maybe they were trying to convince me they were justified in doing what they did."

"Did they hurt you?"

"No, but they promised to. They kept talking about how much fun they were going to have with me once they got to where we could camp. I was so scared."

"What happened when you got to Deep Creek?"

"Nothing. I don't think they had expected to be as tired as they were. The further down we went, the quieter they got. When we made camp, all they did was tie me up and give me my sleeping bag. I had to get into it with my wet clothes. They made a fire, ate, and went to sleep while I tried to be invisible, moving as little as possible to avoid calling attention to myself."

David felt good. All things considered, he was amazed how well everything had worked out. Rebecca was safe with him now and had not been hurt. Then his mind suddenly turned to Austin, and he wondered how he could be so callous as to have thought anything had worked out well.

"Is Austin dead?" Rebecca asked, seeming to read his thought.

"I think so. He was alive when I got to him and I treated him for the wound, but it was close to the heart, and I think he probably bled to death. He lost consciousness just before I started downriver to find you. Even if the wound didn't kill him, a wild animal has probably found him by now and ...." his voice trailed off. It was too painful for him to finish the thought. He wished an additional person had come with them on the hike, someone who could have waited with Austin or gone back upriver to get help while he went after Rebecca.

Rebecca had begun to cry again, and it was apparent that the memory of the previous day was too much for her to think about also. She changed the subject quickly. "They said they had killed you. I didn't expect to see you alive again." She was choking back tears.

"They ambushed and shot me above the Fall, but it was only a superficial wound. I hid behind the Fall until they thought I was dead, either from the bullet or from drowning."

"You've been shot?!"

"It's okay," David insisted; however, thinking about it made the nearly forgotten wound throb again.

131

"I'm sorry I told them you were behind us. I was so scared when they shot Austin that I screamed for you before I thought. They thought we were alone and my hysterical reaction told them about you. When they realized we weren't alone, they decided to get you further down the river. When we passed the Fall, two of them stayed back while the rest of us went on. Later they came back and said they killed you. I thought you were dead. I was so glad to see you back there I started to cry."

"To quote Samuel Clemens, the reports of my death were greatly exaggerated. I'm not dead," David reassured her, "but we have to keep going if we want to keep it that way."

They were passing another canyon coming into the main canyon from the northwest. As with all of the side canyons emptying into the Virgin River through the Park, it was narrow and steep. He could hear as a small stream gurgled its way down the gorge and flowed into the river. David figured they had reached Kolob Creek, one of a series of landmarks that enabled him to keep track of where they were and how much further they had to go. Unfortunately, they had a long way to go to get to safety.

As they traveled on, David became aware of an aching churn in his midsection. The thought of food suddenly brought his attention to the fact that he had not eaten for a very long time. He was famished. He could not remember eating since the lunch of what seemed like days ago.

"Are you hungry?" he asked Rebecca.

"I'm starving! I haven't eaten since lunch."

"Neither have I. My stomach thinks my throat's been cut."

Rebecca smiled. "Well I'm hungry enough to eat the north end of a south-bound skunk," she said, repeating another of her father's stupid ways to say he was hungry. The jokes made both of them laugh for a moment.

"I wish we could stop and eat. But we have to get down the canyon before they wake up and discover you are gone. There is only enough food for one meal for each of us anyway. Let's go on as far as we can."

The little laugh they had joking about eating was not as funny now that they realized they couldn't eat. They traveled in silence, the earlier exhilaration of finding each other having dissipated, and the thought of eating and resting wanted to overpower all other thoughts in their minds. However, negotiating the river in the darkness with nothing other than David's headlamp forced them to concentrate and it soon commanded all their attention. The slick rocks on the riverbed, which were functionally the same as greased bowling balls, made the going very difficult. Rebecca did not have her walking stick and so clung to David during the lengthening fords, which were also increasing in frequency. He had to support both of them in the current. Whenever she stumbled and clutched his arm, the stress on his wound brought a new wave of pain. The aching of his entire body was constant.

Rebecca was having doubts about whether they could make it, or at least whether she could. The canyon was so dark she could see nothing. Even with her father beside her, she was frightened. She was cold, hungry, and her body throbbed from the almost non-stop exertion since the previous morning. "Can't we stop?" she complained. "I'm so tired and hungry." Her words were slurred as if she were drunk.

"No! We have to go on. If we stop they might catch us." David uttered the words emphatically, but he too was beginning to wonder if they could make it. He was so tired he could not think straight, and they were both shivering constantly and uncontrollably. It was becoming more difficult to cross the river even when the ford did not look that difficult, and when walking along the bank they stumbled and struggled just to put one foot in front of the other. They literally had to force their bodies to obey their commands to continue.

Somehow, in the back of his increasingly muddled mind, David suddenly remembered the symptoms of hypothermia. With that, David's mind leaped back to coherence with the realization that they might have escaped death at the hands of the skinheads only to freeze to death in the water.

It was obvious that they were not going to be able to continue walking through the river all night. Rebecca especially was losing body heat. She was smaller and thinner than her father, and did not have the layer of body fat that helped keep him warm. David could feel her body almost convulse with shivering in its failing attempt to maintain its temperature. If he was becoming groggy with hypothermia, she would be much worse. They were also weak from the lack of food and rest. They were just too cold, too hungry, and too tired, and would have to stop, warm themselves, eat, and rest.

"Just for a few hours," he told himself. "Just long enough to catch our breath. We'll rest a little and still be going before the others wake. Even if they run down stream, which they can't, they won't catch us with the lead we will

133

have." He was pleased with the plan, not just because they really didn't have any other choice under the circumstances, but also because it offered adequate justification for stopping in spite of the very real danger which was sleeping just up the river.

In the darkness to their right, on the west side of the river, they soon came upon a large bank. It was too dark to see onto it, but they stumbled up with the hope of finding a good resting spot.

They were rewarded. The bank cut into the rock wall of the canyon some fifteen feet, creating a small alcove sheltered from the river and the night. "The Grotto," David thought, seeing the map in his mind. "We have reached the Grotto."

It was a perfect shelter for resting and warming themselves. "We'll sleep here for a few hours and then continue," he told his semi-coherent daughter. Shivering spastically, he was just barely able to speak the words, and Rebecca's condition was even worse. She could not speak at all and was disoriented, but at least she recognized that they were stopping and was relieved.

There was no time to lose: they had to get warm fast. David's mind fought with his sluggish body, trying to make it to respond more quickly to his commands. After struggling for a moment he was able to get the pack off his back and remove his spare clothes and sleeping bag from the pack. He had only the one change of outer clothing he had brought with him, the ones he had dried earlier, and those he gave to Rebecca.

Even though the waterproofing in the pack was damaged earlier in the day by his pell-mell scramble to get to Austin, the plunge over the waterfall, and the passage of the bullet through the top part of the bag, the inside lining of the bag was still dry. In spite of the constant soaking the pack had taken, the clothes were only damp in spots. The waterproofing had worked.

Instructing Rebecca to change, he went over to the other side of the Grotto, quickly removed his waterlogged clothing, and changed into the dry underwear from the pack. Rejoining Rebecca after she had finished dressing, they unzipped the bag so it would cover both of them. They huddled closely together underneath it, sharing body heat for warmth.

After several minutes of intense shivering, the combination of the dry clothes, the sleeping bag over their now dry bodies, and their combined body heat started to have the desired effect. The intensity of their shivering decreased enough that they could speak.

By that time, they both remembered how hungry they were. David pulled all the remaining food from the pack, divided it equally, and they both wolfed it down, not talking or doing anything that hindered their intake of the glorious calories that gave their bodies the energy to continue. David worried to himself about having food for the next day as they inhaled the jerky, trail mix, and pudding packs. "That's okay," he thought, "we can eat breakfast in Springdale in the morning. I don't need the extra weight on my back anyway."

Finally, the last pudding pack was devoured and their hunger sated. There had been enough food to satisfy both of them. The combination of a full stomach, warm and exhausted bodies, and the late hour had an immediate effect. With the monotonous rushing of the river in the background providing an auditory sedative, they both fell into a nearly comatose sleep as soon as they had closed their eyes.

Chapter 12

Rain in the Canyon

The night passed slowly and without further incident for the three separate groups sleeping in the canyon. The father and daughter in the Grotto slept peacefully, recovering strength while huddled together under the sleeping bag. The men at Deep Creek slept soundly through the night unaware that their captive had escaped. The police team camped just above the Fall also enjoyed a good night's sleep.

Clouds, unseen by any of sleepers in the lightless canyon, had massed silently and stealthily over the park as the night progressed, laden with moisture from the South Pacific and Gulf of California. The storm track from the southwest had not crossed any significant mountain barriers to force the humid air upward into the cold upper atmosphere, so the storm approached with most of its water content intact. Nature was saving it for the mountains of Southern Utah. The cloud cover steadily thickened through the night.

As dawn drew near, the sunlight approaching from the east struck the upper layer of the cloud cover, but only a few scattered photons penetrated the now massive mountain of moisture. On the ground, that night was giving way to day was difficult to discern. The sun would not shine this morning, and in the absence of light, the internal clocks of the exhausted hikers did not wake them.

Near dawn, orographic lift had pushed the moisture high enough to cool lower than the dew point, causing molecules composed of two parts hydrogen and one part oxygen to condense onto minute dust particles and begin their long freefall to earth. It started out as a light sprinkle but gradually increased in intensity. Rain fell throughout Southern Utah, including Zion National Park, but the storm had reserved its full strength for Cedar Mountain. Soon heavy sheets of rain were cascading to earth high in the watershed that funneled into the narrow canyons of the park.

As drizzling rain began to fall into the canyon, it hit the campfire at Deep Creek. Hot embers from the previous night's fire still glowed under a thick layer of gray ash, which crackled and smoked as the shower began. It quickly extinguished what remained of the campfire. The noise of the dying embers and the staccato patter of the rain on their sleeping bags soon woke the skinheads in the camp.

At first, the tired and semiconscious men took refuge deep inside their sleeping bags. It was still dark; they were still exhausted and wanted to sleep longer. In addition, no one wanted to leave the comfort of his bag for the wet and miserable morning. However, the rain gradually soaked through the light material of their bags and a miserable soaking chill replaced the comfortable warmth of the interior. There was no escape from the rain, and sleep was no longer possible.

Bill lay in his bag. The rain had put him in more of a foul mood than normal. He was still exhausted from the previous day's exertion, he was hungry again, and now he was cold and wet, lying in a sleeping bag with nothing but a miserable day staring him in the face as they hiked out of the canyon. Then he remembered the girl, and his attitude changed immediately. He unzipped the soaking bag and crawled out, then turned to the canyon wall where they had left the girl the night before.

He froze in his tracks when he looked toward the rock wall. The green bag, which should have contained the girl, was empty. In the sand next to the soaked, disorderly bag lay the scattered remnants of the ropes that had bound her. She was gone.

"Bart! Wake up!" he shrieked. As he called out, he glanced around the campsite looking for the girl but instinctively knew she would not be here.

Bart was also in a bad mood. He fervently wished that he had picked a more comfortable method of making their political statement. If he had known it was going to rain, he would have stayed home in bed. Bill's cry of alarm brought him out of his bag. "What is it?"

"She's gone!"

"She's what?!"

"She's gone. Her bag was empty when I got up."

"Find her! Get out of your bags, you lazy bastards! Get up and find her now!"

The rest of the group scrambled out of their bags and began running aimlessly around the area looking for the girl.

Bart was in a frenzy. "Where did she go!?

137

"How should we know?" Ed was observing the obvious, but it did not endear him to Bart.

"Find out! And don't sass me again." He pulled his weapon out from under his pillow and brandished it. He was not about to take anything from any of these losers this morning.

"We've got to find her, Bart." Bill was trying to get Bart to focus on the problem at hand.

"Why didn't you wake up and stop her?" Bart demanded.

"I was asleep. We were all asleep, including you." Bill was in no mood to take much more. His tone was low and threatening.

"And who tied her up so sloppily that she got loose?"

"She was already tied when me and Rich got here."

"Bart, you must have tied her. She was tied when we brought back the firewood," Archie remembered.

At first, Bart was angry at this accusation, but then remembered he had indeed tied her. "Well then, how did she get loose?" Bart did not want to have the blame shift to him, so he changed the subject.

"Maybe we should stop running around and see if we can find out something from any track she left in the sand," Rich suggested, who at the moment was the most rational of the bunch.

"He's right! Don't move!" Bart ordered, realizing that anything to be learned from the remaining footprints would be destroyed by walking over it. The entire group froze in place while Bart carefully examined the campsite. Even with the tracks they had made in the flurry of activity upon discovering the girl was gone, what had happened was evident. The bag and cut ropes lay on the ground. One set of footprints came into the campsite and imprints showed where David had knelt in the sand. Two sets of prints then went out, the placement of which strategically missed the placement of the bags the men had slept in. Bart followed the trail to the riverside where the footprints stopped and shoe prints started. The trail then led to the side of the river where they had apparently entered the water. The record in the sand clearly showed that the girl had been helped.

Bart was enraged and ranted violently at everybody in the camp for their incompetence in letting the girl get away. Bill scowled at his brother for having

138

the gall to lump him with the other three in his attack, but he appreciated the gravity of their predicament and kept quiet.

"So who else was in the canyon? Who else could have taken her?" Bart was pacing back and forth now, his brow lined with stress.

"Maybe it was the father." Archie's observation did not cost him anything. He was not one of the two left at the Fall assigned to kill him.

"Yes, maybe it was the father." Bart glared at Bill. "What about it Bill? Did the father rise from the dead and take his daughter right out from under our noses?"

"We killed him. I shot him three times myself."

"And I shot him twice," chimed in Rich.

"It must have been someone else. Yeah, that's right; someone else came in and got her." Bill was grasping for any plausible excuse.

"How many people would come across a campsite, then go straight to the person in the camp who was tied up and help her escape?" Bart responded cynically. "How would anyone other than her father know that we had her?"

"I don't know," was the only lame reason Bill could think of.

"Look, the only thing that makes any sense is that the father did it. No one other than him could have known that we had kidnapped her. Anyone else would have just passed us by and let us sleep."

"But we killed him!"

"How can you be sure? Did you find the body?"

"No."

"How far away from him were you when you shot him?"

"About twenty or thirty feet."

"And you're sure you shot him three times."

"Maybe not. But I know he was hit at least once. The bullet spun him around and knocked him over."

"Great. Just great. I leave you guys to do one simple thing, and you screw it up." Bart was still pacing. He could not believe his brother had bungled a simple ambush so badly.

"Look Bart, we thought we got him. Besides, he fell onto some big rocks. We looked for the body downriver and could not find it. We peppered the Fall with lead in case he was hiding behind it. We even doubled back up to the Fall afterward because we thought he might have survived and was hiding. If he had

139

been alive, he would have come out by then and we would have caught him. What else could we have done?"

"You could have walked up under the Fall and looked for him."

"You're right, we should have." Genuine remorse from Bill was a rare thing, but it was now clear even to him that he had failed his responsibility. At the same time, he was enraged at the man who had made a fool out of him. "We've got to find them. I have a score to settle with him."

"You're damn right we have got to find them. They can put us all onto death row. I just wish it wasn't raining. This is bad enough without rain."

"But Bart, you always talked about how you wished you could have been with General Washington when he crossed the Delaware. It was snowing then, wasn't it?" Archie had that stupid look on his face again.

"That was snow. It was over two hundred years ago. It's not the same thing." Bart was irritated with the comparison.

"But if they could fight for freedom in the snow, couldn't we do it in the rain?"

"This is the twenty-first century, you moron. We don't have to put up with what Washington and his brave men did." This last reply was crisp enough to let Archie know he was crossing the line.

Bart sat down and tried to think through the situation. He had not counted on anything not going according to plan. He had thought that they could take a two-day hike in pleasant weather, anonymously shoot some rangers, and get out before anyone discovered the bodies. Now he was sitting in the middle of the canyon, having killed not a ranger but a boy. Moreover, the boy's sister and father had escaped and might be out of the canyon by now.

The seriousness of the circumstances they were in began to dawn on all of them. They had killed at least one person, and an eyewitness to the murder had escaped, probably with a second eyewitness. The girl and her father had a head start of at least several hours, and if they reached civilization before the skinheads could catch them, the authorities would soon be coming up the canyon to find Bart and his groupies. They could expect to be arrested coming out of the canyon. The stark narrow walls of the gorge began to look like a prison, hemming them in, not allowing digression from a route straight downriver to prison and possibly eventual death. Moreover, this miserable weather had betrayed them. It was supposed to be bright and sunny, but instead it was raining cats and dogs.

"It's raining!" Bart grasped the significance of the rain for the first time.

"Yeah, it's raining. So what?" Bill wondered if his brother was losing his mind. With two people that could positively identify them as murderers getting away, a little rain seemed to be the least of their worries.

"What if it floods?" Bart's only previous worry was in avoiding capture by the police. Trapped in the canyon in front of a rampaging flood was something that he had not even considered. He forced himself to think clearly. They had to get out of the canyon and get out as quickly as they could.

"Floods? What do you mean floods?" Bill had not been warned about this hazard.

"Look at these canyon walls. Look at how close together they are. What do you think is going to happen if the sky dumps a boatload of water on us?" Bart sneered.

"Do you mean to tell us that you brought us here to drown like rats in a flood?" Bill was agitated now.

"The weather was supposed to be good!"

"Yeah, well I'm sure they will write that on our tombstones. What are we going to do now?"

"Let's go back the way we came." Ed's suggestion had some appeal. "The cops will be expecting us to come out of the Narrows."

Bart wondered whether going back up the canyon might be safer. The cops would be expecting them to come out at the bottom. In addition, going through the Narrows in the rain was a foolhardy idea. However, he appreciated the fact that going upstream would be too difficult. Besides, their truck was downstream. They would have to walk for days to get out if they went upriver. "No, we have to go down the river. That is where the truck is. It's the only practical way out."

"And besides, we have to try to catch them before they make it out of the canyon." Bill had not given up on revenge.

"They've been traveling all night. They're already out. The cops are probably waiting for us now." Ed feared the dark converging canyon downriver and wanted to get out by a different way.

"Then they will be waiting at both ends anyway," said Bill. "Do you want to fight your way back upstream against the current of the river? And even if we come out and the cops aren't there, how are we going to get out? You know where the truck is."

After a silent pause, Bill added, "Look, maybe the weather can help us. It could possibly provide cover from the cops waiting for us at the bottom of the canyon. We'll go downstream and find a place to hide till they go by us. Besides, anybody coming upriver will be fighting the river so much that we should be able to slip by somehow. Or, maybe we can ambush them. We should be able to see and hear them before they hear us." Bill thought another chance to successfully stage an ambush might make up for his previous failure.

Rich was thinking about the river. "It's also possible that the girl and her father haven't made it out. The water was cold last night. Maybe they stopped to rest. They must have been as tired as we were."

"You're right!" The thought energized Bart. "And besides, the father was wounded. If so, how fast for how long can he go? He may be dead just down the river from us for all we know." Bart looked at Bill and Rich skeptically. "He is wounded, isn't he?"

"Yes, he's wounded!" Bill snapped at his brother, upset that he mistrusted his judgment or honesty.

"Bart, there is something else," Rich eagerly injected. "If he had a gun, don't you think he would have used it last night when we were all asleep?"

"You're right." Bill was thrilled by this deductive conclusion. "We don't have to worry about him setting an ambush for us."

"All right. Let's go." Bart joined in the others' enthusiasm, and their situation seemed a little brighter than it had a few minutes before. "Maybe we can catch and kill them and get out without being discovered after all. If so, the plan will still have worked, more or less."

They broke camp quickly, stuffing their soaked possessions into their packs without regard for organization or comfort. Because the rain had soaked through all the gear in their packs, there was no advantage to changing clothes. The rain and river would drench dry clothes immediately anyway. They were ready in just a few minutes and without delay plunged into the river and headed downstream. The group quickly disappeared down the river leaving the campsite, the girl's pack and the story that the campsite told intact in their rush to depart.

Chapter 13

Death at the Grotto

David struggled to clear the fog from his mind. He had been tormented during the night with a recurring dream of the '61 flood and the helpless feeling he had experienced watching the wall of water wash away everything beneath him. He could tell it was a dream, and tried to wake himself, but he was in such a deep stupor that he could not wake until he perceived light on his closed eyes. He forced his eyes open and for a moment wondered where he was.

Dim gray light was seeping into the Grotto. He was huddled under the sleeping bag with Rebecca curled beside him. She was still sound asleep and her relaxed breathing and warmth was comfortable and sleep inducing. The memories from the previous day came back, but it seemed distant and unimportant. Gradually, he became conscious of the drumming of rain outside the grotto washing in sheets against the wall of the canyon and trickling down the sides, dripping onto the canyon floor and into the river. The sound was soothing from within the protective shelter of the grotto, like lying in bed listening to rain on the roof. It was so comfortable he almost let himself go back to sleep. Still, in spite of the relaxed atmosphere resulting from his surroundings, he was uneasy. Something was wrong, and his muddled mind tried to figure out what it was.

Rain! David was jolted by the realization of what the sound of the rain meant and by connecting his dream with the present. He could not believe it. How could it be raining? But it was. Moreover, it was morning! He looked at his watch and saw that it was seven twenty-three. They had overslept. He immediately recognized his and Rebecca's predicament.

"Rebecca! Wake up! We've got to get out of here!" Mentally cursing himself for not continuing on the night before, he threw off the sleeping bag, waking Rebecca in the process. He struggled to climb into his still damp clothes while trying to evaluate objectively their situation in his near panic.

"What's happening daddy?" Rebecca was still trying to clear the cobwebs from her mind.

"We overslept. We have got to get going before the skinheads catch up to us."

Rebecca was up putting her shoes on in an instant. "Do you think they are close?"

"I don't know. It depends on how long it's been raining. The grotto protected us while they were sleeping in the open. The rain would have woken them immediately and as soon as they saw you were gone, they would be beating feet downriver. We can only hope it hasn't been raining more than an hour. If so, it's a wonder they're not already here."

Rebecca did not respond. She started to roll the sleeping bag, anticipating packing it.

"Don't worry about any of this stuff. We are just going to leave it." David did not want to take the time to pack. He had finished dressing and was about to leave.

"But when they find this stuff, they'll know we stayed here last night."

David stopped. "You're right. If they know we stayed here, they will speed up and catch us for sure. Pack everything."

David and Rebecca packed as fast as they could, jamming equipment and clothing into the pack, even scooping up the garbage from the previous night's meal. Last, the rolled pack was stuffed into the garbage bag and pack.

"Should we even continue downriver?" he asked her, half thinking aloud. The implications of the rain were fully apparent, and he was grasping at any excuse he could think of to avoid the narrow deathtrap ahead. "Maybe we can hide from these guys while they pass by."

"Yeah, let's do it. Let's hide. Anything to keep from going downriver in the rain seems like a good idea to me."

"The problem is there's only one place to do it downriver from here. Past Deep Creek, where you and the skinheads camped last night, there are only two side canyons that we might be able to backtrack up into and hide. We already passed one of them last night, Kolob Canyon. Goose Creek Canyon is our only chance, unless we try to go back upriver to Kolob creek."

"Why don't we just hide right here?"

"Where? Remember, they're looking for us. There's no place to hide here. Look at these walls."

145

"I don't think I am strong enough to go upriver against the current," she replied.

"I don't think I can either. I am too sore to do it. And I don't think we should take the chance of meeting those guys coming down from Deep Creek anyway."

"Okay, let's hide in Goose Creek Canyon. How far is it?"

David hoisted the pack onto his shoulders, and they started out of the Grotto into the rain with David in the lead. "It shouldn't take much longer than a half hour. It's not too far."

Just as David and Rebecca were exiting the Grotto, a solitary figure with a shaved head came around the rock wall only a few feet away. He was a large and burly man with a sinister expression on his face that told David that he knew he had them where he wanted them. He had a gun in his hand and immediately pointed it directly at David's chest.

Instinct took over. Grasping the staff in the middle with his hands spaced for balance, David swiftly brought it up on the hand holding the weapon as hard as he could just as the man had the business end of the handgun pointed at him. There were two loud almost simultaneous cracks, the sound of wood smashing against flesh and metal and the echoing report of the discharging gun. The handgun flew upward into the air and disappeared over Bill's shoulder.

Bill screamed in agony and went to his knees as the sound of the harmlessly ricocheting bullet reverberated through the Grotto and canyon beyond. He had missed but David had not. The staff had hit the skinhead's hand a split second before the gun discharged and had knocked off his aim.

Not giving Bill any time to recover or react, David immediately pulled back the end of the staff he had used to hit the man's hand and with the same motion slammed the other end with full force into the kneeling figure's Adam's apple. It was a good stroke. Bill dropped backwards to the ground clutching at his throat and gasping for air. His labored attempts to pull oxygen through the crushed throat were in vain, and his violent gasps ended with his body going limp, his eyes staring upward.

"Where is the gun?!" David asked Rebecca. He was elated. They had a good weapon now! He had concentrated on taking the man out and had not seen where it had landed.

Rebecca stood frozen for a moment, her eyes riveted on the lifeless body of the skinhead that had so terrified her the day before. She was astounded that so much could change in not much more than the blink of an eye, and was astonished by the suddenness, speed, and ferocity of the attack. "You killed him," was all she could say.

"Yes I did. It was a choice between him or us, and when faced with that decision I'll take him every time." David had no sympathy whatsoever for the homicidal skinhead splayed out on the ground in front of them.

"But it happened so fast."

"Look honey, this is real life, not a movie. Fights with deadly weapons rarely last more than a few seconds."

Rebecca continued to stare at the dead man's body.

"Did you see where the gun landed?" David asked again, his voice rising with alarm. He grasped Rebecca's arm to get her to come back to the emergency at hand.

Rebecca looked at her father and nodded. "It went into the river!" Rebecca was pointing to the middle of the stream.

Rebecca was petrified. She was horrified at the sight of Bill lying on the Grotto floor. He was the one of whom she had been most afraid; and even though Bill lay motionless on the floor with lifeless eyes open to the rock above she refused to approach him.

David had jumped into the river and was frantically trying to find the gun. But it was to no avail. The gun, wherever it landed, was hidden among the dark rocks on the river bottom and would take time to find. Time that he and Rebecca didn't have.

David climbed back out of the river. "Wonderful. That's just great," he groaned, realizing the direction of his attack had probably lost the gun for them. "Why couldn't I have hit the hand with a downward stroke?" However, there was no time to spend agonizing over it.

Where were the others? They couldn't be far behind, and they had to have heard the gunshot at least. Still, maybe they were far enough away to allow time to once again search for the gun in the water. David went to where he could look upriver, hiding as well as he could. He could not see anyone, but he could hear shouting nearby. The rest of the group was very close.

Looking at the current, David knew it was hopeless to try to find the gun and that even if he could find it he would not be able to go under and retrieve it without the current sweeping him down first. They had to leave now, armed only with the weapons they had started with.

David took Rebecca's hand and they both ran down to the rocky shore and plunged into the current. The river was cold, and they were both promptly soaked from the waist up from the rain. Rebecca clung to David for support while they moved as quickly as they could without being swept downstream.

The skinheads had been traveling downriver for about an hour and a half. Bart was confident now that they would find the girl and her father somewhere in the canyon. The grueling day before and the temperatures in the water and canyon would not let the two get very far traveling at night. Besides, the father was wounded. How far and how fast can a wounded man travel? Assured of success, he had organized his group to systematically search the canyon as they went.

They had passed Kolob Creek and had even searched up that side canyon for several hundred yards to make sure the father and the girl had not backtracked up it to get by them. That had taken about thirty minutes and contributed to the wide separation between them. Bill in particular was a considerable distance ahead of Bart and the others, and the entire group was strung out over several hundred yards. Bill was particularly motivated, and forged ahead of the rest of the group as he was desperate to atone for his previous mistake.

Bart had lost sight of his brother when he heard the faint report of the weapon. He was ecstatic. The sound of the gunshot could only mean one thing: Bill had found them and shot the father. He called back for the rest of them to hurry as he continued downstream.

Bart excitedly crossed the river to where the canyon wall hung over the floor far enough to form an alcove. He rounded the wall expecting to find his brother standing over a dead man but found the lifeless body of his brother instead. At first, he couldn't believe his eyes. Still, the image did not change, and he realized that the man and woman had somehow killed Bill and escaped.

Bart was infuriated. He went out to the river brandishing his gun, and frantically searched downstream for a target while screaming hysterically at the top of his lungs. However, there were no targets, and his maniacal rant was swept away by the cleansing rain. He came back to the body and screamed again, slamming his body against the rock wall of the grotto. He finally collapsed in a rage-induced stupor, recovering his senses only when the rest of the group reached the grotto.

Bart had never been particularly close to his brother, but he was still his brother. But for that relationship, Bill would have killed Bart long ago. What was important now was that the miserable couple who should both be dead had killed someone he felt responsible for. Further, they had escaped again. Part of his anger was directed at his brother. If he had done his job back at the Fall the day before, this never would have happened.

The others straggled into the grotto one by one. Rich was the first, saw what had happened, and checked Bill to make sure he was dead. He was. There was no pulse and his throat had a large bruise on it. He had been hit in the neck with the fatal stroke of some weapon. Ed and Archie arrived, one shortly after the other, and surveyed the scene.

"Did you find Bill's gun?" Ed was worried.

"No." Rich looked at Bart.

"I didn't see it when I got here. Look around for it." Bart was calm enough to talk again, but what he really wanted was to get the jerk that killed his brother.

Rich, Ed, and Archie looked through and around the Grotto for the weapon but did not find it. All three of them were now worried, but Bart's anger was stronger than the fear he felt.

"What are we going to do now, Bart?" asked Ed. He was still in favor of going back upriver.

"We are going to track down that sonovabitch and kill him. What do you think we are going to do?"

"But he must have Bill's gun, and the clip has fifteen rounds in it."

"I don't care. He killed my brother. He's not going to get away with it. Not while I'm alive."

"But what if he kills us?"

"That's why you have a gun, you gutless moron! The idea is to kill him before he kills you! We're all going after him, do you hear?!" Bart had a hysterical look in his eye, and Ed knew that now was not the time to protest.

"Okay Bart, let's do it. But we need to be careful. This guy seems to know what he is doing. All he has to do is hide behind a rock, let us get close enough and he can shoot a couple of us before we know where the bullets are coming from."

"All right! We'll watch for an ambush. Let's go."

"What about the body?" Archie felt uncomfortable abandoning Bill's body on the floor of the Grotto.

"What about it? Do you want to carry it?" Bart was in no mood for Archie's stupid questions.

"Shouldn't we bury him?"

"We don't have anything to bury him with. Even if we did, there is no way to dig deep enough anywhere in this canyon to bury him, and that would give the father and his daughter enough time to get all the way down the canyon! Is that what you want?"

"No, I don't want them to get away. But if we leave the body here, someone's going to find it eventually aren't they? And then the cops will be asking who was with him."

Bart looked at Archie in amazement. Sometimes a rational thought did make its way out of his befuddled mind. "You're right of course; we can't let the cops find the body. But what can we do?"

"Why don't we go now, catch and take care of these two, then come back and take Bill's body someplace where they can't find it?" Rich suggested.

"Not a bad idea. Okay, let's go. We'll come back when we've killed the other two." Bart wanted to catch the curs that killed Bill, and this seemed a plausible excuse to get going now. Soon the group was back in pursuit, leaving Bill's body lying on the grotto floor where it lay. They proceeded with caution, anticipating a firefight when they caught up with Bill's killers.

David and Rebecca had only gone about one hundred yards downriver before they faintly heard the distant sound of enraged and animated shouting from the Grotto they had just departed. The other skinheads had just found their friend, and the implications were obvious. The men knew they were close and they would be coming fast on their heels. David doubted that he and Rebecca would have time to backtrack far enough to hide even if they could find the narrow opening to Goose Creek. If so, they would have to go through the Narrows with four very angry, violent skinheads chasing them all the way.

It occurred to David that the men might think they had retrieved the gun from their companion. This was very good. Misperception could be almost as useful as reality. The skinheads would have to be less complacent about their own security and might go a little slower while watching for an ambush. That was the only advantage David and Rebecca had, and it was a slim one, but it was better than nothing. David only hoped the men would have the presence of mind to notice the weapon was missing. Otherwise, they would come on strong, quickly overtaking their prey.

The two continued down the river, forced by the canyon to spend less and less time on the sides and more and more time in the water. They tried to anticipate the easiest and quickest route, moving as efficiently as they could. They had to be quiet again. If they were heard, they gave away their position and the skinheads would forge ahead faster. Even worse, considering the limited acoustical range, if the men heard them they might be close enough to fire.

Alarmed by the possibility of the skinheads being able to see them even now, David glanced back to look for them and saw no one. He could not see anything past fifty feet. Visibility was decreasing. Focusing attention on the rain, which up to now had been pushed behind other immediate concerns, he could see that it was coming down harder. He wondered how much rain it took to generate a significant flood, or even an insignificant one for that matter. He began to imagine that the water level was rising, and his mind flashed back to another day in the same canyon many years ago. Long repressed, the memory of the quickly rising water level filled him with dread.

"We have to get higher!" he whispered under his breath to Rebecca, frantically searching up and down the canyon for an accessible high point they could both climb to and perch upon. "I think there's a flood coming!"

"A flood?! There's going to be a flood?!

David could tell that this was the first time that any concern about a flood was occurring to his daughter. She got a "what's the use?" look on her face and began to cry. Even worse, she stopped.

Rebecca's reaction forced David to get a grip. He was instantly sorry for the momentary lapse of control. "It's okay honey. I'm so sorry. I let myself get carried away. It would take a lot more water than this to flood the canyon," he said, hoping it was not a lie. Indeed, he saw that the water level wasn't rising. It was still only up to the middle of the waist at the deepest points.

"You're lying. You just want me to feel good before I die."

"No, I mean it. It really is okay. The water is still fine."

"But is it going to flood with all this rain?"

"I don't know. I'm not worried so much about what is falling here as with what's falling on the mountain," he said, motioning in the direction of Cedar Mountain.

"When you were a boy, what was it like? Is the same thing happening?"

"Pretty much. However, the rain falling here is not as important as what is falling in the upper watershed. It rains many times a year, but destructive flash floods are rare. We do need to pay close attention to the water. If it gets cloudy and you see a lot of stuff floating downriver, we need to get to high ground immediately."

"The water looks clear, and I can't see anything floating along."

"I know; that's what I mean. We're okay for now. But we have to keep moving if we don't want them to catch us."

"Yeah, okay, let's go." With that, they started back downstream. David was relieved, both that a flood was not imminent and that they were traveling again.

They had not heard any noise from above since the commotion at the Grotto. This might be a good sign. Maybe the skinheads were going slow, watching for an ambush. Besides, it had been a long time since then and David figured they would have caught them by now if they had been moving at full speed. As quickly as David and Rebecca were going, he knew that four strong young men could move considerably faster than a wounded "old man" and his daughter, both of whom were exhausted. The men must think they had the gun.

David wondered whether he could use this perception to their advantage. Was there a way to fool the men with a fake weapon, perhaps hidden under a shirt? They could wait for the men to reach them, fake an ambush, and demand they drop their weapons. Maybe the men would fall for it and they could disarm them, use their weapons to hold them until the rain stopped. After the flood danger passed, they would then escort the men ahead of themselves downriver, maybe tying them together and partially restricting the use of their hands. David did not think he could tie them up and leave them helpless with the flood potential being as high as he imagined it.

"Get real. You wouldn't get the demand out of your mouth before being cut down," he told himself. These people shot first and asked questions later. He was grasping at straws, trying to avoid the dark narrow canyon ahead with water streaming into it from the river on the bottom and the sky and plateau above. He quickly dismissed the idea. They had to stay ahead of Bart and his gang.

The rain was coming down harder. It had been falling now for at least an hour, which was the elapsed time since leaving the Grotto. David questioned again how long it had been falling before he woke up. A lot of water was coming down. He also speculated how much rain was falling higher in the Narrows watershed. If the storm was this strong for this long, he felt that it must be widespread enough to dump a lot of water on Cedar Mountain. He could feel a flood coming in his bones. He had to force down another powerful urge to climb.

He wondered how long they would be alive. If the flood did not get them, the lunatics behind them would. David began to resign himself to destruction, getting the same look on his face that Rebecca had shown just a little while ago. They might as well get it over with. They could just wait for the men to come to them and it would be over quickly. At least it would be over quickly for him. It would not be as quick or as easy for Rebecca. Anger flared up within him at the thought, and a small shot of adrenaline flashed through his body. He was not going to give up. Those jerks were going to have to catch them. They continued slogging along.

They had been moving downstream for over an hour now, and they still had at least four miles to go to reach safety. Once again, he lamented his decision to stop and sleep at the Grotto. If he had not decided to stop last night, they would have been safe by now.

David began to wonder if he could do anything right. This trip was the worst mistake of his life. Austin was surely dead. If the wound or animals had not killed him, rain and hypothermia had. He and Rebecca were running for their lives because he had not listened to his premonition yesterday, and because he had not brought an effective weapon. Moreover, he had blown the one chance they had to get one by knocking it into the river. He had slept away the opportunity to get down the canyon without being chased by floodwater or murderous lunatics. They were running from his worst nightmare, only too real to him, the terrible destruction wrought by nature on the rampage. Was there anything else that could go wrong? He put the thought out of his mind, not wanting to tempt fate.

David's mind was in such turmoil that he paid scarce attention to what he was doing and his surroundings, and traveled some distance while beating himself up emotionally. The confluence of events that combined to put him and Rebecca into a predicament that would require a miracle to survive, and his ineptitude in not avoiding it, even though all it would have taken was to have made one different correct decision out of many, undermined his confidence in his ability to make intelligent decisions.

"Daddy, what's wrong?" Rebecca asked. She had noticed that David was lethargic and seemed disoriented, and was worried that her father was losing it.

"Nothing honey." Looking at the soaked figure with the worried look on her face standing beside him, David softened his attitude toward himself somewhat. There really was not any choice about stopping the night before. They would have both been dead from hypothermia if they had traveled another half hour in the water. Even now, Rebecca was safe, although that seemed only temporary. He was still alive. Temporary also. In addition, they were still in front of the lunatics. Temporary. Was there anything he could think of that was not temporary? They stumbled on.

His stomach began to grumble again. Breakfast. They were supposed to be eating breakfast this morning in Springdale. He began to imagine the breakfast he had enjoyed only twenty-six hours ago of eggs, hash browns, toast, and orange juice. His stomach growled with the thought. Nevertheless, they had eaten all the food they had last night, and even if they had not, they could not stop to eat now. His stomach would just have to wait.

It was getting darker even though it was morning and should have been growing lighter. The rain continued to increase in intensity and the river continued downward, trying to push them along with it. He wondered what had happened to the high-pressure system that was going to keep the skies clear. It certainly was not over them now. He couldn't help but wonder if this was a natural conspiracy against him.

He wondered how much further it was to Goose Creek Canyon. It should have only taken them thirty minutes from the Grotto. Were they really going that slow? Just then, he became conscious of the fact that he had not been paying attention to their overall surroundings. He had only focused on moving down the river. They had traveled such a long distance since leaving the grotto that they should have reached Goose Creek Canyon by now. Where were they anyway?

David stopped. Looking just ahead, David saw a spring flowing down the western side of the canyon. The water joined the river at a small hole in which trout could be seen swimming from where they stood. Just down the river, he saw the canyon tightly constrict as it bent to the right. It was a view he could not forget. It was the entrance to the Narrows. They were at Big Springs, the steep spring falling from the high plateau above.

David had passed Goose Creek in the rain without noticing it. Now David was infuriated with himself. If they had missed it, it was possible their pursuers would have gone by also. They could have waited out the storm in a high safe location and come out after the danger from both the storm and the skinheads had passed. They might even have been rescued, given the severity of the storm and the fact that they would be overdue. But he had been too busy feeling sorry for himself to pay enough attention to find it.

David wondered if a rescue attempt was possible. After all, the Park Service knew he and his family were in the canyon, and they might send help if they thought they were in danger. At the same time, he knew his hope was futile; the Park Service made it clear that personal safety was the responsibility of the hikers. Still, he had heard that there was a place to get a helicopter down for a rescue and dreamt of a short ride to safety, warmth, and food. Even if it were possible that a chopper would be sent, he didn't know where the helipad was located or how to get to it, and he couldn't wait around for someone to rescue him again. He didn't think they could get a helicopter safely down with the turbulent air in the canyon given today's weather anyway.

David looked up and saw the ledge upon which he had stood so many years before. It was big enough to hold both of them. How ironic it was that the same scenario might be occurring again. He looked at the water in the river, looking for the signs of a coming flood, and listened for the half-expected roar of water crashing down the canyon. "At least that might solve one problem," he thought. "A flood right now would probably take out the skinheads." Still, no roar could be heard, only the constant flowing of the river and patter of the rain.

David turned to face Rebecca, who was waiting patiently for David to take stock of his surroundings. "We are at Big Springs," he said.

"Big Springs? I thought we were going up Goose Creek Canyon."

"We were." The dejected look on his face told Rebecca the bad news.

"You mean we passed it?"

"I'm afraid so."

"Where is Big Springs?"

"At the beginning of the Narrows."

"But I thought we didn't want to go into the Narrows now."

"We don't, but I'm not sure we have any choice. If we go back they'll find us for sure."

"What are we going to do then?"

David did not answer. He knew this was the point of no return. If they went into that dark chasm, the only way out was almost two miles downriver; two miles fraught with danger the entire way. The vision of the muddy wave crashing on the walls played in his mind, and the recollection of all his friends crushed and drowned became real again. Some of the bodies were never found; they were still buried in some unknown sand bank somewhere downriver or had been washed into the cold depths of Lake Mead, never to come up again. He could not force himself to proceed, fearing that he would finally rejoin his troop if he entered the canyon. He continued to hesitate, then remembered something that he had been told many years ago.

"I hear there's a helipad above Big Springs." David was willing to try anything to avoid the canyon below. "If so, there'll be a trail. If we can find it, we can climb out of danger."

"Sounds good to me. Where is the trail?"

"There is a short side canyon just above the springs. That would be the most logical place for a trail to take off from the canyon bottom. Let's try it."

No sooner had David finished his sentence than they heard a shout above them, which brought the urgency of their immediate danger back to where it should have been. David saw a splash of water kick up beside him, and then heard the pop-whiz of the bullet reach his ear a split second later. The skinheads had caught them. Now they would know they did not have the gun and would take care of them quickly. He had delayed too long, agonizing over the inevitable.

"We're going down the Narrows. Now!" He grabbed Rebecca, and together they struggled through the stream down toward the dark canyon, bullets splashing around them. Instantly expelled were all his fears of a flood. As they plunged into and were enveloped by darkness, they heard the gleeful shouting of the skinheads above.

Chapter 14

Pursuit to Big Springs

At about the same time the skinheads were waking downriver, the police woke to the same light drizzle. However, they were expecting it and were prepared, having wrapped their bags in plastic the night before. They had slept comfortably; however, they were concerned about more important things than personal comfort. They got up, donned wet suits, and broke camp.

The team was composed of men with specialty training needed for this particular assignment. The sergeant leading the unit, Jon Leavitt, was a hardened Vietnam veteran who had been a member of Force Reconnaissance. He had also spent many years as a police officer. He was particularly skilled in tracking and interpreting the significance of everything left behind. Gene Blackwell was their sharpshooter; he also was a veteran and a sniper. Dan Gooding was the medic; young and enthusiastic, he was the least seasoned of the group. Last was Marcus Bellingham, who knew the canyon inside out and served as their navigator and communications specialist.

After their gear was packed, they ate a hasty, cold breakfast even as they searched the area for any sign of anyone in front of them. Even though there was not much light from the overcast sky, it was only a few minutes before Gene found a large number of spent cartridges from at least two handguns, one a nine millimeter and the other a forty-five caliber. The cartridges had been very recently fired; they were still bright and free of corrosion. The casings were found behind a rock outcrop beside the river next to the trail that portaged around the Fall. There was no indication of what was being shot at, although the rain might have washed away any blood on the ground.

When the team scoured the area above the Fall for additional signs, much more was found. The recent footprints of six people portaging around the Fall were discerned in the soft dirt. One set of prints was much smaller than the others, probably the prints of the girl. It appeared that two of the group had broken off from the rest and had gone to where the spent cartridges were found. Also discovered at that location was discarded litter from a meal and a well-trampled site where the two people had waited. Last, they discovered the footprints of one person who approached the Fall close to the river but did not walk back out. The prints of the single person were large and so probably belonged to a man.

"What do you make of it, Jon?" asked Dan.

Jon did not need much time to deduce the answer. "We have two guys setting an ambush here," he said, pointing to the trampled area. "They fired a lot of rounds at the guy coming down the river, and he didn't come out. They must have shot him and his body was swept over the Fall." By now, the entire team had gathered around to hear his evaluation.

"What about the girl?" asked Marcus.

"She was alive when they came by here. Her prints go with the group down the trail"

"How many in the group?" Gene was considering how complicated his duty could become.

"Five, not including the girl."

"What now?" Marcus was prepared to proceed.

"Let's try to find the body of the guy they shot. It may be hung up somewhere downstream"

"I guess this means that the father didn't shoot his kid." Dan had three small children himself and was pleased that they had discovered that the father had not gone berserk and destroyed his own family.

"Probably," said Jon matter-of-factly.

Jon also advised his team of the implications of their discoveries for their own personal safety. "We have at least two weapons in the hands of people who have no reservations about using them on innocent people," he observed. "We have to stay sharp. We have to assume all five of them are armed. Fortunately for us, they don't know we're above them." He paused, looking at the debris lying in the grass. "We need to retrieve and bag all this stuff as evidence."

The officers pulled out cameras, tweezers, and plastic bags, then photographed and retrieved all the spent cartridges and debris. They also took close-up photos of each type of shoeprint for future comparison. They worked efficiently, taking care not to contaminate the evidence. When they finished, Dan stowed the evidence in his pack.

As the rest of the team collected the evidence, Jon directed Marcus to call the command center at the Temple of Sinawava. "We need to phone this in and let them know what's heading their direction in case they are so far in front that we can't catch up. Tell them that if we catch them we'll take them to the helipad above Big Springs."

Marcus radioed the Sinawava command center as they started down the trail around the Fall. After reporting what they had found, he received instruction. "The weather is bad," advised the Captain at Sinawava command center.

"I think we figured that out, sir." Marcus wondered if the Captain thought they didn't know.

"Don't be impertinent. I mean the weather is really bad, especially on the mountain. We have reports of heavy rainfall lasting for hours. The flood potential is very, very high. Do you copy?"

"Yes sir." Marcus was willing to forgive the Captain for the comment.

"Keep your eyes on the river. At the first sign of a flood, get to high ground and stay there. You don't need to worry about catching these guys. We'll catch them when they come out down here."

"Yes sir. But are you sure you don't want us to chase them down. What about the side canyons? I know that it's rough going, but it's possible they could get out going up one of them."

"We'll cover those too. We'll watch every possible way out of that canyon. We'll get them."

"Yes sir."

"And Bellingham, this is very important. Under no circumstances do you enter the Narrows. When you make it to Big Springs, climb to the helipad and call us. We will evacuate you from there. Do you understand?"

"Yes sir."

"Advise Sergeant Leavitt. Over and out."

The Captain at the Sinawava command center, Mario Hernandez, was an experienced professional who knew what he was doing. He had started by closing the park to all visitors, both because of the threat of flooding and to avoid confusion with or harm from the homicidal person or persons that the police were trying to apprehend. In addition, he had already anticipated the need for covering all possible exits from the canyon and had posted police units at each of the side canyons with instructions to detain anyone coming out. He

160

had one group of four officers at the end of the paved trail leading upriver toward the Narrows. There was no reason to have them go any further up river. They would catch anyone coming out there.

The team at the Fall, who heard every word that Captain Hernandez said, was concerned and relieved at the same time. Concerned about a flood, but relieved they didn't have to go through the Narrows in the rain. That they were to be evacuated was a true measure of the gravity of the threat. It nearly took an act of Congress to get a helicopter into the Park.

They reached the bottom of the Fall and scoured up and down both sides of the river, looking for more signs and a body. On the south bank, Marcus found more nine-millimeter cartridges. He called Sergeant Leavitt over.

This discovery was alarming to Jon. "Additional rounds fired here. This isn't good. Look around and see if you can find the body of the girl."

The group fanned out on both sides of the river and searched downstream a short distance until Dan came across tracks from the group. He called Sergeant Leavitt to see what could be determined. Fortunately, the tracks were in sand and each set was easily identifiable.

"Well, well, well." Jon was pleased. "This is encouraging. The girl is on her feet walking with the rest of the group downriver, which means they didn't kill her.

"How do we know these prints were made recently? Couldn't they be from another group days ago?" Gene was skeptical.

"Not a chance. Look at the footprints in the sand. Do you see how crisp the sides are and how only a little sand from the edge of the print has collapsed into the print itself? The more recent the print the more crisp the edge will be. Over time wind and weather will eventually wear it down, but these are weathered so little it is certain they were made last night. Even with the rain that has fallen it is evident that these are fresh tracks. Besides, the shoeprints match those we found yesterday."

"That makes sense."

"This means the rounds upstream were fired at the father. So, they shot at him up above and here below the Fall. I doubt they got him."

"No way. That's not possible." Gene could not imagine so many bullets fired without deadly effect.

161

"Yes it is. If they shot a lot of rounds, that means they didn't get him with the first shots. If they didn't get him with the first shots, the guy had time to react. Maybe he was able to get away. It can also mean that the shooters are incompetent and can't hit what they are shooting at."

"You think so?" Gene was not convinced.

"It's a long shot, but it's possible. Let's keep looking. Go back and retrieve the casings we found back at the Fall," he said, pointing Dan upriver. Dan was the youngest and was low man on the totem pole, so he got most of the minor assignments.

While Dan did as instructed, the rest of the team turned their attention back to the search. They were sweeping down the river when Gene cried out in excitement. "Check this out!"

Jon and Marcus rushed over to where he stood. On the top of a large flat boulder lay the paper packaging from a large bandage. The footprints around the rock matched the prints of the solitary man who was apparently ambushed above the Fall. Last, there were drops of blood on the rock, some of which had been smeared, apparently by the person who had sat on the rock to treat his wound. Even Gene and Marcus knew what this meant.

"They didn't kill him." Jon was clearly pleased. "Well I'll be damned. I cannot believe it. I don't know how, but he made it. Call it in now," he directed Marcus. "They need to know to be on the lookout for him."

"He's obviously wounded though," said Gene.

"Yeah, but he was able to treat himself then get up and walk off under his own power. He's not hurt too badly."

"What do you think he is trying to do?"

"I think he's trying to help his kid. This guy has grit. Let's hurry. We need to help him if we can." They continued sweeping down the river while Marcus called in the report.

The news was received at the Sinawava command center with much enthusiasm. All units posted in the Park were advised that both members of the family might still be alive, and were cautioned to be careful not to fire on them.

For Captain Hernandez there was now much more of a sense of urgency than there had been when they were just waiting for whoever shot the boy to come out. The possibility that the father and daughter were still alive and coming down the canyon drastically changed the situation. In view of the obvious danger the father was in, he decided to send the four officers waiting at the end of the Narrows trail up river to where the Narrows ended in the hope that any survivor that emerged could be protected as soon as possible. However, they could go no further. They could not enter the Narrows no matter what. This group started upstream immediately.

The team at the Fall continued, proceeding quickly down the river, while covering both banks looking for any sign. The river was cold, but the wet suits kept them comfortable and they were able to make excellent time. They found nothing unusual until they reached Deep Creek, where they found the remains of a camp from the previous night. The group was careful not to disturb any evidence in the camp until Sergeant Leavitt came up and had a chance to evaluate it.

Jon examined at the camp for some time, moving around the edges of it, and then working his way down to the river as he examined footprints and material. Even though it had been raining, the site was protected by its proximity to the canyon wall. Jon could still read the story in the prints. "He came in and got her out," he announced.

"He did? Are you sure?" Gene was skeptical again.

"Of course I'm sure. Look at the prints going through the center of the camp. Bare feet going in. The ropes binding the girl were cut. Abandoning the girl's gear, they came out, retracing his steps. The prints avoid stepping where the sleeping bags were laid out, so these guys were obviously sleeping when he did it. One set of prints going in, two coming out, one of which is smaller."

"Are you sure they didn't catch him?"

"No way, at least not here. They got out of the camp completely and went to the river. I can't tell for sure, but it seems obvious they went down the river. The reason I'm sure they weren't caught is because of the tracks these other guys made when they found out she had escaped. They started running in every direction. If the girl and her father were in the camp, or even visible, all the tracks would have been pointed in their direction. No doubt about it, they got away." Jon surveyed the scene with admiration for the man who had apparently rescued his daughter. "He went right into the middle of the camp to get her out. And he was wounded to boot," he thought to himself.

163

Jon remembered their need for haste. "Let's hurry and get this site photographed and picked up. Get on the horn and see if they've come out yet. If he got her out last night, they may be close to Sinawava by now." Marcus radioed the latest news to the command center while the others busied themselves with collecting, bagging, and photographing the evidence left behind.

Captain Hernandez was pleased and worried at the same time. It was great that the family had escaped their tormentors, but why had they not reached the safety of the lower canyon yet? He contacted the group working their way upriver to give them the information and to check again if they had seen anything. The report came back negative, although the team was still an hour away from the Narrows exit. The Sergeant in charge of that group communicated that they would keep a close eye out for the family. The team at Deep Creek was advised the family was still in the canyon.

At first, the team traveling up the canyon had an easy time hiking up the trail that ran along the river. But soon, as is all off trail travel in the rugged canyon, their progress was slow and difficult. They had ponchos, but they didn't keep them from getting wet from repeatedly fording the river. They laboriously fought their way upstream to a point where the river emerged from a narrow slit in the canyon wall.

Here the canyon floor was littered with a jumble of boulders and dead trees that served as a grim reminder of the power of the floods that occasionally issued from the Narrows. In a flood, the rapid widening of the canyon dissipated much of the force of the flood, and much of the material carried through the Narrows was deposited here. The team positioned themselves as high up the slope as they could on the west side of the river, and prepared themselves for either a rescue or an arrest. They had seen no one since leaving command center hours before and radioed information to that effect back to Captain Hernandez.

Back at Deep Creek, Sergeant Leavitt was also anxious. "Where are they? How much time does it take to get out of the canyon from here?"

The second question he directed at Marcus, who studied his map for a minute before answering. "About five hours to get out of the Narrows, or seven hours to Sinawava."

"They should've been out by now! Why did they stop? If they escaped last night they should be safe by now." Jon was frustrated by the apparent contradiction between what the evidence here at Deep Creek told him and the fact that the family was still not out of the canyon.

"How do you know? Can you tell what time he came in and got her? Maybe they started from here in the late morning." Marcus was mentally calculating how much time had elapsed since the family had likely escaped from Deep Creek.

"Could be, but I don't think so." Jon was convinced that the escape was made early in the night because the father almost certainly was close behind the perpetrators after he was shot.

"Maybe they went up one of the side canyons. If so, we might not see them for a couple of days." Marcus was trying to think of all of the possible explanations for the family's delay.

"I hope you're right. Still, we have to assume the worst. And the worst scenario that we can help them in is if they slept overnight downriver and started out just in front of the guys that are chasing them." Jon, realizing that he had stumbled upon the most likely explanation, paused before thinking aloud, "I bet they stopped at the Grotto."

"You could be right. You know, it was pretty cold last night. They may have had to stop to keep from freezing." Marcus had the same thought when Jon mentioned the possibility of them sleeping overnight in the canyon.

Jon looked at his wet suit. "Of course, they couldn't have gone on all night. I'm sure they don't have comfortable wet suits to help them retain body heat. Yeah, you're right. Are we ready yet? We may be the only chance they have. Let's get going."

The team had finished collecting and packing evidence and started down the river again. The knowledge that two lives might depend on their speed spurred them on, and they traveled as quickly as they could. In less than thirty minutes they covered the distance to the Grotto.

Concerned that they might find the group of gunmen they were chasing still at the Grotto, Sergeant Leavitt had the team group up. He organized their entry into the grotto as if they were bursting into a drug dealer's home, minus the door. Giving the order to move, the team suddenly piled into the hollow in the rock wall. Just as abruptly, they stopped in their tracks, surprised by what they found. The Grotto was bare except for the motionless, outstretched body of one man.

"Check him out," ordered Jon.

Dan moved to the side of the body. He checked the neck of the man, feeling for a pulse. There was none. "He's dead, Sergeant. There's no pulse."

"Any idea how long ago he was killed?"

"Not long. His body is still warm. My guess is a half hour or so."

"What killed him? A gunshot wound?"

Dan examined the rest of the body, including rolling it over on its side and checking his back. "No, it was something else. There's no blood from an entry or exit wound." Dan continued to examine the upper torso and head of the dead man, looking for the cause of death.

"Could this be the father?" Gene asked.

"You tell me. Do you think it is?" Jon wanted Gene to deduce the answer to his own question.

"Probably not."

"Why not?

"He's younger than I would expect the father of two teenagers to be. In addition, his head is shaved and he has multiple tattoos. He is a skinhead, and you don't see many middle-aged skinheads."

"That's good. Besides that, he wasn't killed with a gun, which we know that the group trying to kill the father possessed and had no qualms about using. Plus we know the father is wounded, and this guy has no other wound."

"I think I know what killed him. Take a look." Dan pointed to the man's neck where a dark bruise had formed. "He took a hard blow to his neck. It looks like it crushed his larynx, so he probably was asphyxiated."

"Look around and see if there is anything else in here" the Sergeant directed the rest of the team. They examined the site, looking for clues that might tell them what happened. They were easy to find.

"I have impressions here where two people must have slept last night," Gene said.

"It looks like they were walking out when this guy came in." Jon was tracing the muddle of tracks made by both groups, trying to make sense of them. "The father's prints start out, then twist sharply right here," he said pointing to the upturned dirt. "He must have turned his body abruptly."

"I bet he hit the guy with something right when he walked in," observed Gene.

"You're right. Good work. So it looks like the father and daughter slept here then killed this guy who walked in on them as they were leaving. And that may have been only a half hour ago. Why did he kill him?" Jon wondered.

"Can't tell for sure with what we have here. But he must have been threatened. The guy probably had a gun," offered Marcus, who was examining the tracks at the entrance.

"Could be. Any sign of a gun?"

"Not that I can see."

"Look, here is another shell casing," interrupted Gene as he retrieved the casing from the top of the sand floor. "Someone did fire a gun."

"It may have been one of the other perpetrators, but I don't think so. That would only make sense if there was a different body here," Jon reasoned.

Dan was now examining the soles of the dead man's shoes. "Look," he said, "this dead guy's footprints match one of the guys who staged the ambush at the Fall, and we know he was armed."

Jon was more certain now of what had occurred. "That means the father probably has this guy's gun. He must have been able to win a fight in these close quarters. Why didn't he stop here and use his weapon against the others?"

"One against four is not good odds. And maybe he doesn't know how to use it," Gene suggested.

Jon wasn't convinced. "I don't think so. Remember, he owns weapons; one of our initial concerns was that he had shot his son with his own nine-millimeter. In any case, he certainly knows how to use something as a weapon that enabled him to kill this skinhead even though he had a gun. And he knows what floods can do in this canyon, which is even more reason for him to try to get the drop on these guys."

"Maybe he went on with the idea of doing it in a better spot." Gene was thinking aloud.

167

Jon nodded in agreement. "That makes sense. After all, that is what they did to him last night. In any case, we need to call this in. The guys downriver need to know the father may be armed. And I don't want anyone getting shot by mistake."

Stepping out of the grotto into a now severe rainstorm Marcus radioed Captain Hernandez with the latest information. Even with the advanced state-of-the-art equipment they had brought they were so deep in the canyon and there was so much rain that the communication was garbled and barely coherent. Still, he eventually got the message across. The Captain took the message, but then had some instruction of his own for the team and asked to speak to the Sergeant.

"Yes sir, what is it?" Jon wondered why the Captain wanted to talk directly to him.

"Sergeant, you need to stop where you are now and get to high ground."

"What was that? You're breaking up." It was true that the message was difficult to understand, but it was communicated.

"Get to high ground and stay there. We can't evacuate you in this rain and wind, and we have confirmed reports of flooding upstream."

"I can't understand. We'll relocate and call you back." Jon turned off the radio.

Mario was angry with Jon. He knew that his message got through and that Jon was disobeying his instructions. But the only thing he could do now was to advise his teams that one of the perpetrators had been killed and that the father might be armed, which he did.

Back at the Grotto, Jon scrutinized his men. All of his team members were married and had kids. He had five grandchildren himself and he wondered if he should obey orders and stop, but decided to poll the team.

"You heard the Captain. He wants us to stop and wait out the rain. We can hunker down on high ground and wait out the storm, or we can chase both groups down the river, at least until Big Springs, in the hopes of catching them before they enter the Narrows. But no further. If they enter the Narrows, they're on their own. What do you guys think?"

"I think we should continue, at least for now. So far, these two have made it. We owe it to them to help if we can. And besides, we're so close." Marcus voted aye.

"We may be the only chance they have. These guys will kill them, especially after they killed one of their own. We can't leave them twisting in the wind." Dan also voted aye.

"There's still time. The river is still clear for now, and we'll have some warning of a big flood. Let's catch up with them." Gene, who had checked the condition of the river and concluded that a flood was not imminent, made it unanimous.

"Okay let's go. But watch the water."

The team proceeded downriver amid the increasingly heavy downpour. The river water soon became murky, and the team began to worry more about a flood than about the threat of the men they were chasing. Nevertheless, the combined effect of the hope of reaching their goal and the adrenaline produced by the knowledge of imminent danger propelled them down stream at an incredible rate of speed.

Just prior to reaching Big Springs, they heard the faint report of gunfire. Drawing their weapons, they proceeded cautiously, looking for any sign of ambush. This was a precautionary measure; they did not seriously think they were in danger from attack because there was no way the perpetrators could know they were behind them. Yet, they had to be cautious. Jon assumed the perpetrators fired the shots at the father and daughter. If that were the case then the father and daughter had been alive at least until a moment ago.

Rounding a bend in the river, they saw Big Springs descending from the plateau above; just downriver was the beginning of the Narrows. Standing at the entrance, peering into the darkness were four men, all with drawn guns. All of them had shaved heads and numerous tattoos, and their attention was focused downriver. They were arguing among themselves.

Jon motioned the others to be quiet, and then pointed with his finger directing the others to creep up on the group. The others understood, and silently moved closer by carefully walking from one vantage point to another, taking advantage of the limited cover the terrain provided. The team soon crept up close enough to hear the skinhead's debate.

"Why didn't any of you hit them?" snarled the man who was clearly the leader.

"They were too far away," one of the others whined as he kept his eyes focused downriver.

"The rain threw off my aim," said another who also looked intently at the canyon below.

"Did you hit them Bart?" the third asked.

"That's beside the point. I can't believe that all of you could miss such easy targets after firing so many times." Bart was clearly not happy with Archie's question.

"Now what? Should we go back and get Bill's body?"

The question angered Bart. "Of course not! We're going after them! They're just in front of us going downriver. If we go after them now we can easily catch them. If we go back to Bill now we don't have any chance of catching them before they reach safety downriver and we'll be arrested as soon as we get out of the canyon ourselves!"

"But Bart, what if it floods?"

"I don't give a damn. We are not going to let them get away just because we're afraid of a little flood. Do you understand?"

Jon decided to make up their minds for them. "Police officers! Halt! Drop your weapons!" he shouted at the top of his lungs. However, before the officers could react, Bart and his group simultaneously sprang forward into the darkness of the canyon, shouting recriminatory accusations among themselves as they went. No shots were fired.

The officers hurried to the Narrows entrance and stood looking into the darkness that had swallowed the four men. Jon looked at the mouth of the canyon, then at his men, then back at the canyon. "Now what?" He asked the question aloud but he was really asking himself. The others stood silently, pondering the danger that lay down the river.

"Call Sinawava. Tell them that both groups just entered the Narrows. See what they want us to do." Jon knew what the answer would be, but did not want to accept it.

Marcus tried several times, but try as he might, he couldn't raise the command center. The sheer rock walls and rain combined to make contact impossible. The latest intelligence report would have to wait.

Jon faced the rest of his team and cleared his throat. "It's clear," he started, "that both groups, the family and the skinheads, are just inside the entrance. The family is running from the skinheads, and the skinheads are now running from us in addition to chasing the family. If we continue, we might catch up with the skinheads before they can catch the family. If we stay here as the Captain ordered, the families' only chance is to reach the team waiting downriver before being caught." Jon hesitated for a moment to let the significance of his words sink in before resuming.

"The order to get off the river bottom was given to us when we were at the Grotto, before we knew they were just ahead of us. If we could talk to the Captain, maybe he would change his order," Gene offered weakly.

Jon looked up, searching for any hint of blue sky beyond the falling rain and ominous clouds. "I wonder how many inches of rain have fallen this morning. It has to be a lot. Even worse, it's likely that the rain is heavier on the mountain. One inch of rain there means at least a three-foot rise in the water through the canyon. If we go in and a flood hits before we get out the other side we'll die in addition to the others, and our deaths won't help anyone." He paused again.

"Even if we go in after them, there's no guarantee we can capture them. If we do catch up with the skinheads, the canyon is so narrow and constricted that the possibility of one of us being shot is more probable than not, especially because the skinheads now know we're behind them. The odds of complete success, which is all of the skinheads killed or captured with no injuries to us, in a firefight in such close quarters is not good. Even if we can catch and disarm the skinheads, there is no way to warn the possibly armed father of who we are before he shoots at us. He probably won't believe us even if we identify ourselves as officers." The last pause gave the men time to make up their minds.

"What do you want to do now, given the circumstances?"

"I think we should go," Gene offered, although with considerably less enthusiasm than what he displayed at the Grotto.

"I do too." Dan looked down at the river as he said the words. Jon knew he was lying because of his tone and demeanor.

171

"I'm with the rest." Marcus's voice cracked with stress.

Jon knew they didn't want to go; he didn't blame them because he felt the same. However, even if he had, he knew it would be a futile effort. Captain Hernandez would never consent to their entering the canyon. For good reason, they had to stop here and get to the helicopter pad. The other team was waiting downriver in the direction that they would be expecting help to come from. The family would just have to make it on their own through the Narrows.

"Turn around, let's go back and climb. There's a trail just upriver to the left."

The men looked at Jon with a combination of mild resentment and relief. The vacant expression on his face told them he had made a firm decision and that any further discussion was futile.

The team reluctantly turned from the Narrows entrance, and forged back upriver to where a slight trail angled up a short side canyon. Soon the trail ascended a slope with a series of switchbacks that hugged the canyon wall. The team carefully made their way upward to the safety of height. Five hundred feet above the canyon floor there was a level spot just large enough for a helicopter to safely land upon where they stopped and waited. The adventure was nearly finished for them, as they stared over the side of the cliff to the increasingly roiled river below.

Jon ordered Marcus to contact Sinawava again, and this time the effort was successful. Jon advised Captain Hernandez that his team was waiting at the evacuation point, but that both groups had just started down the Narrows. Marcus and Jon spent several minutes detailing the events that had occurred since their last communication to ensure the Captain had all the information he needed.

Upstream the canyon was churning. The continuous cascade of rain had finally soaked the ground and vegetation, which then had started running off in small trickles, which joined other trickles, which became rivulets joining other rivulets, which became streams joining other streams, which joined with the already swollen river on the canyon floor. The combined weight of thousands of tons of water responding to the irresistible force of gravity flowed faster and faster and in doing so picked up first loose soil, then small rocks, then large rocks, then large boulders, and finally trees torn from their roots, all propelled down stream by the now raging torrent.

All of the groups involved in the drama were set in their final positions, as if some elaborate chess game was nearly at checkmate. The command center at the Temple of Sinawava waited, wondering what was happening up the river. The team stationed at the mouth of the Narrows watched for anybody to emerge. The team above Big Springs waited patiently for the helicopter evacuation that could not come until the storm had passed. Meanwhile deep within the Narrows two solitary figures were frantically running ahead of four others who were just behind them and steadily gaining, while further up the canyon the raging torrent of water, rock, debris, and mud began to crash down the canyon toward them all.

Less than an hour and a half after the skinheads had disappeared into the Narrows, Jon and his team saw the torrent approaching. It was the biggest flood they had ever seen. The fifteen-foot high wall of water born projectiles came crashing down the canyon, wiping out everything in its path as it came. The noise of the destructive mass of roiling water, even high above the river, was deafening. It swept into the Narrows, increasing in speed proportionate to the constriction of the flood because of the funnel effect of the same amount of water being forced through the constricted canyon. Marcus informed the command center of the event, who in turn advised the guard teams and the Sheriff's office in St. George.

Jon sighed. "How long did you say it takes to get through the Narrows?" directing his question at Marcus.

"Two and a half hours at best. And that time is with favorable conditions." Marcus didn't need to add that current conditions were anything but favorable.

"And how long ago did they start through the Narrows?" Jon knew the answer, but hoped he was wrong.

"Only an hour and a half. We have two inexperienced hikers in the middle of the Narrows with a fifteen-foot wall of water bearing down on them. Nothing can save them now."

The others stared down at the churning brown mass of water at the bottom of the canyon and contemplated the terrible set of circumstances that seemed to have lead to the demise of an innocent family. They were grateful to be alive themselves, saved from a violent death by the wise decision of Sergeant Leavitt.

For himself, Jon was relieved that he had followed his Captain's instructions and had not chosen to follow the others into the deathtrap. Still, he was crushed that the father and his daughter were forced to choose between different means of death; either to be murdered at the hands of the skinheads or crushed in the narrow canyon as an indifferent mass of water and debris swept over them.

Jon had to force down self-recrimination. His training had taught him to remain objective and detached from the circumstances of his work. Still, he was human, and could not help but wonder that if he had done things differently his team would have been in a position to help the family before it was too late. If only he had started a few minutes earlier this morning, or had only pressed forward faster. Nevertheless, there was nothing that he or his team could do about it now.

Jon looked again at the boiling river below and mentally calculated the time it would take for the flood to go halfway through the Narrows. The wall of water should be reaching them just about now. He stared helplessly down at the ferocious river, visualizing the terror on the faces of the father and daughter at this moment, just before the wall of water swept over and crushed their fragile bodies.

Chapter 15

Emergency in ICU

The vigil Marie kept was the longest night of her life. She stayed by Austin's side and tried to sleep while resting her head on the side of his bed and holding his hand. She did not want to miss any movement he made, but her position was very uncomfortable so she drifted between a fitful sleep and a semi-conscious waking in which facts and fears mingled and were muddled together. She couldn't easily distinguish between her dreams and reality. Sometimes she forced herself to wake up completely to see what was going on, but each time she found herself in the same place, despondent that the events of the previous day were not some horrific illusion, but happy that the nightmares of accomplished doom for her family were not real.

Austin did not move all night, and his pulse rate gradually declined. Marie did not notice because the drop in the rate occurred over a long period and so the beeping pattern emitted by the heart monitor did not perceptibly change. Only the nursing staff monitoring the electrocardiogram, charting the result, and waiting for the inevitable emergency to come, noticed the slow rate of decline.

Marie woke for the last time when Audrey returned early in the morning and insisted that Marie go and eat breakfast. Marie was too groggy to argue with her and quietly agreed to go. She again found the cafeteria and ordered something, plopping down at a table with the intention of sleeping until her order was ready. No sooner had she laid her head on the table she was awakened by the call of the hospital intercom asking her to pick up the nearest phone. Alarmed, she asked the cafeteria staff where the nearest phone was and rushed to it. She knew she shouldn't have left Austin! What had happened? The voice on the end of the phone line did not have a message from hospital staff, however. It connected her to the sheriff's department, and a gruff voice came on the line.

"Is this Marie Peterson?" the officer asked.

The sudden shift in the direction of concern was startling. This call would be about David and Rebecca. Her first impulse was to hang up the phone. It

175

was better not to know what was happening than to find out they were dead and lose all hope. She resisted the impulse and answered.

"Yes."

"We have some news of your husband and daughter," the officer began. "Our team has found evidence that both your husband and your daughter were alive this morning."

"That's wonderful. What did you find?" Marie could barely contain her joy.

"It may not be as wonderful as you think. Can you come over to our office and talk? There's too much to try to explain over the phone."

"I can't leave now. My son is in critical condition. Can't you tell me over the phone?"

"The team found a camp where several people spent the night. They also found cut ropes and an abandoned backpack. We think it belongs to your daughter. It appears that a group of five men held her prisoner; however, someone else, probably your husband, may have rescued her. The team is sweeping down the canyon now and hopes to find them soon."

The news was like a breath of fresh air. Marie was ecstatic. David and Rebecca were alive. Suddenly a question came to mind that was troubling. "What about the other group, the ones that were holding my daughter prisoner? Where are they? Were they captured?"

"No. We have not caught up with them yet. We can only assume they are ahead of our team, trying to get out of the canyon."

"Does that mean that the kidnappers are between my family and your team?"

"Not necessarily. Your family may have gone up a side canyon. On the other hand, they may have a very big lead and may be almost down to the end of the Narrows. Your husband is apparently an intelligent and resourceful man. Don't worry; things are looking much better than yesterday. Of course, the kidnappers may also have gone up a side canyon too."

"Is there anything else?"

"That's it. If you give me your cell number, I'll call you if we get any more news."

Marie gave her number to the officer and thanked him for the good news, then hung up and started back to the cafeteria. At first, she was overjoyed at the news that David and Rebecca seemed to be okay. But soon, knowing they were still in the same canyon with the people who had shot Austin the previous day, she became nervous. She had a tendency to fear the worst anyway, and yesterday's events had reinforced the inclination. She began to visualize her husband and daughter frantically running down the river with a band of drug-crazed psychopaths trailing close behind, shooting indiscriminately whenever they got close enough to fire. The vision was unsettling. However, as she got her breakfast and began to eat, she reasoned that David was smarter than a bunch of drug-crazed psychopaths, if that was what they were, and that he was either way ahead of them or had successfully hidden from them. She forced herself to accept this logic, finished her breakfast, and returned to intensive care.

Austin's condition seemed to be the same, and Marie felt a need to get outside for a breath of fresh air. Aunt Audrey agreed, and indicated she would get her immediately if anything happened. Marie left the unit and wandered outside.

It was daytime now, but the sky was dark from the low, menacing cloud cover. In the distance, she could see flashes of lightning and hear the accompanying thunderclaps. The atmosphere had an electric edge, and the smell of rain was in the air. She noticed that the thunder and lightning was from the east, toward the park. The realization that it was probably raining in the park right now compounded her worries, but she again forced herself to accept the notion that David and Rebecca were safe somewhere. She was now so tired that she wasn't thinking clearly. She stayed outside for just a few minutes until a light rain began to fall. Looking to the east, she said another prayer for the safety of her family, and went back inside.

When Marie got back to intensive care, several people who had not been there before were talking to Aunt Audrey. As Marie approached, she could see a camera crew from a news station, plus another group taking notes.

"Oh, no, media," Marie said to herself. "This is just what I need," she thought sarcastically. The thought of facing a group of news-hungry jackals in a feeding frenzy almost caused her to spin around and run the other direction, but Marie knew that they would hang around Austin for news, and she had to get past them to be with him. She would have to face their questions. Trying to clear the cobwebs from her mind, she proceeded to the small but unruly cluster of people, who surrounded and directed their attention to her.

177

Immediately a steady stream of questions assaulted her from all sides. She answered questions continuously for an hour, explaining several times over what she knew about the previous day's events, wondering if anyone was actually listening to her responses. It seemed the questions would never end, but she gave as much detail as she knew, including the information she had been given that morning by the police. Eventually the reporters exhausted all of the different angles they could use to ask the same question and were finally satisfied. Just then, her cell phone rang and she pulled the phone from her purse and answered it. The reporters fell silent and listened, hoping to get some new information from the call.

"Is this Marie?" The voice on the phone belonged to the same officer she had spoken to earlier that morning. She welcomed the voice; she was at first confident he would have good news, but as soon as he spoke she realized from the tone that the news would not be good. The officer was speaking slowly and deliberately, carefully avoiding saying something that would alarm her. She was seized by an intense fear that the news would be of her husband and daughter's death.

"We have some late news on the situation in the park," the officer began. "Just a few minutes ago, we received a message that the officers in the park caught up with the group of men who had apparently shot your son and kidnapped your daughter. The team came upon them shortly after hearing a number of shots fired. When the officers came up behind the men and ordered them to give themselves up, the men bolted and ran down the river." Here the officer paused as if he considered whether to continue.

"Did the team catch up with them?" Marie asked. She wished the officer would tell her the whole story and be done with it.

"No. The team could not continue down the river. It was at the entrance to the Narrows, and they had been instructed not to enter."

Marie could not believe what she heard. She was furious. "What?!" she exclaimed. "The police are going to let them catch up with and kill my family!! Is that what you are trying to say? Just because someone has decided that your officers shouldn't go into the Narrows, my family is going to be killed?"

The officer, although clearly on the defensive, continued with his deliberate approach. "They couldn't go into the Narrows because if they did the current was too strong for them to be able to get back out in time."

"In time? In time for what?"

"There has been a constant steady rain since early this morning, and the team saw evidence of a flood. They could not go in because there was not time to get through the Narrows to safety. They had to stop."

With this last revelation, Marie understood what the officer had been telling her in a roundabout way. If there was not enough time for the police to get through the Narrows, certainly there was not enough time for David and Rebecca to get through, having been chased into the Narrows only minutes before the police had been stopped. David and Rebecca were going to die, either by the hand of the killers who had chased them in, or by an impending flood. "Are you sure a flood is coming?" she asked, grasping at any straw she could find.

"About an hour and a half after the exchange at the Narrows entrance, the officers witnessed a wall of water come down the river, taking everything with it. I am sorry ma'am, but an hour and a half of traveling down the Narrows would have put them just past the middle, with no way to get out of the way of the flood. I don't think your husband and daughter could possibly have made it."

Marie was in shock. She fumbled closing the phone, and her face was pale. She had no more straws to grasp, for the news left no room for any doubt. She had been so optimistic just a short hour ago. Now there was no hope left.

The reporters, having heard Marie's end of the exchange and seeing the expression on her face, figured out what the news was. They began to pepper her with new questions anyway, trying to ascertain the details about what had happened. Marie was too stunned to respond. She walked listlessly back toward intensive care, toward the only remaining member of her family.

As she approached Austin's room, she could see another swarm of people. They wore hospital and surgical garb, and huddled around Austin, working frantically. Aunt Audrey was outside the room, watching with a grim expression.

Marie's heart fell. She raced to the unit and tried to get to Austin but was prevented from entering by a nurse who took her back into the hall and explained that her son had gone into cardiac arrest. She insisted that Marie stay out of the way for her son's sake. Marie leaned against the wall and slumped to the floor burying her face in her hands.

Chapter 16

Flight in the Narrows

"Are you okay?" David asked softly after they had fought their way into and down through the darkness of the Narrows some distance. Immediately after entering the opening, they had hit a deeper spot in the river. For some time the water was up to David's neck, and he had paddled forward, the pack riding high on his shoulders, his feet barely touching the bottom. Rebecca struggled to keep her head above water and her feet on the bottom as well, but the water was over her head and she had gone under even with him holding onto her.

"Yes," she whispered just louder than the sound of the water. "I'm okay. The water was over my head. I had to paddle a little." Shouting could be heard a short distance up at the entrance of the Narrows.

"What about the bullets? Were you hit?" The skinheads had stopped shooting at them when the darkness of the canyon had enveloped them.

"No," she answered. "They were splashing around me but nothing hit. I thought I was going to die. What about you?"

"I'm okay. Either they are lousy shots or they were a little too far away for the handguns." He hoped that it was the former.

The deeper water had swept them swiftly down the river for about fifty yards. David was surprised at the speed with which the current had taken them with relatively little effort. The pack had buoyed them both up as the current had swept them down. They had then struggled another fifty yards in the dim light through water up to the middle of their waists. They were now moving down about a hundred yards from the opening.

They were in a real river now. They had started the day before standing in what was only a large creek with the water up to their ankles while Marie took their picture. Augmented by sources like Deep Creek and Kolob Creek as the flow descended over the relatively short distance they had traveled, the Virgin had become large and deep. With limited exceptions, it now filled the entire floor of the canyon from wall to wall.

180

They were in the water almost continuously now, and the Virgin stretched on with a rolling surface only occasionally broken by rocks or thin bars of sand. The walls arching over the canyon floor almost gave the impression that they were descending into a cave, constricting and channeling them as they continued downriver. As he looked at the walls, David began to feel like they were converging, trying to close in and trap them. He began to feel claustrophobic and briefly contemplated going back in spite of the danger upriver.

"Not a chance," he told himself. "Even if we could fight our way back up against the current, we would still have the skinheads chasing us down. We can't go to them." He resigned himself to the inevitable and allowed the current to help carry them into the bowels of the canyon.

David looked back to see how close his pursuers were. He could see four small dim figures standing in the water, silhouetted against the gray light just out of the opening, but they were not coming in, at least not yet. Maybe they were too frightened to enter. The skinheads did not have quite the motivation that David and Rebecca did. He turned and continued, stumbling along downriver with Rebecca right behind and clinging to David for support.

They were safely hidden in almost nighttime darkness now. The Narrows only gets direct sunlight for a few moments before and after noon. Other than the time when the sun is directly overhead, the light is always dim and visibility is limited. This overcast and gloomy weather made it even worse. They could only see a few hundred feet ahead, which was bad, but that also meant that the skinheads could not see further than a few hundred feet either, which was good. They had temporarily escaped and they were extending their lead.

As they were going around their first, bend in the river since entering. David looked again and saw the four figures still outlined against the gray light. He hoped that they would not enter. Maybe they could get away. Maybe the skinheads had decided not to chase them. David could easily believe that. Only a fool would be in this canyon in this kind of weather unless forced to do so. He turned and continued, stumbling around the bend only a moment before a commotion behind them resulted in the silhouetted figures plunging into the darkness of the Narrows entrance toward them.

Obviously, the rain was still falling, but in the deep narrow shaft, not much fell directly from the sky to the river. Instead, torrents of water cascading down

181

the sides of the rock walls splashed into the Virgin, especially where the walls arched tightly overhead. The scene would have been truly spectacular had it not been so dark, wet, cold, miserable, and terrifying.

David couldn't remember being so wet for so long in his life. He and Rebecca had been in the river, the rain, and now the cascades of falling water all morning. They were surrounded by water on all sides, and he wondered if it would be necessary to evolve gills to breathe in the water-laden atmosphere. They had been completely soaked since leaving the Grotto, and it was obvious that they would remain so until reaching the car at the Visitor's Center. David wondered how long it would take them to become waterlogged. He imagined what it would feel like to be dry again, and once again wistfully yearned to be quietly resting at home.

They were going faster now, letting the current push them. They looked for drowned sandbars or rock shoals where the water was shallower and followed them as far as they could. The locations of these were predictable from the surface of the water and from the location of bends and turns in the canyon. Any turn would force the brunt of the current against the wall into which it flowed and would scour out deeper sections from the floor, while depositing the material in the middle of the river or on the opposite side downriver. The water over a shoal was choppy and the water over the holes was smoother. They utilized this information to avoid the holes.

The water had become deeper, either because the channel was constricted or because increased water from the storm had caused the water level to rise. David knew the river was normally deeper here, but he did not know how deep. All the rain that was falling now had to affect the already high river level. He could not remember anything about this section of the canyon from the 1961 hike because he was carried through most of it after the flood had wiped out his troop. He began to pay close attention to the average level of the water on their bodies through the straight flat stretches of the canyon. So far, it seemed to be just up to mid-waist.

The thought of the 1961 trip triggered a new round of anxiety. He began to wonder if the skinheads had waited at the entrance because they had heard the same ominous noise he had heard so long ago. Even now, they could be climbing for the same ledge he had sought refuge on years ago, hoping to escape a deadly wall of water that was about to crash through the canyon with them trapped on the floor. If so, David and Rebecca's lives would be snuffed out in but a few minutes. He caught himself listening for the expected roar in the distance, but he could only hear the normal sounds of the river and cascading water as they sped along.

Gunfire and fear are remarkably invigorating. Before David and Rebecca were obliged to enter the canyon with bullets splashing around them they had both doubted whether they could continue. Moments later, they were moving with renewed energy, going faster than they had ever gone. The adrenaline had helped, but that should have quickly worn off, and yet they were still going strong. David could only suppose that they had both caught their second wind.

David could now hear shouts echoing against the walls and realized that the skinheads had entered the Narrows in pursuit. His spirits sank at the realization. Rebecca looked at him; he could tell that she had also heard the shouting. David and Rebecca exchanged a silent acknowledgment of the danger behind. The skinheads might be catching up, and they were back to silent running.

As they traveled through a wider section of the canyon, David and Rebecca were hindered by a number of massive boulders lying on the floor of the canyon. In addition, there were numerous tree trunks lying askew, some of which were splintered like matchsticks. It was evident to David that this was the site of a recent (in geologic terms) avalanche.

The stark evidence of the inevitability of gravity's irresistible force brought a new danger to David's mind. Although the chance of its occurrence was very slight, the way this trip was going he would not be surprised if the worst-case scenario transpired. Like all of nature, the canyon was dynamic and changing. Occasionally, within recorded history, massive sandstone slabs have broken off the canyon walls and crashed to the floor, creating massive shock waves which destroyed every life form in their path. Wind speeds of up to two hundred miles an hour result from the shock of the collapsing wall with devastation reaching a fair distance down the canyon from the slide. Typically, these avalanches occur after a major storm or flood has undermined the foundation of the wall to a point where it collapses.

David looked at the walls of the canyon, undercut by the river, arching high over its bed, and wondered how much more of the wall would need to be eaten away by erosion before it finally succumbed to gravity and came crashing down.

And what would it take to trigger a landslide? Would the sound of a gunshot be enough? If the skinheads got close enough to see them and get a clear shot, David did not doubt that they would fire. Knowing that the sound of a gunshot often started avalanches on snow slopes, he imagined the same vibration might trigger what was, over time, inevitable, a slide that would obliterate everything and everyone within miles of the slide inside the constricted canyon. Although he knew that sandstone is considerably stronger and sturdier than snow he did not want to take a chance. He didn't want the skinheads firing in the canyon if it could be avoided. Besides, the skinheads might actually hit one of them if they got close enough to fire. Even considering how lousy at shooting they were, that was a considerably greater possibility than a sandstone slide. He and Rebecca had to stay ahead of them. He decided to tell Rebecca, even though the chance was slight and it would give her even more cause to despair.

"Rebecca, we have to stay ahead of them at all costs" he whispered.

"No duh" Rebecca responded, looking at David as if he was an idiot.

"No, not because the skinheads will kill us. I just thought of something else that we need to worry about."

"Oh yeah, that's just what I need; something else to worry about." Rebecca was now glaring at her father.

"Sometimes pieces of the canyon wall break off and fall to the floor. I don't suppose I need to tell you that wouldn't be beneficial for us."

"No, I don't suppose it would. But what is the chance of us being under a collapsing rock? These canyon walls have been here for a long time."

"Yes, that's true. Unfortunately, it's not just a problem for those under the rock. The avalanche could generate a shock wave that would wipe out everything within miles of the slide. It would not be a good idea for us to be anywhere near it."

Rebecca looked at David with a mystified expression. "So what are you trying to tell me? How are we supposed to know when there will be an avalanche?

"Of course we can't know. But the way our luck is running, I think we should not give the skinheads a chance to fire at us just in case the vibration from their bullets might cause these waterlogged walls to finally collapse. I wanted you to be aware of the possibility.

Rebecca was really discouraged about this prospect. The expression on her face was a mixture of resignation and disgust. "I think right about now is a good time to finally tell you that your hike stinks" she said.

"I don't think I'll disagree with you right now."

They both pressed forward, but it was not fast enough. In spite of the motivation that David and Rebecca had to stay ahead, it was clear that the skinheads were catching up. The shouts reverberating from the walls were getting louder and closer. David and Rebecca either had to go faster or find someplace to hide. Yet, there was no place to hide; the smooth vertical walls offered no refuge. The skinheads would look in any possible hiding spot anyway.

"Maybe we could hide under the water," David suggested to himself. "We could wait at the side around one of the bends where the current isn't so strong. When they come we can go under and hold our breath long enough for them to go by."

The foolishness of the idea was immediately apparent to David. First, the water was not as deep where the current was light. Second, the skinheads would be spread out, and they would need to hold their breath for many minutes for all of them to go by. Third, David wanted to stay ahead of them anyway. The threat of a flood was all too real, and he knew they had to get out of the canyon before the skinheads and stay ahead of them. Last, the pack was too buoyant; it would not let them go under water.

Just then Rebecca sighed. "I wish we had a boat so we could just float down the river."

"Wait a minute!" David softly exclaimed aloud. He had a flash of insight. "Rebecca, you are a genius. Why didn't I think of this before? The pack floats! We can float down the river nearly as fast as the current." He remembered fighting the floating pack yesterday when trying to reach Austin and how high on his back it had ridden at the entrance just a short time ago.

"But I don't have my pack! What am I going to do?" Rebecca whispered. She looked at him as if he were going to abandon her.

"We can both hang on to my pack! It should be buoyant enough for both of us."

"You think one pack will hold both of us up?" Rebecca had a disbelieving look on her face.

"I think so. At least I hope so. What do we have to loose by trying? If it only partially works, we will go faster than we are going now. We have to get ahead of these guys. This might work!"

"Anyway," he said with a mischievous grin, "The worst thing that can happen to us is that we'll drown like rats on a sinking ship. That's not so bad is it?"

Rebecca flashed David one of her scathing looks to let him know she was not at all amused. Laughing, he took off his pack and positioned it in front of and perpendicular to them to maximize the surface they could grasp. He tried to figure out how to attach the staff to the pack and quickly stuffed it under the straps holding the top down. The result was sturdy enough to hold them.

They moved out into the main channel where the water was deepest and hung onto the pack with both hands. Rebecca grasped the straps with one hand and the top flap with the other while David hung onto the straps and the side. David instructed Rebecca to float feet first with him, holding the buoyant pack in front of them so their bodies curled underneath it. That way they could better guide themselves and use their feet to push away from obstacles in the stream.

Rebecca suddenly had a terrified look on her face. "I can't do this," she whispered. "I don't want to drown. Let's keep walking."

"You won't drown. If we keep walking they will continue to close the distance and we will die. This can work. It may make the difference between life and death. Give it a chance."

Rebecca was still terrified, but she maintained her position and prepared to start.

"There they are!" The menacing voice was only fifty yards away, rounding a bend in the river.

"Get your feet as high in the water as you can!" David shouted to Rebecca. There was no need for silence now.

David leaned back in the water as far as he was able and tried to get his feet as high as he could. Rebecca did the same. With their feet just clearing the bottom, they began to float feet first down the canyon. He heard the whiz-pop of the guns and saw bullet splashes on the river's surface. However, the skinheads were too far away, and they only had David and Rebecca's heads and a small portion of the pack for a target with little light. The skinheads only fired a few rounds to no effect before Rebecca and David drifted out of sight and range.

"It's working!" David gloated gleefully. "We're going to beat them!"

Rebecca was not quite so sure. She was looking down the canyon into the darkness with her feet off the bottom, drifting with the current. "I don't like this!" she exclaimed, the high pitch of her voice betraying her fear. "Let's go back to walking."

"We can't! Remember, they just caught up with us. We've got to go as fast as we can. Just keep your feet high in the water. Keep your feet forward and backstroke with one arm a little to control your movement. We'll be okay."

"All right. But this is scary."

"It will be a lot scarier if they catch us." Rebecca did not argue with that.

"Look to see where we're going," David instructed her. "Remember to watch for large rocks under the surface and use your feet to push us away."

They were floating quickly downstream now. David wished that he had thought of this before. They probably would have been out of the canyon by now if they had started floating from Big Springs. They both watched for submerged boulders and rocks and tried to steer away from them by paddling with their free hand. Even so, several times they hit rocks or scraped the bottom, resulting in smashed and scraped toes, legs, and body parts. There was no serious injury, though David thought they would be black and blue for some time.

Where before they tried to find the shallowest sections to travel, now they searched for the deepest channel and the swiftest current. Occasionally they had to stop floating long enough to cross short sections of water where the entire width of the channel was too shallow to float or to traverse from one deep section to another, but most of the time they were able to continue drifting with the river.

If the circumstances had not been so frightening, David thought this could have been fun. He could imagine doing this under a sunny sky without crazed lunatics chasing them. "They could make a ride like this at a water theme park," he said.

"You have got to be kidding!" Rebecca chided, turning her face to look at him as if he was some kind of alien creature. "Nobody would ever do this! This is crazy! Why would anyone want to kill themselves at a theme park?" Apparently, their tastes in amusement park rides were dissimilar.

They were floating just slower than the current. Both of their bodies were being pushed by the current at a rate less than they would have been pushed if they were floating separately. However, they were still moving a lot faster than they had been while walking and David figured they had opened a safe lead on the skinheads.

When David and Rebecca were hiking they had worked their bodies and generated heat, but now they had been floating in the cold water for over thirty minutes. They were both cold and shivering again. The potential for hypothermia seemed to David to be almost as high as it had the night before when they abandoned their chance to get out of the canyon at the Grotto. However, this time they could not stop. Even if they didn't have the immediate threat of death behind them and wanted to stop, there was nothing they could do to get warm by doing so. Their only hope was to make it out of the canyon before their body temperatures dropped so low that they became physically impaired.

Neither David nor Rebecca wanted to be in water again as long as they lived. Their skin had shriveled from the constant immersion, and their trembling had impaired their ability to guide themselves, so with increasing frequency they bounced painfully against submerged rocks. Their legs hurt, and the effort of keeping their feet off the bottom was taking a toll on their strength. Their backs screamed in agony from the constant effort. "Maybe this wouldn't be such a great attraction at a theme park after all," David observed aloud.

In spite of their pain, the comment was funny under the circumstances and David and Rebecca both laughed as they continued floating.

Suddenly as they floated they realized that the rain had stopped. Just ahead sunlight shown on the upper wall of the canyon, bathing the canyon wall in a beautiful orange light. It was beautiful, not just because of the break in the weather, but also because there was hope that they would not be caught in a flood after all. At the same time, the canyon in which they descended was still ominous, with water cascading down the canyon walls and the river flowing downward into darkness.

"How much further was it to the car," David speculated to himself. "Will we make it?"

"How much further is it to the car?" Apparently, Rebecca was wondering the same thing.

"I'm not sure." David tried to calculate how far they had come. They had probably been about half way down the Narrows section of the canyon when they started drifting, and they had been drifting with the current just over thirty minutes. As the river was flowing at about five miles an hour, he figured they should be passing the mouth to Orderville Canyon any time now.

If so, that would be a relief. About an eighth of a mile downriver from Orderville Canyon, the canyon widened and the there were once again places to climb above an impending flood. Or did Orderville Canyon join the main canyon an eighth of a mile after the Narrows ended? David could not remember; that would be even better if the latter were true.

Either way, it seemed that if they could continue floating unimpeded they could make it to the paved trail that came up from the Temple of Sinewava in a half-hour. David questioned whether they could float for another thirty minutes. Then, after they reached the path they would still need the strength to walk to the ranger station, presumably with the skinheads hot on their trail. David was confident that the Park Service would have closed the Park to visitors, so he and Rebecca could not count on help until they got to the end of the trail.

"I think we have another hour to go before we reach the Temple of Sinewava," he advised. "I think we're about a quarter mile from the end of the Narrows, and it's just over two and one half miles from there to the ranger station. We should reach it in an hour."

"But I can't do this for another hour! Can't we stop and rest? We must be miles ahead of them by now." Rebecca was pleading.

"No. Rebecca, you have to keep going. I know this is the most difficult thing you have ever done, but your life depends on it. Hang in there."

"But I don't think I can do it."

"You have made it this far; you can make it the rest of the way. We only need to continue floating until we reach the paved trail. That should only take around thirty minutes. Look, we have to get out as soon as possible, and floating is the fastest way out. I regret that we stopped and rested last night. If we had gone on, we would have been safe now. We can't take the chance. We don't know how far ahead of the skinheads we are. You never know, they might be drifting with the current too."

189

The realization that the skinheads could be floating as they were was alarming. David suddenly realized that he had become complacent about staying ahead of their pursuers. Too complacent. He speculated whether the skinheads were just behind them drifting with the current at the same speed they were, or even worse, faster.

"Do you think they are?" The fear in her voice told David she was as worried as he was.

"I hope not."

Just as David finished the sentence, he heard a shout two hundred yards upstream. Rebecca screamed instinctively. David's heart sank; the skinheads had apparently seen them floating and copied their action. He and Rebecca had been caught, and he had no more tricks to save them. There was no way they could win this race. The skinheads had been just behind them all the time, slowly gaining on them while David and Rebecca had been literally dragging their feet.

Suddenly, David understood why the man behind them had shouted, which had given away the skinhead's advantage of surprise. In the distance, far up the canyon, he could hear a low, menacing rumble. At first, it was barely perceptible, but it grew in intensity almost immediately. The river was rising and the speed of the current increasing, at first just barely discernible, but clearly rising just the same. The water carrying them was now dirty and clouded. Pine needles, twigs, and pieces of bark began to float by. David had heard and seen these signs before. His worst fears were materializing. A wall of water was on its way down the narrow channel, speeding murderously toward them.

David and Rebecca could hear panicked shouting upstream. Most of the men were about three to four hundred yards behind them, but the closest skinhead was now only about one hundred and fifty yards away and he was rapidly closing the distance. The skinheads had figured out what was coming down the canyon, and were trying to escape it.

Still drifting, David resigned himself to the inevitable. If his calculations were correct, they were at least an eighth of a mile above where the canyon widened. They had not passed Orderville Canyon, which was about that distance from the end. He also knew that Orderville Canyon, if they passed it

190

now, would not provide refuge. It would be flooded also, and did not have a climbable surface near it's entry into the main canyon.

The rumble was increasing in intensity as they drifted through what seemed to be almost a tunnel, the channel having narrowed to only forty feet across. They could no longer touch the river's bottom; it was completely gone now, a result of the combination of a deeper channel and the rising and murky water. While being unable to touch the bottom was disconcerting, at least neither David nor Rebecca had to strain their backs for the last few fleeting moments of their lives.

Emerging from the narrow gorge, they came out into what was comparatively an expansive open area. There was a wide bank which sloped a considerable distance up the side of the canyon. Large rocks littered the bank and river bottom, and several large uprooted trees had been deposited on the canyon floor by old floods. They were out of the Narrows! In one breathtaking second, David realized they still had a chance. It was imperative that they get out of the water immediately and up high enough before the wall of water and rock arrived.

"Swim to the side!" David shouted the instant he realized where they were. They fought their way to the right side, where the bank was thinner and had fewer obstructions. Reaching the river's edge, they tried to scramble up, but tripped over each other's feet and fell exhausted to the bank. David's bruised leg was now really hurt. He had strained something. The pack was now a hindrance and David threw it off to the side.

"We've got to get up and climb!" David shouted. "We have to get above the flood level or we'll be crushed." David and Rebecca scrambled up toward the rock cliff some sixty feet away. Climbing up the rocky bank, they headed directly toward a large sandstone slab, about fifteen feet high, which was lying up against the slope of the canyon at an angle. Reaching it together, they started to climb up the slab.

Behind them, the din of the crashing flood reverberated through the canyon and the water rose swiftly, overflowing the bank and inching up the slab they were ascending.

David's leg suddenly gave out and they tripped and fell the precious few feet they had climbed. David landed on his back in the muddy water with Rebecca on top. He felt a sharp pain in his ribs and he could hardly breathe. In addition, his long forgotten wound forcefully reminded him that it was not good to have someone land on it.

"We only have one more chance! Let's try again," he encouraged, trying to forget the crippling pain in his leg, ribs, arm, and body. "Start again." They climbed together, trying to hurry. It worked this time. Just as they reached the top of the slab lying against the canyon slope, the roar of the flood and the dull pounding thumps made by boulders bouncing along the walls and floor of the canyon reached a terrifying crescendo.

David heard shouts both in front and behind him. Looking up he saw a figure in a police poncho scrambling toward them, motioning to his rear. Turning, he saw one of the skinheads had also emerged onto the floodplain and was running directly at them with his gun out, aiming and firing on the run as he splashed through the water covering the lower bank. The skinhead was only forty feet away, and he was quickly closing that distance.

"That's Bart, their leader." Rebecca whispered.

Bart emptied the gun without hitting either David or Rebecca. He changed the clip in the weapon while running and continued toward them, quickly closing the distance. He reached the sandstone slab that David and Rebecca were climbing and scrambled toward them. He had the weapon in his hand as he climbed though he did not fire. Apparently Bart wanted to ensure he was close enough that he could not miss with his last remaining rounds.

"You killed my brother!" he screamed. At that instant, Bart raised the gun at point-blank range, pointed it directly at David's heart, and fired.

"You killed my son," David returned calmly but firmly as he ducked down, placed one hand on the rock, and kicked out with both feet. He hit Bart solidly on the chest with both feet just as another shot rang out; the police officer who was now close had fired a round. David and Rebecca watched as Bart simultaneously sailed backwards into the air and grabbed his stomach with his free hand. Blood issued between Bart's fingers, and he landed in the muddy water at the base of the boulder.

For a brief moment, he didn't move and David and Rebecca eyed the body with short lived relief. But then Bart struggled to his knees and again raised his weapon, aimed it directly at David, and started to pull the trigger. At the same instant, another shot rang out from the bank above them and Bart was knocked backward from the impact of the bullet. Simultaneously, a horrendous wall of muddy water spewed from the canyon's mouth, enveloped him as he screamed in anger and anguish, snapped his body like a dried twig, and swept it along with the mass of roiling water.

The relief that David and Rebecca felt was short-lived. The flood swirled around the rock and slope, instantly transforming it into a minor nub protruding from a sea of water. It was going to cover them completely. They were not high enough.

The poncho-clad officer was now trying to reach them. He extended his hand, but David and Rebecca were too far away and too low. It was impossible to take advantage of the help the officer was attempting to give them.

David looked at the rock they were stranded upon, and recognized a slim opportunity to help himself and Rebecca, but knew they only had an instant to act before the water would take them. Moving to the side of the slab away from the flow of the water, he dropped to the rock and thrust both of his hands as far as he could down the crack between the slope and the slab. He then tightened both of them into clenched fists. His fists became an anchor in the rock.

"Hold on!" was all he had time to say to Rebecca before taking a deep breath. She put her arms around his stomach and locked her hands on her wrists just as the muddy water swirled around and then completely buried them.

David was holding his breath. He hoped Rebecca was also. The force of the water tore against their bodies, and David thought that his arms would be yanked from their sockets. David could feel Rebecca holding on for dear life, but it seemed that the flood was determined to dislodge both of them from their anchor. The incredible pressure on his hands and arms was excruciating, and his chest was in agony as he held his breath for what seemed like forever. He could feel the slab shudder when a large object smashed against the other side of it. He hoped that it would not give. He prayed the water would quickly subside so they could breathe.

The officer who had shot Bart was only a few feet above the rock. He watched as the flood enveloped the father and daughter, but just before the brown water covered them, he saw the father jam his hands into a crevice and the girl grab him around his waist. Initially, he thought it impossible that they could withstand a current that splintered tree trunks like matchsticks. He was anguished that he could not have gotten too them a few seconds sooner and helped them up. If he had not been forced to take time to shoot the crazed man who was shooting at them he would have.

Then he noticed a pattern in the current just below the rock. To his surprise, just down from the rock he could see debris floating upriver opposite the downward force of the flood. The floodwater just below the rock was re-circulating around in an oblong circle. Floodwater flowed upstream next to the bank, hit the rock, was forced out toward the flood, then hit the powerful current of the main flood, and was bounced back into the circle. The current in the eddy was violent and powerful, but only a small fraction as powerful as the force of the flood in mid-stream.

His mind leapt to the vision of the two lying on the ground, the father's hands anchored in the crevice, and the daughter's arms locked around his waist. He looked intently, trying to see through the opaque floodwater. He could see nothing, but had a powerful impression they were still just a few feet below the surface where he last saw them.

By this time, his three companions had joined him. "Give me a rope," he demanded.

"What do you think you're doing?" The team leader was incredulous. "You can't help them. They're dead already."

"I don't think so. I think they are hanging on right there." He pointed at the place where he last saw them. "They are being protected by an eddy behind the rock. We don't have much time. Give me the damned rope!" he demanded again.

The team leader grabbed the rope and handed the end to the officer. The others knew what they had to do. While the officer circled the rope around his waist and tied a one-handed bowline, the others circled the rope around a large rock, then braced themselves with the rope in hand prepared to use leverage to keep the officer from being swept downstream. The rock was above the eddy so they could pull the officer out of the flood in the direction of the upstream eddy. Thus they hoped to keep the current from carrying the officer and those he was trying to save away. The whole process took less than twenty seconds.

"Keep the rope tight. One jerk means to give me a little slack. Two jerks means pull me back." The officer looked at the water. It had been almost a minute since they were submerged. Were they still there?

194

He jumped into the water feet first just below where he thought they were and toward the bank. He was counting on the eddy to push him upstream toward the couple. It worked. He felt someone almost immediately.

David was ready to give up. He felt Rebecca's grip around his waist loosen as if wrestled from his waist, then suddenly she was gone. "I might as well go too," he thought. However, his hands refused to relax, and they stayed anchored in spite of his attitude. His lungs burned, and he wondered why he didn't just get it over with. All he had to do was let go, push out the stale carbon dioxide from his lungs and take a deep breath of water. The revolt of his lungs would be short lived, and then it would be over.

Against all reason, David's survival instinct forced him to hold on. In spite of the agony in his chest, the wrenching of his fists and wrists, and the buffeting of his body, his physical being was determined to stay alive. If only he could last until the initial wave passed the water level might drop just enough for him to breathe. Then suddenly, as if some subconscious order from his mind was given without regard to his conscious will, the muscles in his hands involuntarily relaxed, and he began to free float along the rock outward toward the channel. At the same moment, he felt what seemed to be arms wrap themselves around his body and anchor him against the current.

David felt himself rise in the water instead of floating downward. "I must be disoriented," he thought. It was illogical that he was not drifting with the current, but was still fighting against it. Or rather was being pulled through it. Yet, it was no use; he could hold his breath no longer. He succumbed to the irresistible reflexive desire of his respiratory system to push out the stale air from his lungs, took what he hoped would be a breath of air, but water came in its stead. He tried to cough it out, but only more foul tasting water took its place. David panicked, struggled for seconds, and then lost consciousness.

The effort by the men on the rope was enough; the officer emerged from the river with David in his arms. They both sprawled on the bank. Rebecca was also lying on the bank coughing, and the three officers on the bank lay exhausted from the exertion of pulling the combined weight of two people out of the raging current twice.

Trapped in the Narrows

The officer tied to the rope had felt David's final struggle just after he let go of his air. He felt for vital signs, and while there was still a pulse, he could detect no breathing. He immediately began mouth-to-mouth resuscitation, bending David's head back, pinching his nose, and breathing into his mouth. In less than a minute David began to cough up gulps of brown water.

Epilogue

Finish

Lying on the bank with his eyes closed, David was only dimly aware of movement around him, but he knew he was still alive because of the pain. Every square inch of his body hurt. The wound in his arm hurt. His ribs hurt when he breathed. His leg hurt. His hands and wrists were lacerated and bleeding. His entire body was a mass of bruises, bumps, and contusions. Even undamaged muscles ached from the constant exertion over the past two days. He coughed violently, still trying to eliminate the offensive guck that he had swallowed from his system. Then he heard Rebecca coughing to his side. Suddenly, he felt great.

David opened his eyes. He couldn't remember how he had gotten out of the flood. Yet here he was, lying on the bank with the warm afternoon sun beating down through partly cloudy skies onto his battered body. The warmth of the sun infused strength into him, as if he was getting his batteries charged by the comforting life-giving light that bathed his body with energy.

David and Rebecca lay on a rock with police officers scurrying about them. The officers had removed their wet clothes, put dry ones on, and went to work rubbing their skin to warm the two nearly blue bodies sprawled on the sandstone slab. Both David and Rebecca were returning from the brink of death.

As he became aware of the officers working to revive them, David became conscious that their ordeal was over. They were safe now. There was to be no more escaping from skinheads, no more running from floods. The water level was still high and the river would continue to be too dangerous to traverse for the next twenty-four hours, but the flood had crested and the danger had passed. The four officers, David, and Rebecca had only to wait until the water level dropped enough to allow passage back to the ranger station at Sinawava.

The flood had wiped out all of the skinheads. Bart was shot when he attempted to shoot David and Rebecca. The others didn't make it out of the canyon. The roiling mass of water swallowed them and swept them away. Only two of the bodies were later recovered miles downstream, partially covered by freshly deposited sand.

The next twelve hours were confused as David drifted in and out of consciousness. He wanted to stay awake and talk, but was unsuccessful. He was dimly aware through the fog in his mind of people bustling around him. Finally, he awoke the next morning and stayed awake. There was food to eat and water to drink. After eating, David felt stronger. Rebecca had awakened a few hours before David, and had eaten while David was still sleeping. All of their injuries were relatively minor, and neither one of them would have any lasting effects from their ordeal.

The water level in the river had returned to its normal high flow and, as the inclement weather system had cleared the region, it was deemed safe to go down the river. The officers were trying to figure out how to get them down. Rebecca was unable to walk from a foot injury she had received while under water in the flood so she would need to be carried.

David insisted he was strong enough to travel on his own. His wound was treated and his legs felt good enough to walk on. Twenty-six hours after the flood, the group started down toward the command center at the Temple of Sinawava.

Progress was slow, and not just because Rebecca's stretcher was difficult to carry downriver. David was not moving at his normal pace either, but least he was moving. The normal travel time of two hours from the mouth of the Narrows to the paved trail took four hours instead, with many rest stops for everyone along the way.

They finally reached the paved trail along the river. It was a surprise when they finally reached it. After walking around two large meandering bends in the river, they came back to a southward heading where the trail began, the first sign of civilization that David and Rebecca had seen for three days.

The rest of the hike was easy. David had walked it many times, sometimes wheeling his father before him in a wheelchair. The entire trail was familiar, and he ticked off the landmarks and trail turns as they strode along.

Indeed, it seemed that the closer he got to the parking lot, the more his energy level rose. Even with the bruised and beat-up body, he felt good about what he had accomplished, especially under the circumstances. His walk became firm and he stretched his legs and lengthened his stride to normal, forcing the aching muscles in his legs and back to extend. They began to pass small groups of people walking up the trail, apparently aware of who they were, but who kept a respectful distance from the group of police officers carrying the stretcher and escorting him.

He was walking the last leg to the parking lot when he remembered Austin. How long had it been since he had recalled that his son was dead? In the fight to survive all of his thought focused on the struggle at hand. David was wracked by the thought of what had been taken from him. No one could ever take his son's place. Considering the outcome with Rebecca, he knew he had made the right decision the day before yesterday by abandoning his son.

They reached the last stretch to the parking lot. A knot of people was waiting at the lot, and as they came into view they all swarmed toward them. A number of reporters thrust microphones in his face and fired a barrage of questions at him. He did not answer. He was too despondent about Austin to speak to anyone. He continued walking, forcing his way through the mass of people.

Someone was working her way toward him from the opposite direction. It was Marie. She reached him and hugged him so tightly that he cried out from the pain in his chest and arm. Then she loosened her grip, and they stood there in each other's arms resting their heads on the others neck while the press continued to pepper them with questions. Rebecca and the rest of the group continued on to the waiting ambulance. David and Marie silently held each other as they gently rocked back and forth, oblivious of the crush of people around them, grateful for the opportunity to be together again.

Eventually they broke the reunion embrace. David looked into her bright sparkling eyes, wondering how she would react to Austin's death. "I'm sorry honey," he said. "I lost Austin. I had to leave him to go after the guys who had taken Rebecca."

"No you didn't. He's at the hospital in St. George, and he's going to recover," beamed Marie. "I just got word from the hospital two hours ago that his condition has been downgraded from critical to serious and that he is awake and recovering. Even better, he's hungry, which seems pretty normal to me."

"You mean he's not in the canyon? What happened? Who did it?" The rapid-fire questions burst from David. The knowledge that Austin was safe changed everything. A rush of euphoria swept over him.

Both David and Marie peppered each other with questions as they reached the parking lot, boarded the ambulance, and rode to the hospital, with one police officer on board to debrief them. The ambulance drove the route to St. George without sirens or lights as the sun set behind Pine Valley Mountain in a clear and cloudless sky.

THE END

www.ingramcontent.com/pod-product-compliance
Lightning Source LLC
Chambersburg PA
CBHW031428250626
47155CB00004B/1671